African Compass

New writing from southern Africa

2005

Published by Spearhead
An imprint of New Africa Books (Pty) Ltd
99 Garfield Road
Kenilworth 7700

www.newafricabooks.co.za

First edition 2005

ISBN 0–86486–580–5

Cover design by Nic Jooste, Comet Design
Text design and typesetting by CBT Typesetting & Design
Printed and bound by MSP Print

HSBC/SA PEN Literary Award

Prize winners 2005

1st   **Pius** by Elizabeth Ann Pienaar
2nd   **Compass** by Farhad Abdool Kader Sulliman Khoyratty
3rd   **Ice with water** by Fatima Fiona Moolla

Honourable mention   **A Joburg story** by Darrel Bristow-Bovey

HSBC
The world's local bank

Contents

Contents

African Compass – New writing from southern Africa 2005 is the first book launched as part of the three-year series of the US$10 000 HSBC/SA PEN Literary Award. It follows a five-year series of 'New South African Writing' published by South African PEN in the sixties. This time we have spread the net wider. Our targets for these awards are young writers who are citizens of any country in the Southern Africa Development Community.

The chosen genre for the series is the short story and this volume contains a selection of the best from 373 entries. The upper age limit of writers was 40, their work had to be original and previously unpublished, and it had to be written in English. The whole selection process maintained author anonymity – initial readers, members of the editorial board and award judge, Nobel Laureate JM Coetzee, did not know the identity of the authors throughout the process. John Coetzee read all the stories that were shortlisted for the book and chose the prizewinners from these.

Writer and South African PEN member, Alexandra Fuller, comments: '. . . it is long past time for us who are Africa-seeded to elbow our way to the front of the world's bookshelf'. This implies a touch more force than writers are prone to exert, but it is important that the work of African writers be heard globally. The writer has a crucial role to play during times of turmoil in the world – in developing societies particularly. He or she has the power to reflect in writing a shared humanity, to build respect for individual dignity and integrity, and use the power of imagination against the power of those who wish to polarise the world into West v East or North v South. There is only one future for all humankind, one truth, 'one world' as the PEN Charter states, and writers should explore this with creative energy in the hope that shared principles will rise above the traditional responses that divide us.

Amin Maalouf, PEN member (Lebanon and France), writing in a recent edition of *PEN International*, mentions the need to re-imagine the future and says that this is not a task that should be left only to political or religious activists:

. . . It is precisely the task of poets, essayists and novelists. It is up to the writers of the six continents to strike the right notes, to find the right balance between

universality and diversity. Universality of fundamental human values, diversity of languages and cultural expressions.

It is ultimately up to us to determine whether our century will go down in history as the century of suicide or the century of imagination, the century of human folly or the century of human wisdom, the century of the bomb or the century of the pen.

Tribute must be paid to HSBC Bank plc who agreed to fund this literary award and reach out to encourage the 'century of the pen'. Also tribute to Brian Wafawarowa of New Africa Books, who shook hands on a proposed publishing agreement and advocated encompassing the larger region of all SADC countries.

When Antonio, apprentice to Michelangelo, asked how he might emulate the master, he was told: 'Draw, Antonio Draw!' We say to young people of our region 'Write! Africa Write!' There must be future 'masters' of the written word in southern Africa, and this series is intended to search them out and encourage them in the early days of their careers. Rest assured, some names in these volumes will become renowned, and they will remember who gave them a start to their careers as writers.

Congratulations to the prize-winners of the first award! As I write this, new stories are coming in for the 2006 edition. Who knows what treasures we will find?

Keep writing, Africa!

Anthony Fleischer
President, SA PEN
June 2005

Comment from Nobel Laureate JM Coetzee

There was a rich variety amongst the twenty-six finalists for the 2005 awards. Some of the stories still bore the marks of the school classroom, others were obviously by seasoned hands. Some were sophisticated in style, drawing confidently on the extravagances of contemporary postcolonial fiction, others were still fully faithful to the example of Somerset Maugham. On some the influence of the television script was clear, while others remained resolutely literary.

If there was one dominant failing, it was that few of the authors seemed to be reading each other. That is to say, few seemed to be conversant with the kind of writing that other southern African writers of the new generation are doing, and few were therefore in a position to give their own handiwork a clear, cold look to assess whether it was truly novel, whether it truly made a contribution to new southern African writing. Even among the twenty-six who reached the last round, too many were content to employ stock characters from the contemporary repertoire, to fall back on stock situations, stock dialogue.

There were four offerings that stood out.

Pius is a moving account, from several perspectives, of the last days in the life of a victim of murderous violence. The language is vivid and poetic. I look forward to more work from its author's hand. It is a worthy winner of the first prize.

Compass is an African life-story – 'African' in the widest sense – rich in humour and allusion, eclectic in style. It takes second place.

Ice with water is the story of the death of an old man in hospital. Its language is modest, and the element of fantasy is beautifully controlled. It takes the third prize.

Honourable mention goes to *A Joburg story* for its well-crafted dialogue.

Pius

Elizabeth Ann Pienaar

'I've got a funeral policy.' He tells me, first thing.

They always say the police, the police don't do their jobs. Fock. Fock them, I am sorry, I am sorry because this time here we are, quickly, the man from the Zenex phoned and we came and when I got out of the car I saw first thing, he'd lost a lot of blood. He was a giant. He was talking, can you believe, he was lying there nearly, maybe dying and he's talking on his cellphone. So I phone the ambulance and I think he's a giant, maybe that's why there's so much blood, maybe he's not so bad. Maybe it's just the dark, you know, it isn't so much blood. The sergeant shakes his head, then gets right back in the car and reverses a bit so we can shine the lights on him. He talks to me, when he finishes softly, softly, on his cellphone. He tells me they were very young, he says they were like his kids, like his second born, maybe twelve, maybe thirteen, just children. We wait and more people come and he tells me about his job driving he says we must tell his company he will be late. Then he stops talking, his face twists, and his eyes open and close quickly. The sergeant gets out the car and his face is like thunder, I know this man is angry mad, he looks at his watch then he phones the ambulance again and shouts, he fluks them in Afrikaans.

Then he starts to shiver, the big man. He shivers and shivers. I try to hold his hand, the one hand that is free, he's fallen on the right one and I can't move him. But he won't let go of his cellphone. He closes his eyes and he tells me he's waiting for his wife. The man from Zenex comes with a blanket and covers him. He still shivers so much. I go and phone focking again. The ambulance. You know they always say it's the police we don't do our job but here I am and they don't come. Even when he stops shivering, we are still waiting.

A mote floats in the air. Dust upon nothing. There is more of nothing than there is something. In the atom, there is more space between than there is mass formulated in structure. It is the space between: that holds everything. The space where there is nothing.

The space the rational construct bounds, yet cannot reach. The unknowable. What happens when we die? We go to the space between. And then we can't come back to tell. Keeping the unbounded bound. A good construction, keeps itself from tumbling down.

On Thursday he told me where his funeral policy was.

On Saturday he slept late. He woke up just half an hour before work. So he was going to be late. But I let him sleep, I don't know why I didn't wake him, I don't know how he slept even though the light straight above him was shining, and I was cooking, the pan was making its own sh hss shss sounds, and the television was on. I let him sleep. I watched him while I cooked for him. He looked like he was happy, sleeping. He looked like there was no worry inside him. He looked clean and shining like when I first knew him, he looked like our last born, big and strong.

When he woke up he just said 'I'm going to be late.' No shouting, no, no cursing and slapping things around, he just put his new shirt on quickly, and came to the pan and took a sausage before I could even put the plate with the pap next to him. He ate standing, scooped a few mouthfuls, then he took another sausage and opened the door and said 'I'll see you tomorrow.' Then he went out and I noticed his new shoes were still in the corner. Near the cupboard where he kept an old shoe box full of papers, including the funeral policy.

I sat down with my own plate, I sat on the bed to watch the television, but even with the television on I could hear all the Saturday night sounds around me — the radios in the corridor, someone playing Mandoza, someone talking, news I think, some young guys shouting. I went to the balcony to look out, nearly nighttime but still fading light, and down in the street, lots of people, lots of people. I thought I saw him, my husband, running through the people, to get his taxi. Perhaps he would not be late. My husband is a very good man. When he doesn't have his problem. This time, things are different. Now, with this job, I think he has stopped his problem. He is serious, these last few months. He gives me money for the children. He goes home to his mother. He prays. He wants to do the ceremony for his dead father, this year, he says, and when I say next year we will have more money, he still says, no, let's make things right for my father now. He is serious these last few months. I think he is different now. It is only a temporary, this job, and only nighttime, but it is a job. And even though he has a job, there has been no problem.

So when he phoned me, I was surprised. If he woke up, maybe quarter past six, it was quarter to seven that he phoned me. 'Come quickly,' he said. 'They have shot me.'

Yellow light seeps like a stain across the horizon. Each day we start again from scratch. Natal. The past is untouchable, the future indiscernible, mere speculation, rational construction upon the continuum of consciousness, flimsy human order upon the firmament of unending chaos.

On Thursday I told her where I kept my funeral policy.

On Saturday I slept late. I woke up at quarter past six. To the brightness of the fluorescent light, the yellow light like sun, caught. And the television. And the sound of her frying. 'I'm going to be late,' I told her. I barely had time to wash, I slept in my white vest, so I just dressed over, I put on my new check shirt, but my old shoes even though I had a new pair standing in the corner near the bed. Old shoes for work because when you drive all night, you want to be comfortable.

So I took my wallet and my phone and as I took a mouthful of the pap and sausage, for some funny reason I remembered telling her, yesterday late, to go, Ma, go down, please and get some more air time for me. She did. Even though she'd just come in, and I could see she was very tired. My wife. Beautiful. Inside and outside, a clean light, my wife. She forgives me, a lot. Still, it is her place.

One more mouthful of supper then I had to run out of the yellow light, out of the warm close smell of our place, our bed and our small stove and our one chair and our television on the low part of the cupboard. Out of our smell into the open corridor, the shine of noise from so many people in the corridor, some radios, some news some music some young guys being cool for the new girl in the corner flat, the night was sharp in the way it touched me, so much light shining off the blackness, and from up here you can see the lights of the city looking South. Where I had to go.

Down. Go down four flights because the lift doesn't work, and then run, I had to run, still chewing her sausage, through the streets, pushing through the people. Tonight they all seemed to shine, like a light ran off them, all the people parted like a stream of water in so many flowing colours, as I pushed through them. To get my taxi. Squeeze in, middle row, I watched the lights of the highway thick, yellow, the outline of the man next to me, his head kept getting caught up in the yellow flow. South.

The taxi stops near an open flat piece of land. I can see the darkness hovering over it, but not quite touching yet, there is still a thin strip of daylight at the edge of the land, glints of silver reflect the stubby new grass in the taxi headlights. The others all go in the opposite direction, into the bright halo around the Zenex garage, and beyond that, the warm night, I don't know where they go to, other night shifts. Like mine.

I have to walk across the open land. The new growing grass is crunchy under my old shoes. Just across this open patch, there's my compound, the fence is shining, shining, as if I can see the electricity running through it, I know I can't really, but I think I can. Like I think I can see the guard in the guardhouse, built out of precast. But not really. I know can't really because it is still too far away, the factory from which I must drive their slow beasts, their heavy steel cows with stomachs bloated by gas. I must drive their giant beasts through the darkness. Because they are slow and carry a dangerous load and must not take up the road at daylight.

I must drive at night because I cannot get a job driving in the sunlight. I have made a lot of mistakes. Just being a man. My wife forgives me. I cannot get a job easily because a job brings me money and money brings me the poison. When you drink too much poison you fall down. I have been a man who does not stop until I fall down. Until the money is gone again. And there is nothing to give to my wife because they say to me this is a job you cannot do, not even on the lonely roads through the emptiness to Cape Province, no you cannot drive if you drink. But perhaps it is the driving that makes me take the poison. Alone. And with so many other women. My beautiful wife. She is a clean light inside and out.

I was thinking of her when they came for me, it felt like I had been walking for so long, for so long, and the grass shining up crunching under my feet, it seemed that there was more and more sparkling silver light coming up from the grass, just slightly wet from the nighttime cooling. But also it seemed I could get no closer, no closer no matter how much I walked. To my compound.

They shouted to me to stop. Two of them from behind, they ran out to me and they hit me on the back of my head. Two other ones came from the front. I could see how they lifted on tip toes to hit at me. They were so small. They were so young. I am not so young, but I am not small. So when they shouted for my wallet, I swung my arm out, I felt — 'these are young worms.' They fell. One on his back, one hit his head on the shining sharp grass and even in the dark I could see blood. One rolled, onto his knees, and one ran. There was a lot of thick sound hitting me, like a shambok of white whipping my ears, they were cursing me, then some fingers slipped against mine as I held my wallet, these were so thin and slippery, and I know the sound from my lungs was like a wave, I was very angry at these cheeky fingers. I flipped the wrist till it cracked.

But there were five of them, my beautiful wife, and it was the number five who stood back from my fight and let loose the streaking gold light through the dark. I could see how this yellow thick light lodged. Somehow I stood above and beside and inside and I could see how it stopped in my chest and the gold started to spread through me, inside. Just as the red blood spread out. They shouted like cracks in the blackness, and as I fell I rushed back inside. The one who stood back came towards me. He looked down at me from eyes like orange sand. The strange thing, my wife, is not that he was in age like our second born but that he was like a shadow in the shadow. It was as if he was only paper and then only thick air because I could see the open sky and the starlight slipping right through him. He stared. There was nothing in the eyes that made me think he was sorry. He prised each finger from my grip on the wallet. Calmly, he took my ATM card out, then he held the wallet upside down. I watched the few silver coins floating down, floating so slowly I could count them — there were four. Then he dropped the wallet on the ground.

I watched, I heard but I could not move. Could not make myself move. There was a lot of red thick blood underneath me. He walked around me, and began to undo the laces of my shoes. First he pulled my left shoe. I could see the effort, the strain in his face, he struggled, but then he pulled it free. I watched and by the time he took the second shoe off, he was not even a shadow in the shadow, I could not see him at all anymore, but, you know, they were my favourite shoes. A big big sound, a sound like water falling over a cliff, came up, came from inside me, came out from me, and it crashed right over them. Then it sounded like small birds, shrieking, and they all ran, then I was left alone on the ground. Far far away, the light of the compound twinkled on the horizon. That was when I found I could move my left hand. And that I still had my cellphone. With air time.

So my beautiful wife, I phoned you. And I waited. For you to come, as I told you, come quickly, they have shot me. I waited. Inside and outside and above my fallen body. I waited when the police car came. I waited with the policewoman for the ambulance which never came. I waited and the thick yellow light spread from the edge of the world, closer and closer, yellow light like sun, caught. I tried very hard to wait for you. Inside, beside, above. But it became too hard, so hard, a man from the garage came and put a blanket over me, there were lots of people now, then the policewoman phoned for the ambulance again, and then I found I could not go inside. So I waited beside and above.

I waited and all the people got more like paper, then like air until I could see the yellow light flowing right through the police car and the policeman, a white man, and the policewoman staying next to me and the man from the garage. 'I am waiting for my wife,' I told them. But they did not answer me. I thought of our last born my boy who is made big like me, but with your face, and like you, beautiful, inside and out. And then you came pushing through and the crowd parted like a stream of water, and even though I went straight to you and said 'I am here, I have been waiting,' you went straight to the blanket, and the sound that came from you cut the air like a blade and then the yellow light that had been rolling in rolling in from the horizon, reached me, the yellow light like sun.

A mote floats in the air. Dust upon nothing in a slipstream of light, dancing, the light cast upon the unknowable chasm, the emptiness. Somewhere the wings of a butterfly beat and rippled the empty air, the chasm folded, and refolded, and one was no longer there.

And one was.

Compass – Or How Grandpa Conquered the West

Farhad Abdool Kader Sulliman Khoyratty

Para Guillermo
Amistad para siempre

It was the time when 'Abba' meant 'father' and not yet a group of four swinging and swaying Swedes. The Sixties (according to the Western calendar – evidently) was giving in to the Seventies (according to the Western calendar – evidently). Grandpa (nana, dada, abuelo, granper – *many mouthfuls for a small, slight, slim, short man, vertically- and compass-challenged) was ailing as I was leaving Mauritius. He sat me down next to him on his bed during what was both the sacred and emotional moment when lore is handed down by the patriarch across generations to guard against the ravages of time, and the ridiculous moment when generations shout serious nonsense across chasms of space and time. Grandpa was suffering from his usual asthma or whatever it was Darth Vader suffered from. In between wheezes, his philosophy poured out, a link in the complex history of East and West, or perhaps North and South, or whatever . . .*

I have always enjoyed little private jokes on my own. It is at such moments that I feel most at peace with myself, as though I have finally taken my life in my own hands – it is a bit like the escape and choice provided by suicide. No less; no more. Sometimes, I ask vegetable sellers in Germany for aubergines, in English but with an affected German accent. Sometimes it is in Dakar and I adopt a Wolof accent in my French as I ask for cloth.

Lately, the joke was on me. I was travelling to London from the Canaries on a cheap flight, mostly with lager louts and assorted British hooligans, loud but 'salt of the Earth' all in all. Spotting my Indian looks on the plane, the only non-shellsuited, yuppie-looking man on the plane asked me for 'Uh corry, mate!' and guffawed. 'Oh! How recherché!' – affected pedantry, colonial bourgeoisie was all I could aspire to in turn. I wanted to explain how, technically, I was African, how, effectively, most of the world was ideologically European, how, after all, I didn't know what being anything was at all anymore. I gave up because it took too much energy and he wasn't worth it. After all, it was a joke, inn't? – which was good enough but not good enough.

But that was now. This is the Seventies. I walked along Charing Cross Road, in my colourful flares and an open shirt framed by a large collar revealing a huge chain and a shamelessly hairy chest, looking at books in the bookshop windows, browsing: I had nothing specific to purchase and nothing better to do. I responded to a paranoia that had grown into a virtual fetish of mine: I asked about Mauritian literature: was there a special shelf for it? No, there wasn't. I should try under African literature, or perhaps Indian? Or maybe French? Surely, under 'Commonwealth literature'? Maybe Travels, or Tourism? In order to know who you are, you first have to know where you are. The price for being everything at the same time: invisibility? I was trebly lucky, so trebly lucky – Mauritian, Muslim and African: nowhere and everywhere at the same time, everything and nothing.

'Taariq, my boy, the Vilayeti, the foreign folk lure you with material riches. They have a mirror. They show you your face in it, but it isn't really your face, it is that of another, impish. Then they steal your soul away, and pack it tight inside the mirror. And you grow paler and paler.' Wheeze! Wheeze! Wheeze! *Pause for a puff at the made-in-Britain* Salbutamol. *'You'll look just like them: pale, dead. Their women wear make-up to hide the soullessness of their death-masks.'*

I could safely call Las Canarias, northwest of Africa, southwest of Spain, my home, since I had lived there for twenty years, more than I had in Mauritius, in Plen Vert, east of Port Louis, northwest of Mauritius, southeast of Africa. I had jumped across Africa, from one end to the other, southeast to northwest, both places that were Africa-but-not-quite-yet-who-knows-what-is Africa. In Las Canarias it was useless trying to explain where Mauritius was let alone what being Mauritian was. As if I knew what it was. They will remember me forever as the Mauritanian or the Indian (Hindu most said, for Muslims were Arabs). And who gives a shit? (*'Tauba! Tauba! Tchi! Tchi! Tchi! Tchi!'* *Grandpa would have been indignant – Muslim Indian words at the service of bourgeoisie – that Seventies word for 'civilisation'*). I am that I am.

I remember following Consuela to Las Canarias. Back/forward to Africa. I gave up a degree in Cartography at Leeds, north of England, south of Scotland and simply packed my bags and left, never to return to complete it. I allowed the unsmiling laws of gravity to dictate my life and fell into the warm lap of islands of the Canaries, west. We lived, Consuela and I, for twenty round years on the seafront, on the Avenida Maritime del Norte, in Las Palmas de Gran Canaria. Then, one day, we visited Tenerife, South of Gran Canaria. The dream stopped, and reality started . . .

'In America (generic term for the West) *these women wear plumes on their private parts, and their mouths, pointed like beaks, painted with blood, will suck all the life out of you, and throw you up, an empty bag of skin; they shhhhuck you up.'* The sucking sound he made was decidedly gruesome.

In Tenerife, Consuela fell in love with the most boisterous East London, Southern English thug, a walking caricature, perfect villain for my piece. He was called Ferdinand (they called 'im Ferd'). Consuela and I never married, which had not bothered me until then: the decade of Flower Power was barely over so a contract sealing each other as each other's property was far too passé, chérie! Besides, Consuela was mad, I thought. Here I was, the one that women fell for . . . with my beautiful, tanned, brownish skin and my Island smile, chez Blendax©, my hair done chez Brylcreem©, just for you lucky ladies out there! How *could* she? It shouldn't have been like this – it was too easy. Falling in and out of love, not like back home. But behind the tall stories we humans tell each other and our own selves around campfires is a heart of darkness. The Horror! The Horror! Hearts of darkness out of Africa!

Instead of beating my shamelessly hairy chest or covering my greasy hair with ashes, however, I diverted my attention to her hair: I became obsessed with Consuela's hair. I began to realise I had never loved her. I had slept with a stranger, woken up with a stranger, cooked my soft Mauritian rougay and liquefied spicy gazpacho for a complete stranger. It was her hair that I loved. I loved the provocative severity of her hair tied in a bun. I loved her flowing hair dancing against canicular mornings. I loved her hair when it curled wet against her face after a swim. Calendar poses. I progressively remembered that that was the only reason I had ever loved her, that had she lost all her hair, all my love for my Delilah would have been *deSamsonised*. No bald Consuelas for me, no *cantatrice chauve*!

'They use their hair to lure men, like sirens did to Illis Bhai. But Illis Bhai (Ulysses) *was faithful to his wife to the end. Hair is like Shaytan the Snake – it ties you up, crushes your bones and swallows you whole. Beware women who can sit on their hair.'*

I'm not sure whether Ulysses was faithful or just very good at telling tall stories to cover his heart of darkness. Here's mine: Consuela was turning, in my mind's eye, into a wave of hair whose form and whose shine was asking for it, Your Honour. I, however, refused to play the Othello, and shed everyone's blood on life's stage, which will no doubt evoke the contempt of both Mauritian and Spanish men. I was no Moor from the South. Muslim, but not that kind of African. Which kind? The non-jealous kind. That's not a kind . . . Which kind of

Moor, then? Othello the 'real man' or Boabdil the 'woman' who lost Granada for the Muslim world? Which Muslim? Which African? Which Indian? Which Mauritian? Which caricature? Which stereotype? Choose wisely my son, or become invisible.

At night, as I would see Consuela off to meet her Ferdinand, I would lie awake and dream of the hair. If only I could convince her to cut all her hair off, I felt, I could let go of her completely. If only I could convince her to leave me that long shininess . . . Then, she could join her Ferd' for all I cared: I would caress the sensual hair, and we would all live happily ever after. THE END.

But no, she wouldn't.

'They will never be yours. In America, women are the men and men are the women. Are you a eunuch?' Rhetorical question.

When Consuela returned, happy, but sometimes bruised up by her sweet boy Ferd', I would pretend to be fully asleep, and even not to mind her nocturnal adventures in the mornings, playing it all very English. But I did: for she always brought her hair with her, and it was her hair I loved after all.

One such morning, when the love of my life hadn't returned yet, in my showers I re-discovered (like myopic Christopher Columbus) an old, half-forgotten pleasure, a New World of Indias where I was two: masturbation. I realised (I now had a ready flow of time on my hands) that it was the form of sex that was nearest to philosophy: it dealt with what could only be grasped by the proponent of the discussion, mostly enjoyed in solitude, viewed suspiciously and misunderstood by the moral majority, was mostly to do with the mind and a fair dose of imagination, and if practised in excess was said to lead to blindness. Was I (like myopic Christopher Columbus) the first to have discovered this? Mostly, I discovered that the Consuela I loved was no less than myself I loved; it was a Consuela I wanted, a Consuela I had wanted and therefore invented. As Voltaire might have put it – had he known Consuela – if Consuela did not exist, Taariq (*moi*) would have invented her.

'You are already half a eunuch. You refuse to grow a beard, like our people do! Do you think men would have been given the capacity to grow one by the Almighty so we might get it shaven, so we prance around like girls?' He clears his throat of phlegm and spits.

I now know that the Consuela of my mind will always be there. But there was still the small matter of the hair. I decided to take things in my own hands once again sotospeak: I decided to mentally construct another Consuela, created in the image of her loose hair. I named her Carmencita. She crept quietly into bed with me as soon as Consuela

left for her lover. She came from the North of the North of Tenerife,
that is, northeast of Gran Canarias. Yes, she came from Southern
Spain, Andalucia, the East's West and the West's East, Europe's South
and Africa's North. Andalucia: a whiff of oranges bursting with golden
eroticism, a kerb, a junction, a roundabout, an accident, a collision, a
crash, an exclamation. I remember the animal scent in Carmencita's
hair as the bun gave way and flew into the breeze on a beach in
Malaga. I remember the summer of '78 as we visited the white marble
of the Alhambra, whiter still against her gypsy skin, darker than mine.
Mine: Indian, north of Gujeraat, south of Kashmir, east of Pakistan,
west of Uttar: Punjabi. We shared the same angular nose, soft straight
hair, shady skin, fiery eroticism, love for rootlessness, flamenco and
the *Kamasutra*. We also shared Africa, transit but also origin. We could
but dream of weaving our combined darknesses into the whiteness of
the Moor's civilised stone and turn the delicate building into a Tantric
temple of writhing bodies, bodies as impossible as desire. What happy
caricatures we were, free of Nuance!

*'They had no roots, no culture, no food. So they came to us. All the way round
the world.'*

Carmencita and I had once both been African, but: you
Gypsy/'Gyptian, me Morisco/Mauritian. I had gone North, and she
had gone West. No, we had not gone anywhere, it was a *shoah* within –
we had been brought by our ancestors: rejected children, jealous and
defiant. We were children of a First Rape, a Papa Europe our Mater
had then been forced to marry (she was Indian), children of the rapist
and the raped – small wonder we were confused! I remembered Mer-
imée, and Bizet, the two Frenchmen who, like me, had invented Car-
men, and began to feel like the frail French soldier who was cheated,
and then killed, by one of her incarnations. Was there a real fire in
Andalucia that singed, burnt and then killed? An auto-da-fé for heretics by heretics?

Wizened fingers had pointed, loose-skinned and phallic:

*'Europe's girls no good. They give good time easy easy. Then they take your
soul easy easy. And they devour it. West is Wild. Girl in West is like Pony
Express.'*

I loved the rhyme and decided to concentrate on the promise of the
'good time easy easy' first. But Andalucia beckoned, like a bloodthirsty
siren, with a middle finger, and took all you had and killed and left, la
Belle Dame Sans Merci. Beautiful Andalucia, like a ripe fruit under a
summer sun, but with dagger-like incisors crimson yet still alluring –
like red lipstick. I had learnt to recognise her, for I knew of her: she
had defeated me before, sent me back to Africa, burnt me and my

Jews, and got an Italian to redraw a map that made me invisible. But
there was also the man in me, drawn to hair, unthinking, and also the
French soldier in me, and that tragic romantic part still wanted the
locks of hair that made a soft but self-assured bun. Who is me? Which
is me?

*'They are practical to the bone. Love is nothing. We Indian people cry a lot in
films, don't you see? They leave their old in homes. Dustbins!'*

Consuela became ferocious as she realised she was losing both Ferd'
and I. Ferd' had casually informed her that he was going back home,
thank you ma'am, and, by the way, had *uh woif* by the name of Isabel
waiting for him (they called her Bel!) – oh! Truly, what Eastender
villains they were! Consuela called and asked me to come and save her
from Tenerife so we could go back north to Gran Canaria. We would
then return to the comfort of where we were before.

But new territories had been discovered; History would never be the
same again. 'Time was of the essence' and had taken over from Space.
I advised her to proceed to Las Palmas on her own. I was visiting
friends in Seville and would then proceed to visit my parents in Mauritius, prelapsarian. She decided to play the quiet Desdemona, sensing I
would now always travel with Carmencita and was never going to miss
her again:

'Jew go to Moorishus. Jew ghav fun!'

I pondered over her pronunciation of Mauritius: neither East nor
West, was it something Moorish? Or forever other, was it Jew? Was the
answer to be found in Al Andalus/Andalucia, where West had reasserted its difference from East, or even Constantinopoulos/Istanbul
where East had reasserted its difference from West? Mdina in Malta or
Antioch in Syria? Or Jerusalem, everything at the same time? What
language to use? Kiswahili, a language that linked East to South? Or
Morisyen, North and South? Or Brasilian, a language of the North
given a Southern soul? I decided the answer would probably be found
in Carmencita's arms, and proceeded to yet another philosophical
cogitation over why (the gist of which I will spare you).

*'There is the devil himself in human form. It is called woman in heat. You
will meet it everywhere in America. If you meet it do not even talk to it! Woman
in heat is surrounded by film-people and writer-people. This is what you see in
cinema. Cowboy never marries woman in heat. You find such, with writers
where you least expect them. They are devils, and will sell you for a cheap price.'*

That night, I was in Gibraltar, north of Africa, south of Spain,
Africa's North and Europe's South, neither here nor there, except
on coloured maps and for shiploads of migrants from Africa. I stood

on the balcony of a grand *parador* overlooking the dark and angry sea.
I wore an embroidered, golden, silk gown, Moorish and Hollywood-
ish. A crescent moon pierced the sky with the white despair of the
jilted *femme fatale*. I looked at the Rock and remembered with a mix-
ture of strange, excited expectation and nostalgia, that smelt of the
old, of sandalwood and incense sticks, that it was named after a General Taariq of barbarous Barbary, my namesake, grand conqueror of
Spain (did he discover it too, like myopic Columbus?). Scratch this
name though to see a time when the Rock had no name, before it was
tamed, before it was 'civilised', before it was reduced, stuck to a continent, force-fed an identity like a duck readied for foie gras. Heart of
Darkness.

'You are full of crap, Taariq,' snorted Carmencita, reading my mind
(she was Gypsy, remember?).

'What does a gypsy know about poetry?' I asked, not quite knowing
what I was saying.

She grabbed a sword and rushed to me, shouting:

'We, the epitome of rootlessness and namelessness, don't know anything about poetry? We live poetry with our bodies!'

'You are full of crap, Carmencita!'

'I will defend my people's name to the death!'

We were such happy colourful caricatures, opera figures, panto-
mimes . . . I ducked sideways and with operatic grandeur, Carmencita
fell into the sea, impaling herself on the sword before she did so with
surgical precision. From the next room, I saw a head pop out, balding
and comical; I recognised it as belonging to an irritable Indian writer
of some renown, a Salman Rushdie, who had declared to me his decision to write about Southern Spain once he had completed his
present novel. He said that novel would be a sensation. Oh, yeah? I
thought, with one Afro-American wise-girl sceptical hand on ma hip.
He added it would be a historical link between East and West, and
about North and South. Oh yea? Every writer thinks he's kinda special.
But then, what is East, what is West, what is . . . No time for all that – we
had a whodunnit at hand. And I was travelling not just Space but
Time.

I asked, nonchalantly, with a casual hand gesture stroking my thick
Seventies sideburns the wrong way, thinking how I looked a bit like
him (daddy?):

'Did you, perchance, hear anything fall?'

'Fall!' He looked at me strangely 'That's brilliant! That's how my
next novel will begin: with a fall! A plane falling.'

'On a building? Or two?'

'Just fall. No, *The* Fall.'

He rushed in, and I knew he hadn't seen a thing. Today's writers are weird, I pondered. They fill pages with a lot of junk. No grip on plot. No editing. Just then, the clocks struck midnight, Postmodernism's monstrous kicking legs were emerging from the humungous fundaments of the world, no one knowing what to name it and I joined my hands in a namasté. Time to say goodbye; time for rebirth. Curtains to the pleasure principle, Freudji! *L'enfer c'est les autres*, Sartre my bwana? True, and to be is to act. And it is a dangerous world out there, so now I have to return to myself, foetal position. Erez, my land, my Yerushalayim, mine! Safely. Is moving back moving forward? I suddenly decided I wanted to see my parents (especially my mummy) in Mauritius and therefore to leave the very morning. Back/forward to Africa.

'Marry your kind. Our women will be yours ever. Cook for you, clean for you. Not complain.' The appeal in his eyes made me realise that the old relic was genuinely afraid for me. It made me want to hold him and kiss him, but one cannot be too effusive with a patriarch, however old. 'We have more beautiful faces: large deep eyes, a healthy glow on our skins, proud noses, and . . . shiny hair. What more can you want?' Did he say 'Hair'? Prophetic words, transgression of Timespace, Tchi!Tchi!Tchi! . . .

I heard, as I reached Mauritius, two hours' longitudes away from Ferdinand and his wife Isabel. At midnight the night before, Consuela had taken a ship due north (an hour longitudinally) to Britain. She had decided to leave me and was to cohabit with the couple. The idea of joining in with all three of them sounded kinky and fired my imagination, but I suddenly discovered my old Plen Vert prudishness and resisted asking them if I could join in. Let them, I thought, resolve their Battles of Trafalgar and avenge the Armada together. Or what if they said to me: no entry to the Union? I skulked to Mauritius.

'Buy Mauritian; buy Muslim. Buy Pepsi© . . . Marry Mauritian; marry Muslim. Then you know where you are. We have morals. They have no sense of direction. No compass.'

I could see a crescent, large, grey, proud, slicing the sky with gusto. Suddenly, it knelt down as the fanatical cross of a sword plunged into the bull's back, and the proud crescent dug into the soft arena. I shook the image off my mind: where I came from had never anything to resolve. How could it? It simply did not exist: it was neither Oriental nor Occidental, neither North nor South. They called it African and it wasn't ever too certain. In fact, no one knew where it was. In fact, it wasn't sure where it was. Indeed, as I was walking down the Place

D'Armes in Port Louis, I suddenly saw the palms of the Avenida Maritime del Norte. I saw Carmencita. I called her. She replied, in Morisyen, in only one composite, writhing exclamation:

'*MwamoYildis!*'

'Your name is Yildis?'

I scanned a smorgasbord of human languages. Should I say Hajime Mashite, but no she wasn't Japanese. Or ask: you Ashkenaz or Safarad? Halwein caste? Shona or Ndebele? Why was I complicating matters? In fact, it was all kismet, Bollywoodish and we followed the Script: Turkish name, dark face, Mauritian, Muslim, no wedding rings, but, above all, the same hair. I winked up at God the Great Matchmaker and she thought I was winking at her. She smiled timidly, concentrating on her open sandals and hennaed toes, every inch ready for fertilisation. An older self, sitting inside me melted into grainy Urdu poetry, delicate, like listening to a beautiful dream.

'Will you marry me?' I asked.

Here's how we do things, I thought, satisfied. No complications. No sitting in bars feeling lonely and rejected. No uncertainties. No adultery. No drugs. I'd returned to Mauritius, the moral centre of the world (for that book, I should have looked under 'Ethics'. . .). I was back full circle. Having sought for magnetic Norths, I was back where I started: with my true North.

Grandpa is no more: I am now a grandpa. I now suffer from asthma, inherited from civilisation. I hate contemporary music and the way these young people have no respect anymore. And I speak in italics too . . .

Ice with water

Fatima Fiona Moolla

'Nurse. Nurse. Nurse!'

He shouted with irritation, his staccato punctuated by the impatient prodding of the buzzer.

It took just a minute or two before he heard the light tapping of her heels on the glossy disinfected floor and he saw the tidy silhouette against the blinding corridor light.

'Yes, Papa, what can we do for you now?'

'Thanks to God it's you sister and not one of those young foolish ones who don't know how to treat a sick man. With their ridiculous spiky hairdos and big clumpy shoes they have no place in a hospital. In the mortuary maybe but not in the hospital. They're the cloven-hoofed ones you should be on your guard against, devils with no patience for a sick man, no none at all.'

'Yes, Papa, yes, but what is it now?' she soothed with a look of quiet forbearance.

'It's this chicken, sister. It's this chicken that looks like it was kept for me from the Old South Africa. How's a man supposed to eat this? And these vegetables! Not like they had to pick them and clean them, just emptied from a freezer bag and still burnt, burnt! You've given me a lunch of rubber and soot. Take it away! Take it away! If this bloody disease doesn't kill me then your food will.'

'Alright, Papa. If the food doesn't suit you then have the dessert. It's jelly, I'm sure that will go down nicely.'

'Jelly, bloody jelly. What do you think I am, an infant? If it's not enough that you've got me in a scratchy bloody nappy and a baby nightie, now you want to forcefeed me jelly too.'

'I'm sorry, Papa, but this is all there is.'

'OK, I suppose it's not your fault. Get me water then – no! not water, get me ice, a nice glass of ice with a little water.'

'That's better now. I'll be back in a few minutes.'

Breathless once again after this little exchange, he allowed his back to slump against the crackle of the plastic protected pillows and he looked in the direction of the window. The combined effect of the dust and the rain and the wind had traced a pattern of dirt against the window, like a dull, grey version of a child's kaleidoscope. Through the lace of dust, he could, if he wanted to, see the slope of the Peak where the wildebeest cavorted and where the wind seemed to inscribe mystical messages in the knee-high, swaying grass. But he was not one who had had the leisure (or the inclination) to notice the beauties or wonders of nature, except, perhaps, for one occasion, when struck by the brazen extravagance of a bougainvillea in unadulterated bloom, he questioned his wife's motive for planting puny bloody pansies year after year, when she could have cultivated this shocking pink splendour. And he was not one for puzzling over signs and mysteries. Life carried its meaning on its face. One needed only the intelligence to perceive it.

His was a life of accumulating knowledge and facts, solid knowledge and robust facts: the first president of independent Congo, the drama of the Bolshevik revolution, the successes and failures of the Gandhi dynasty, current fluctuations in the stock market, the comparative cost and fuel consumption of the latest automobile models. And all self-taught, he ruminated to himself as he lay his balding, bleeding, flaking skull against the pillow. This was the first time today that he was not driven to cursing or crying by the itching. It was like ants, like the large black ants of the Highveld creeping just beneath his skin. And then he scratched. He scratched with his nails; and when they were worn down, he scratched with whatever was at hand, a hairbrush, a pair of scissors. In areas his skin looked like distressed leather – oxblood – the colour all the rage at the designer décor warehouses just further down the main road. All self-taught, he comforted himself. Out of school in the Northern Transvaal dorpie his parents had settled in and contributing to the family coffers at age nine. But determined in the deep dark days of Apartheid to educate himself. He read, read every newspaper he could lay his hands on, listened to every radio news broadcast, became intimately familiar with almost every book on the public library shelves. Not novels, mind you – stories were a luxury he'd leave for succeeding generations.

But after all that, after all that hard work and achievement to end up with this bloody old man's affliction, when, whichever way one looked at it, he was not old. He had a lot more verve and wit than men half his age. Categorically, he was not old. In fact, in some ways, he felt reborn, just like this nation of his was supposed to have been reborn with its rainbow and its Babel of languages, a melange of which now wafted through the open ward doors. The voices combined the cadences of the irregular exchanges of the people outside the ward doors and the controlled rhythms of the dialogue of the afternoon soap operas on the television set. But then, perhaps this disease was his distinction. It certainly seemed to strike only the good men, like himself and his soul mate, that chuckling, mischievous but good-hearted gnome in his vermilion and black garb of pastoral office. He counted himself in good company. But still, to lie here day in and day out in his diaper and without his dignity – that took some getting used to; and some fighting against.

But he did not care for this avenue down which his thoughts were being marshalled.

'Nurse! Nurse! Nurse!'

Again the barrage and the buzzer, again the silhouette against the light. This time however, the profile was short and stocky, like a collection of sausages bunched fortuitously together into head, abdomen, arms and legs. As the image, almost the inverse of a photographic negative, imposed itself on his consciousness, for a split second he recoiled. At the mercy of bloody functionaries. This was a tough one, much like his chicken portion at lunch. But if he could dispose of that, he could deal with this one.

'Yes, Papa, what's your problem now?'

'It's this place Nurse (she was no 'sister' of his), it's this place. The problem is this place. It's like bloody Grand Central Station here. People coming, people going, people talking at the top of their voices. And if that's not enough, then there's also the noise from your TV. And this is a place where I'm supposed to rest and recover – what a bloody joke! It's like bloody slapstick comedy. Every time I shut my eyes, I get slammed in the face with a pie!'

'Why can't you relax, old man, like Mr Zabarowski there next to you. This place would be a lot quieter if we didn't have you shouting and buzzing every couple of minutes.'

'Relax! Relax! You want me to relax. That's your way of saying play dead, like this decrepit old collection of bones here next to me. Yes, but of course it would be much easier for you lot if we all just lay here with tubes sticking out of us. Then you could have your good gossip and your tea and your Romany Creams and watch your *Sewende Laan* without any disturbance.'

'Old man, you are trying my patience. Since you have been here, you have been nothing but a nuisance. Don't you realise it's time for you to make peace with yourself and prepare for the hereafter? And while you're about it, leave the rest of us in peace also.'

'Peace! The hereafter! What interest have I got in the hereafter. My only concern is the herebefore – I must get out of here before you kill me!'

'Papa, now please just calm down or I'm going to tell that new young doctor to sedate you. It's almost time for the ward round. Now shush! Here he is coming.'

'Good afternoon, Sister. Good afternoon, Papa – I believe that is what everybody calls you.'

'Yes, yes, that's fine.'

'I see from your records that you are eighty-four.'

'Oh, is that what it says? Actually, I'm eighty-two. The last two years with this disease, you can't call that living.'

'I'm glad to see you haven't lost your sense of humour.'

'Yes, yes, I've lost everything else, but not my sense of humour, never my sense of humour. We couldn't live in this world without one, could we? We couldn't do without our sense of humour?'

The doctor rummaged around in his folders for a few minutes, and then yet again he tolerated being poked and prodded.

'How are you coping with the pain? Is it still under control, or would you like me to increase the morphine?'

'No, it's fine, I suppose it's fine.'

'Well then, I'll see you tomorrow.'

'Yes tomorrow, there's always tomorrow.'

They left his bedside and moved over to the adjacent one. He saw them reading reports, consulting with each other, lifting one limp wrist of the body in the bed alongside his and compressing it, pricking the tip of a dry, withered finger, squeezing to get the recalcitrant drop inside. He lay and he watched, was it five minutes, was it ten minutes or was it fifteen? A strange thing occurred. Before his very eyes, the tableau before him became bleached of colour. The insipid creams and greens of the floors and walls favoured by state hospital decorators together with the more meretricious hues of the blooms brought by weary relations and stuffed into old jars and tumblers seemed to run together and seep out of the scene. Stranger and stranger, he thought. All the colours around him mixed and transformed into their original state – white. All the shadows became black.

He watched them, the doctor and the nurse, after a short or long while (he wasn't sure), walking off into the light of the corridor. They must have been chatting. Their mouths were moving, but he heard nothing, just a distant ringing in his ears. How ridiculous, he thought. The time had come for him to move on. There was nothing more that they could do for him. And, more significantly, there was nothing more that he could do for them. He wished to leave. He wished to depart. He wished to go. Farce, he thought to himself, that is what all this had become, a grand farce.

He considered for a moment and then resolved on what had to be done. Not at all difficult for a thinking, resourceful man like he was. They thought they could restrain him in this bed, no this cot, no this

cage with its bars and railings. But, of course, it escaped them that it
also had wheels. They could not have failed to notice, however, its
horn. He certainly had used it often enough to summon them to his
attention. Like the automobiles now dim in his memory, its side step
was its running board.

Perfectly composed and in control of all his faculties, he slowly
manoeuvred himself out of the bay that had been allocated to him.
Fortunately, it was almost time for the tea trolley to be wheeled in, so
the staff nurse had opened the second of the ward's double doors. He
eased himself through the doors and around the corner with the
grace of a Senna or Schumacher and edged towards the long, wide
expanse of Hospital Avenue. Surprisingly, no one saw him. He
certainly didn't expect the complacent corpse called Zabarowski
to sound the alarm, but the nurses, surely, should have seen
him. But to the credit of the scriptwriters commissioned by Auckland
Park, they were engrossed in the noiseless chatter of the little
square box.

He carefully negotiated all the byways that led to the openness of
the hospital's main corridor and effortlessly began to cruise down. As
he gained momentum, he had the leisure to look at the children's
paintings that lined the walls, naïve splodges that optimistically suggested fish or frog or playground or happy family. The decorators certainly got this one thing right. They did make him feel lighter and
happier, from the first time he arrived, despite the pain and the itching and the irritation of the catheter. They were brightly coloured
then, but now in the monochrome of his present vision, they seemed
to have lost none of their charm. They flew past, picture after picture,
like the fleeting images flashing by, seen from the back seat of a car.
He raced past the porters and the visitors who on one or other pretext
had managed to sneak past hospital security when the preordained
hour for visiting had not yet arrived. But really, there was no need for
speed, the element of surprise or subterfuge since they seemed not to
see him. Just a sharp turn to the right and through the big glass doors
and he was out!

Freewheeling now, down the hill. It struck him that he was on the
wrong side of the road, but it did not seem to matter to any of the
other motorists in the cars that he passed by. What exhilaration! This
must be the joy of a childhood of adventures and cycling down
inclines, a childhood which, unfortunately, he had missed. He passed
the cemetery with its solid, architecturally impressive walls on his right
and thought with derision of the boxed souls who had allowed themselves so impassively to be taken. He was going to head north now back

to where he came from. As he shifted speed he thought to himself: this life, what a bloody Charlie Chaplin show!

Sister Cornelissen returned to ward 3E after a considerable while. There had been no ice in the freezer of the kitchenette closest to the ward, so she had to take the lift to the lower level. She returned now, tapping a little tattoo on her neat little court shoes she knew the old man so admired. Funny, she thought to herself, so old, so near death, but he still noticed little things like shoes. But perhaps it was death precisely which made all the little things in life all that much more precious. She entered the ward and approached the bed. Good. The old man was sleeping now. Clearly a deep and peaceful sleep because he seemed hardly to stir. Pity he couldn't have that beatific look on his face when he was awake. Always a challenge.

She gently put the thick glass tumbler on its thick china saucer down on the metal cabinet alongside the bed. She did not want to wake him. Then she went back to the nurses' station to tidy up before the multitudes of visitors arrived.

The ice lay like large unpolished diamonds in the clear matrix of the water. In the warmth of the ward which retained the heat of the November sun that had shifted past the windows a while before, little droplets condensed on the outside of the glass, which soon ran in little streams onto the saucer. The ice slowly melted and transformed into water, its prior or later state, depending on one's vantage point. Gradually, the matrix and the matter became one and through it one could see clearly.

A *Joburg story*

Darrel Bristow-Bovey

'What's this street called?' said Rob.

We looked at the street and then we looked at Rob.

'Seventh,' I said.

'I know Seventh,' said Rob. 'Obviously Seventh. Seventh what?'

We thought about that. It was a good question. 'Seventh Street,' said Mershen. 'The streets go down, avenues go across.'

'Right!' said Rob triumphantly. 'But then why's that programme called *Sewende Laan*? *Laan* means avenue!'

'Maybe it's a different Sewende Laan,' I suggested.

'No!' said Rob, more triumphant. 'At the credits, they show *this* street.' He jabbed his finger streetwards. 'In fact, the overhead shot starts just about exactly *there*.'

'So what's it, then? Seventh Avenue?'

'I don't know,' said Rob. 'That's why I'm asking.'

'When we go,' I reasoned, 'one of us can walk up and see what the sign says.'

'Good idea,' said Rob.

'Not me,' said Mershen. 'I'm parked down the road.'

'Me too.'

'Me too,' said Rob, which seemed to more or less end the conversation.

'Maybe,' said Mershen slowly after a while, 'the Seventh Avenue on *Sewende Laan* isn't supposed to be a real street. Maybe it's a fictional street that just *looks* like this street.'

'Mmm,' said Rob.

'Uh,' I said, and with that we took another drink.

There was nothing very unusual about that night. We were out too late at the Ponta Linga Linga, Rob and Mershen and me, and there were no girls left in the place and Seventh Street or Avenue was closing down but we were still drinking more in that tired, sorry way when you think that maybe if you stall a little longer, get a little more drunk, something will happen. That's the thought: if only I were a *little bit more drunk*, something fun might happen.

I know it was a weeknight because we all had work the next day and also because we only ever sat around drinking that late on weeknights. Down the street the other bars were closing and the waiters across the

road were putting chairs on tables. Cas was at a table in the corner,
talking with some girl who'd seen one of his plays once. The Ponta
Linga Linga Bar and Restaurant is Cas's place. We asked him once
what Ponta Linga Linga means and he said it's a place in Mozambique, which makes sense because there's a tatty map of Mozambique
stuck to a wall, and a potted banana tree, and a mural of some palms
and a beach and there are some Mozambican bank notes sticky-taped
behind the bar.

If Cas hadn't been talking with that girl who'd once seen one of his
plays he'd probably have shooed us out because it was way past closing
time. Rob was drunk. I knew Rob was drunk because every time Cleo
passed us he looked at her breasts as though it was the first time he'd
noticed them. Cleo wasn't her real name but everyone called her Cleo
because the first night she worked at the Ponta Linga Linga the other
waitress's name was Chloe. If that makes any sense to you, you're probably a regular at the Ponta Linga Linga.

So we were sitting there at the bar, just talking a little, and that not
much, when the guy came in. He was just a guy, not especially tall,
head shaved bald, but he was wearing a kind of oversized shiny tracksuit and that attracted our attention. It was shiny purple and he wore it
with new white Nike trainers, so he looked like a drug dealer. Not a
real drug dealer, not a Joburg drug dealer, but like in a Spike Lee
movie or a rap video. I'd guess we all thought, *Why does this guy want to
look like a drug dealer?*

Cleo looked up from wiping a table and said, 'Sorry, we're closed.'

The guy raised his hands with his palms open toward her and said,
but mock shocked: 'My sister, no!'

He wore a big smile and he said something to her in Sotho or maybe
Sepedi – I know it wasn't Zulu or Xhosa because I know a little Zulu
and Xhosa has more clicks – and she said something back in, I suppose, Sotho or Sepedi, and he said something again and she said
something again and then she let him in.

He came up next to us at the bar. We nodded and he nodded and
Mershen said 'Heita', and the guy nodded again and said ' 'ta'. I could
see Mershen filing that away. Next time, I knew, he would just say ' 'ta'.
The guy ordered a drink and rolled the ice in the glass, looking at it,
like you do.

By this time I had lost interest in the guy, but Rob was squinting at
him and rubbing his forefinger and his thumb together, like he does
when he's trying to think of something.

'Don't I know you?' said Rob. The guy raised his eyebrows.

'I don't think so,' said the guy and held out his hand, and they shook hands so we all shook hands. We said 'Hi, I'm David' and 'Mershen' and 'Rob', but he didn't say his name, which I thought was a little bit odd, even then.

'Didn't you work on *The Early, Early Breakfast Show?*' Rob persisted, still squinting. 'Don't I know you from there?'

'I'm not in television,' said the guy, which made me like him even though he was wearing a shiny purple tracksuit and – I could hardly believe it – around his neck in the open V of his tracksuit a gold chain with big gold links. Now, I'm not trying to be funny, but come on.

'Oh,' said Rob. 'I thought I knew you from *The Early, Early Breakfast Show.*'

Then I knew he was very drunk, because Rob doesn't ordinarily like people to know he was involved in producing *The Early, Early Breakfast Show. The Early, Early Breakfast Show* was not a success. People laughed at it, but not in a good way. Rob always said that it was the only TV show in the history of TV shows that never got any of its producers laid. It never actually got anyone involved with it laid, which is unusual because in my experience it's not how good the thing is that gets people laid, just whether it was on TV.

So we sat there and drank some more of our drinks. The guy finished his and ordered another with a hand movement that I thought was very cool. Some people are cool – I'm not, and Mershen isn't really and Rob only is sometimes – and this guy was. We didn't say anything for a while, mainly because we'd run out of things to say.

Finally Rob said: 'Are you sure you weren't on *The Early, Early Breakfast Show?*' Weren't you the guy who dressed up like a piece of toast?' and the guy shook his head with what looked like honest regret and said, 'Sorry.'

'So what do you do?' I asked, to keep the conversation going.

'You should be on TV,' said Rob.

The guy just smiled and shrugged and took another sip of his drink. He gulped the first one but this one he sipped. I noticed he had a gold watch. I hadn't seen a gold watch since my father's gold watch. The guy noticed me staring at it while I tried to remember what my father's gold watch looked like.

'Nice watch,' I said.

The guy nodded and smiled again. He was a good smiler, it was an easy smile.

'You're not a drug dealer, are you?' said Mershen all jokey, sitting next to Rob, furthest from the guy.

The guy threw up his hands like he did with the waitress. 'I'm not from Nigeria,' he said and we all laughed, also him.

'Pity,' said Mershen and we all laughed again.

We finished our drinks and debated whether we should have another and I said I had to work tomorrow but then the guy ordered drinks for all of us, again just by moving his hand. Ordinarily Cleo likes to pretend she hasn't seen hand movements, especially late at night when she wants to go home, but this time she served up. We looked sneakily at Cas to see if he would object but he was leaning across the table, speaking low to the girl who'd once seen one of his plays. He was touching her hand with his finger, making a point, and I heard him say something – I swear – about deconstructing bourgeois conventions. He glanced at us and looked a bit embarrassed, not because he was touching the hand of a girl who wasn't his girlfriend, but because he thought we might have heard him say something about deconstructing bourgeois conventions. Then he lowered his voice even more.

When a guy buys you a drink you should make some conversation with him, but we didn't really know what to say. I was about to say to Rob, 'Why did someone dress up like a piece of toast?' just for conversation, like, when Rob said to the guy, 'So if you're not in TV what do you do?'

I thought the guy might get annoyed but he just smiled again, big and easy, and turned sideways to face Rob.

'I do jobs,' he said.

'Jobs?' said Rob.

'Right,' said the guy.

'Yuh?' said Rob encouragingly.

'Yuh,' said the guy.

'What kind of jobs?' said Mershen. It wasn't like any of us to take such an interest in what a guy did for a living, but this guy had a way that made us curious.

'Jobs,' said the guy again.

'Jobs, like . . .?'

The guy smiled into his glass then he raised it to his nose and sniffed at it.

'I kill people,' he said.

I wished he hadn't said that.

In the silence that followed I thought maybe I hadn't heard right, but then I felt a little lurch in my stomach and I thought, *I don't like this guy.* I still think that.

I don't know if any of us really wanted to say anything more, but when someone says something like that you can't just ignore it.

'What sort of people?' said Mershen.

The guy smiled kind of proudly. 'Anyone,' he said. 'All kinds.'

I'd had enough of talking to the guy in the shiny purple tracksuit. I don't like that kind of joke. Outside I could hear the car sounds of Seventh emptying and I remembered I had work to do tomorrow and I started to feel tired and my clothes smelt of cigarette smoke.

'Whoever I get told,' said the guy.

'Fuck off,' I said to that, half like a joke and half meaning he should fuck off. But Rob and Mershen seemed to find him funny.

'You're a hitman?' whooped Mershen.

The guy shrugged again. Besides smiling, he was also a frequent shrugger.

'So you, what, you get told to, uh, to, uh, to *whack* someone,' said Rob, and I don't think he was believing him, but you could see he really liked using the word 'whack'. 'And then you – what? – you go and you, you *whack* them?'

'Then I go to his driveway and –' he made a gun shape with his forefinger and thumb and jerked his wrist to indicate the recoil. 'Like a hijack.'

By now Mershen wasn't finding the joke funny either. He frowned and leant back on his stool. But Rob, gee. Rob was drunk.

'So do you know these people?' he asked. 'Who you whack?'

'Not at first,' said the guy. 'But then I get to know them. Watch the house, see when they come, when they go.'

I looked around for Cleo to call for the bill but she must have been outside in the stockroom.

'Sometimes,' said the guy, 'I meet them before.'

'You meet them?'

'Pass them on the street, sure, maybe ask directions. I like meeting them before. To get a –' the guy rubbed his palms together in a circle, 'a feeling.' He looked across at Rob.

'Look,' I said to Rob and Mershen, levering myself from my barstool, 'I'm going to get going.'

'Just wait a minute,' said Mershen, 'we're going too.'

'I'm not listening to this.'

'Just hang on a second, let me finish my drink and we'll . . .'

'Sometimes,' said the guy conversationally, 'I maybe bump into them in a bar.'

If I could I'd just leave this part blank to show the silence then. It wasn't total silence, there was still Cas's voice low at the table behind us and the sound of Cleo clinking bottles out the back and a car going by outside, going by, going home, but it felt like it. It felt like total silence. We looked at the guy, me and Rob and Mershen.

'What?' I said, not friendly.

'Sometimes I maybe bump into them in a bar. Say hello. Buy drinks.' He shrugged and rubbed his palms together, looking at nothing in particular.

'What're you saying?' I felt myself getting properly angry.

He shrugged again.

'No, fuck you, what are you saying?' I said and I stepped toward him so I was standing right over him.

'Dave,' said Rob grabbing my arm.

'Fuck you,' I said to the guy, and my voice was getting louder. *What are you saying?*'

I don't usually get aggressive when I drink and I don't usually want to get into fights, which is good because I can't fight, but I wanted to fight this guy. No, I just wanted to hit him.

'Hey!' said Cas from his table but I didn't turn around, I kept staring at the guy's face although he wasn't looking back at me, I kept staring at him like maybe Joe Pesci in *Goodfellas* or like one of those Latino gang movies with Edward James Olmos, but I wasn't trying to be like in a movie, I was wanting to hit this guy, just hit him, just keep on hitting him until I couldn't see him any more. The guy just carried on looking away, all casual, and I couldn't tell if it was because he was scared or because he really wasn't. Rob stood up between us and said, 'Dave, leave it, leave it,' and he steered me down onto his barstool and he sat down on mine. I looked at Mershen and his eyes were open wide but not because of me. He was staring at the guy.

'What *are* you saying?' said Rob, and although he still sounded drunk he sounded a little bit less drunk.

The guy just shook his head and shrugged and raised his hands again, palms open, like to say, 'I'm not saying anything, I'm just sitting here.'

'So when you get your – your orders,' said Rob, all casual, 'who are they from?'

'A guy,' said the guy, 'who gets calls from people.'

'What sort of people?'

'People who don't want other people around any more.'

'Like what sort of people?'

'People.' His eyes flickered. 'Say, someone who doesn't like you.'

'Me?' said Rob, his voice suddenly very high.

'Anyone.'

I thought this was all bullshit and I said so, I said 'This is bullshit', and Rob looked at me but he looked back at the guy. The skin around Rob's eyes was tight and grey and he was holding his glass so tight his fingertips were white. I hated this. I hated this guy coming into our lives in five minutes and doing this to us, I hated it, because of course it was bullshit, of course it was, but how could you not be scared, this guy in his purple tracksuit, this guy?

'So what do you do after you've bumped into them in a bar?' said Rob softly.

'Sometimes I buy them a drink, and then I go home and then we only meet again one more time.'

'And other times?'

'Other times . . .' the guy pursed his lips then sucked them then pursed them again. 'Other times, sometimes, we make a plan so we don't meet again.'

'A plan, like . . .'

He spread his hands, just slightly. 'I am a businessman.'

'For Chrissake!' I said.

'How much?' said Mershen.

The guy seemed to be counting something in his head. He said, 'Six.'

'Six?'

'Two each.'

'Guys!'

'Is that an offer?' said Mershen.

'Guys!'

'Is that an offer?'

'It's an offer.'

It was a nightmare.

'When?' said Rob.

The guy said, 'Now.'

'My ATM limit is a thousand,' said Rob.

'Me too,' said Mershen. 'And I've already drawn today.'

'As much you can now,' said the guy. 'I'll collect the rest tomorrow.'

'From where?'

'I'll come to your house,' said the guy and his voice and his eyes were very flat.

'You don't . . .' Rob started, then stopped.

'Where you live in Auckland Park,' said the guy to Rob. And then: 'I won't worry your wife,' he said to Mershen.

They just stared at him. Mershen's mouth was slightly open.

'I'll let you decide,' said the guy. 'Five minutes.' He got up and walked out the back door to the little concrete courtyard where the toilets are. He passed Cleo in the doorway and as she came in I asked her for the bill. Behind us at the table Cas and the girl were kissing, leaning into each other, like goldfish. One of Cas's girlfriends once told me he only ever kissed her in public. 'He's afraid of intimacy,' she said. Rob and Mershen were looking at each other.

'What?' I said when I saw this look going on. 'What? You're not!'

They kind of raised their eyebrows and didn't say anything.

'Come on!' I said. 'Some guy walks off the street and says he's been hired to kill you and you give him money? What are you, children? Come on!'

'You're very fucking confident,' said Rob.

'If some white guy had sat down next to us and said he was a hitman, would you give him a second thought? Guys, now, come.'

'I would if he was Eastern European,' said Rob, thinking. 'Like, Russian, or, you know, Bulgarian.'

'Or Lebanese,' said Mershen.

'Or that kind of Afrikaner,' said Rob.

'With blue eyes,' agreed Mershen.

'Joost eyes.'

'So anyone, basically,' I said, 'who isn't white and speaks English?'

'Who'd ever hire us to be a hitman? We'd be fucking useless,' said Rob, which was a good point.

'I wouldn't believe an Indian guy,' said Mershen thoughtfully. 'Indian guys, not really.'

'I don't know,' I said there. 'Those guys in Durban who run the clubs, I wouldn't . . .'

'Are you telling me I don't know Indian guys?' said Mershen, who is himself an Indian guy.

'You're from Joburg, you prick,' I said. 'You don't know them in Durban.'

'Look,' said Rob, 'what are we going to do?'

'We're not giving him fuck-all,' I said. 'This is a scammer. He's an actor. He's the guy who dressed up like a piece of fucking toast, and you want to give him money.' It pleased me to hear the words I was saying.

'He knows where I live, Dave!'

'And that I'm married!'

'You're wearing a wedding ring, you knob, and as for you, if he worked on *The Early, Early Breakfast Show* he'd easy know where you live. You're always slipping home next door from the set because you've forgotten your cellphone or you're fighting with Leigh-Ann or something.'

'You think he planned this?'

'No,' I said. 'I think he walked in for a drink and saw you and thought, "Ha, ha, there's a cunt." I'll tell you this, if you give him money now he's not stupid enough to come to your house tomorrow when you're sober and have thought about it. He'll just go home and laugh with his buddies for the rest of his life about what a cunt you are.'

'But what if it's not me who's his job? What if it's you?'

I wished he hadn't said that.

Just for a moment the breath stopped in my chest, just a moment, but for that moment it was harder to fight down what I'd been fighting down, this big thing, this fear that came from nowhere and made me want to cry or beg or something. This wasn't just being afraid, it was *fear*, like something there, something inside you you didn't know about, not even a part of you, just using you to come out.

'I'm not his job,' I said, 'and nor are you. He hasn't got a fucking job, the fuck.'

I hated the guy in the purple tracksuit. I'm not an afraid person but now this fear, this *thing* . . . I couldn't tell if it'd been there all along and he'd woken it or if maybe it's not from inside at all, maybe it runs through this town under our feet and through our skin and the air like dark electricity and this guy just conducted it, just brought it down and focused it in one place. I hated him for it.

'You're right,' said Rob.

'Fuck right, I'm right.'

But none of us moved. Outside Seventh was dead, the cars were all gone. Seventh is too dark with no people in it, the yellow streetlights aren't enough. I tried to remember the guy's face. If I had to describe him for the police I wouldn't be able to. He was just an impression, a shiny tracksuit, a shaved head, a smile, a pair of spread hands. He was more an idea than a guy.

'You can stay if you like,' I said. I dropped two hundreds on the bar. 'Are you staying?'

Something passed between them.

'No,' said Mershen.

Rob got up too and they left money and we all hurried outside onto the dark sidewalk. We stood there a moment, the three of us, and breathed the air.

'Fucking scammer.'

'Fuck 'im.'

It was dark out there, we couldn't see each other's faces.

'We shouldn't, like . . .'

'What?'

'We shouldn't, like, do something? Teach him a lesson?'

'Oh for fuck's sake, who are we? *Teach him a lesson?* We couldn't teach ourselves a lesson.'

'Right.'

Even in the dark we were looking away from each other, looking at our feet, over our shoulders.

'OK,' I said, 'my car's down there,' and we shook hands like we always do and I took off down the road. I turned at the corner with Second where I'd parked and when I looked back Rob and Mershen were still standing on the sidewalk outside the Ponta Linga Linga. They were standing there, and it looked like they were saying something to each other, then at last they turned and walked together up the road, and I went into Second and found my car and drove home.

It felt good driving home. The lights on the freeway were good and bright and the wide, empty lanes felt safe, like day. It felt good because I'd beaten down the fear. My heart felt light, I thought: *I can live in this town. I've got what it takes.*

But that was a couple of weeks ago and since then my heart's not so light, because the next morning I remembered that conversation I had with Rob and Mershen before the guy came in, about the name of the street and the sign up the road. I remembered that their cars were down the road, the same way as mine, not up the road where they walked. The only thing up the road was the corner café but that was closed, and also the ATM and that was still open. And I wondered whether maybe they'd drawn money so that they could buy a pie from the all-night Shell shop on the way home, or just maybe whether they'd taken their money back into the Ponta Linga Linga.

And I know it's nothing, but I haven't spoken to Rob or Mershen since then, or maybe it's that they haven't spoken to me. I've driven past the Ponta Linga Linga a few times and I even went in but I haven't seen the guy again. And the thing is I want to see the guy again because I know it's just the fear but two nights ago when I came home I saw a blue car parked a little way up the street and I don't know if I've ever seen a blue car parked there before, and although it didn't look like there was anyone in it, still I'm thinking maybe of going tomorrow to my bank in Sandton City and drawing out some money and keeping it on me or maybe in that alcove in the dashboard behind the gearstick because, look, I know it's just the fear, I know it's just the fear but it's two grand, right? Right? I mean, what's two grand? What's two grand, anyway?

You should have called me Narcissus

Nicholas Dall

The walk to the shops is not long and Herman knows it well. He takes a short cut through the park, avoiding the multicoloured steam engine on which he used to play as a child, and waits at the traffic light on Belvedere Road. He lurches over the pavement and taps at the tarmac with his cane. Herman makes this journey every morning and he waits for a familiar hand to help him. Eventually a hand takes his, but he does not recognise it. It is not the hairy calloused hand of Kevin the shopkeeper; nor is it the brittle, veined hand of Mrs Collingwood the estate agent. It definitely isn't the hand of a gardener or a labourer. This hand is soft and cold and its fingers are slender peninsulas. The hand leads him across the road and its owner does not speak as it loosens its grip. Herman clutches at it desperately. The hand has only four fingers and he does not want to let go of it.

'Excuse me, but I'm not going the same way as you.' The woman's voice confirms the beauty of her hand.

'I'll come with you.' Herman forces himself to let go of the hand and he stuffs both of his hands in his pockets, out of mischief. 'I'm not in a rush.'

'I have a hair appointment.' Herman hears the rustle of paper-shuffling. 'It would be very boring for you.'

'Your hand.' Herman takes his hands out of his pockets and clasps them in front of his chest. 'I'm a sculptor.'

'That's great.' She laughs. 'I really need to be going.'

'Don't go.'

'I have to.'

Herman tries to distil his thoughts, to boil off the impurities. 'I have to sculpt you,' he stammers and holds out his hand. 'I'm Herman, by the way.'

She shakes his hand. 'Selena, nice to meet you.'

'When can I sculpt you?'

'You don't even know me.'

'I know, but I also know – '

She cuts him short. 'I don't do this sort of thing. It embarrasses me.'

'Just give it a try . . . please?'

'You're a stranger, how do I know I can trust you?'

'Trust me? All I want to do is sculpt you.'

'Look, it's been really nice meeting you, but I don't have the time.'

'But,' Herman is getting desperate. 'Over the weekend.'

'I'm terribly sorry, but you'll have to admit this situation is more than a little awkward.'

'Yes, yes, I know I'm coming across as a bit of a psychopath –'

'I wouldn't go that far.'

'As slightly odd, then, but it's only because I felt something in your hand that I've never felt before.'

'I think I prefer the psychopath … this spiritual stuff's not my scene.'

'Oh God, it always comes out the wrong way. I know what I'm thinking, but as soon as I try to explain myself it goes pear-shaped.'

'Okay, I'll give you one more chance: what is it that makes me different from everyone else?' Selena is inquisitive.

'It's not something concrete. It's just, what's the right word, a bond. Don't you feel it?'

'I'm an engineer. I don't believe in that kind of thing.'

'There's nothing to believe in, it's just that some people work well together.'

'Why me?'

'There's no answer to that,' Herman feels like he is beginning to sway her. 'Just give me an hour of your time, and we'll see if my hunch is right.'

'What the hell.' She hasn't had someone pay her this much attention since her accident. 'I'll do it.'

Selena is already late for her appointment and they exchange phone numbers and addresses.

* * *

The moonless dark is blacker than blindness. Herman goes to bed but he does not sleep. He rises before the birds, and showers and dresses and waits for her. She arrives at ten o'clock, as promised. They greet one another.

Herman controls the avalanche of confusion and focuses his attention on the act of creation. 'Let's go to my studio, we don't have much time.' Herman allows Selena to lead him up the stairs, but once they are inside he assumes control. He is at work and he will not let anything get in his way. He shows her to a chair which he knows is green. He takes her hand and holds it; rubs it. At first it is rigid, but in time she allows him to squeeze and caress it. He searches for the stump, the point of entry, but finds it missing. The hand has five fingers. He reaches for her left hand, but she draws it away.

'Please . . . my right hand is more beautiful.'

'I don't think so.'

'I can't do this.'

'Please don't go.'

'I don't understand.'

'What is there to understand?'

'Why are you doing this?'

'I know that I will never see you. I only know your hand and the sound of your voice. These two things are all the explanation I need.'

'I speak just like any other girl from Cape Town, and I lost a finger in a construction accident.' Selena stands up from the chair. 'And you think that this makes me more beautiful.'

'But there's more to it.'

'I think you're just a freak.'

'I can hear that you think you lost more than your finger in that accident.'

'Well then why don't you find someone without all of my flaws?' Selena's thoughts race: who does this guy think he is? Okay, he's blind and he's a sculptor and it's all terribly melodramatic, but he can't read my mind. I'm fine, I love my work, I couldn't care less about my finger. And what can he do about it, anyway? Sculpt it back to life? Selena is trained in rationality.

'You promised me an hour. Time is running out.' Herman pushes her downwards, back into the chair. 'Let me try and show you what I mean.' He takes her left hand and tightens his grasp. He runs his fingers along its smooth surface, scrapes over her knuckles. It is cold like soap-stone. He opens her fist and holds each finger individually, memorising the taper and the segmentation, the texture of the skin, the shape of the fingernail. Each of the four fingers is unique: the steep knuckle of the thumb; the index finger which is slightly wonky at the end; the absolute straightness of the middle finger and the lateral scar on the ring finger – a watershed which separates fertile and arid. Herman devotes the most time to the absentee. He does not stroke or rub or knead the wound. He sits on the arm of the chair, hunched over Selena's lap and holds the hyphenated digit in silence. In time, Herman breaks the pose and brings the hand to his nose. He smells apples. Selena has just eaten breakfast.

Selena sits down and Herman finds his way to his workbench. His head trembles as he sniffs the air and takes a piece of soapstone from the crate beneath the bench. He is not in a rush but his chisels are sharp and he wastes no time. The stone seems softer than ever, as if the natural fault lines and hairline cracks are not there by accident. The dark silver blade glistens in the sunlight and Selena's tea is untouched, cold. Herman reaches for a smaller, more delicate chisel. Slowly, quickly the stone becomes her hand. It is still rough, but warmer than its human counterpart, as it accepts the sun's heat. Selena looks at the abrupt gnarl that is her wrist and she knows that she wants to see it become her arm. Herman stops working. He takes the stone and holds it just as he held Selena's hand hours before. The beeping of his watch breaks the dusty silence. 'Selena, that means it's lunchtime.'

'Already?'

'It's one o'clock, my mother will be waiting.'

Selena plucks at words, tries to return to reality. 'I'd better be off then.' She stands and gathers her handbag. 'I'm meeting someone at half-past.'

Herman is too flustered to show her to the door, and he is the first to descend the stairs.

* * *

Selena takes her regulation fifteen days of paid leave and arranges to spend the time with Herman at her family's holiday house in Paternoster.

There is a wind blowing as they pack in a hurry. Selena drives and the wind is even stronger. It is a dry, dirty wind in busy streets. Gradually the roads become emptier and the wind becomes cleaner and they are happy in this distant world. They drive through the bird sanctuary in the West Coast National Park.

'I love this place,' she says.

'I remember it. We used to come here when I was a kid.'

'I haven't been for ages, I always drive past it on my way.'

'We used to come for the spring flowers.'

'You should see the lagoon.'

'Flat and grey.'

'And covered in flamingos.'

'I don't remember the flamingos.'

They walk out to the hide on the boardwalk and are alone in the middle of the water where the wind has stopped blowing. Selena looks into Herman's eyes; or at least at her reflection in his sunglasses. They kiss up against the coarse poles. The flamingos are pink and so are they, but they do not worry for they are in a hide. They drive on to Paternoster.

They do not have the energy to unpack the car properly, as it is laden with limestone (sculptures: completed, uncompleted and not yet conceived); two nine-kilogram gas bottles; and all three of Herman's toolboxes.

They sit in the front garden, overlooking the hard crescent beach and braai the snoek that they bought at the fish market. They share a bottle of red wine.

After supper they unpack the car. For two months Herman has sculpted Selena whenever time has allowed and her busyness over the past few weeks has given him the time to polish and perfect all of his half-finished projects. They are laid out on the floor and Selena, the complete article, lies next to them. The earliest fragments – her hand, elbow, torso and hair – are joined by new recruitments: a brittle balsa-veined ear, a diagonal swathe from breast to coccyx, and a mahogany navel. Selena has seen each item individually, but this is her first chance to appreciate the entire menagerie. Herman is more than a mirror, more than a mountain pond's reflection. Herman sees, creates, her as perfect.

He sits in the box armchair behind her. 'What shall we sculpt tonight?'

Selena is in no doubt. She stands and places her naked left foot on the arm of the chair. She takes Herman by the hair and eases his face towards her foot. When his nose makes contact with her toes, his hands rush to join in. Selena closes her eyes and allows herself to be sublimated by his attentions. She has always loved her feet: so small and so pink. She loves to bunch her toes and pirouette; to pretend she's five and she needs something from her father. She asks for favours with her left foot, achieves balance with her right. She still buys children's sizes. Her feet will never grow up. Herman explores her foot with his fingers, memorises its bumps and creases; crevices and slopes. The awkward pose does not tire Selena and she holds it for as long as Herman needs. Eventually he announces, 'Get me my tools, and some stone.'

'You must choose the stone,' she objects.

'No, you must.'

'I don't know what to look for.'

'You'll know.'

Selena goes to his toolboxes and gathers the tools that she knows he will need. The apple-crates of stone leer at her and she does not know where to start as she gropes her way through the hunks of grey and black. She shuts her eyes, and allows herself to feel the grain and the sinew of each piece. Her hands settle on one right at the top of the crate. It doesn't shine at her like a thumb-sized nugget in a prospector's pan, but she thinks she has found the piece. She takes it to Herman.

He holds it and inhales its powder. 'I told you you'd know.'

They say no more and Herman gets to work. Surely this is love: the silence of the night broken only by the sound of steel on stone and wave on shore. Two people who do not need to speak to be happy. They say that is what love is. Herman tries to purge the memory of Selena's foot, but still his hands move. He is a conduit for the stone's reformation. He is powerless to resist.

Selena never shifts her gaze. She watches as the stone becomes her foot: a physical and emotional replica. Herman sculpts a foot that could only be hers. Bunched asparagus toes, archless sole, creased heel, voice of a pleading child. He understands the personality of her beauty, could converse with every part of her body. No one can feign this.

The last words they exchanged.

I don't know what to look for.

You'll know.

A blindfolded search.

I told you you'd know.

They know. Time sinks to the bottom of a swimming pool and they too are submerged. It must be late when they get to bed. They do not make love but they sleep like they have.

* * *

The next morning Selena rises early and takes the completed sculptures into the garden, one by one. She strains under the weight of some of the larger pieces – in particular an abstract representation of her tangled hair, and the polished ellipse of her torso – but she does not rest until they are all on the lawn. She arranges them in a circular shrine that overlooks the beach.

She enters the shrine – picking her way between her left elbow and her right shoulder – and sits at its centre. Surrounded by her fragmented self she takes stock of events. The sculptures remind her of her beauty and give her peace. She is grateful to Herman for having forced her to reconsider, for making her understand that there is more to life than an obscene salary and a company BMW. She has not had a boyfriend since her days at UCT and she knows now that she was never in love with any of them. The shrine proves that Herman loves her.

* * *

They sit on a log on the beach, and are silent for a long time. Eventually Selena slaps the log and speaks, 'Could you sculpt me out of this?' Selena is afraid that she has asked a stupid question.

'What's left for me to sculpt?' Herman laughs. Over the last few weeks he has sculpted her tirelessly.

'You could sculpt all of me.'

'I could try.' Herman lifts Selena from his lap and crouches next to the log. He runs his hands over the log which has been rubbed smooth by the sea. It is as long as him, and there is a round knob at one end which must have been a branch once. He is still for a long time. The sun has set and he has not said a word. He rubs his face against the damp wood. It smells of the sea. Selena is happy to be quiet. Herman is at his most handsome when he is working: she does not even notice the scarring around his eyes or the roots of his black hair which are visible through his pale skin. 'It might well do,' he announces.

'Great.' Selena rushes to embrace him. 'We'll get it tomorrow.'

'Now,' he insists, 'I want to sculpt you now.'

Selena remembers that the darkness means nothing to Herman.

They drag the log up the beach and into the lounge. It dirties the carpet but they do not care. Selena lies on the floor next to the log, resting her head on her hands. She is at once angelic and alluring. Herman lies beside her and his hands move over her body like ghost crabs when the full moon is out. They scuttle frantically, stopping irregularly to excavate and explore. Their beach is camouflaged by irritating clothing and they claw and scrape at this. Selena is soon naked. Now the crabs are unhindered and they travel. Over the white mussel shells which are her shoulders, through the corrugated dune valley of her back, around the neat sandcastles of her bum and lower to her bow-shaped driftwood shins. He knows her body so well. Far better than any man who can see. But still he rubs and smells and feels her for hours. He suckles her ear and inhales the smell of her neck. He massages her scalp and untangles her hair gently. He traces the shape of each of her ribs and kisses the sharp twin peaks of her pelvic girdle.

Neither person says a word and they do not have to. Finally he gets up and begins to sculpt. Selena is comfortable in spite of the cold stone floor and she does not move. Her body remains loosely curved, neither outstretched nor bundled up.

Herman starts at the smooth end of the log and he sculpts her feet. He loves her feet almost as much as she does. Selena's eyes do not shift as he chips away at the desiccated wood. She waits patiently, transfixed, as he replaces his chisel with a sharper one. He moves up and onto her shins, her thighs, her mesmerising navel. He has never sculpted so much of her, and Selena shivers with excitement as she watches herself grow from the bottom up, like a plant. Her replica is brittle and pale: smooth, bubbling marzipan. Her breasts take shape and they gleam in the lamplight. He sculpts her nipples like bloated dog pellets, and she lowers her eyelids in surprise. This only serves to confirm his accuracy. The log tapers, towards the creased knot, to form her neck, and she waits for him to move onto her face. But he sculpts her hands instead, taking special care with her left hand. He has always loved it more than anything else about her. The log lies in the middle of the room – lifelike and life-size – apart from the rough knob which rests on her hands. Herman stands up and Selena realises that he has finished. When she looks at the gnarl it is even more beautiful than her face.

Selena drags herself along the smooth polished tiles, to her wooden counterpart, and kisses it on the bursting split which she imagines to be its lips. She presses her nipples against the wooden dog pellets and brings her maimed hand round to shelter in the small of its back. While she lies there she can hear Herman putting his tools away. He never breaks this routine.

His voice plucks her from the embrace, 'Let's go to bed.'

She moans in agreement, and strokes the sculpture along its length as she first kneels and then stands. She kisses Herman and hooks her thumb into the back pocket of his jeans. They walk up the stairs so attached, and Herman undresses and gets into bed. He waits for Selena as she closes the curtains. The moon is about to set over the ocean. Selena does not bother to put her negligée on and she clambers on top of Herman and strokes him through the sheets.

'Herman. I love you.'

'I love you too, Galatea.'

'You're too kind.'

'I'm not.'

* * *

The sun has not yet appeared over the hills and Selena sits in the middle of her shrine. She can no longer avoid the thoughts that have been gathering like storm clouds: she is bored by Herman, she has nothing to say to him. He's still sleeping, as usual, but it's even worse when he's awake. Ever since he sculpted her for the last time, he's been nothing more than a self-satisfied lout. He sits around the house, content in the fact that he has created what he terms 'the sculpture I've always dreamed of'. It *is* amazing. She can't deny that. But that's not the point . . . you can't just give up on your life's ambition at the age of twenty-five. She knows more than ever now that she's going to go back to university and finish her PhD. Whatever it takes, she'll do it. She's not going to waste away. Maybe it's just the fact that he's got so much talent which he isn't using that irks her. Maybe they're just very different people. But she knew that all along, that's what attracted her to him in the first place. She always saw him as her rock, as a solid landmass that she could tether herself to. Now it seems as if he's sinking ever deeper, and he's dragging her with him. She knows he's proud of her, and he keeps on telling her that he loves her. When they first met she remembers being attracted to him because he had a thirst to understand her completely. Now that he thinks he has achieved this, it leaves her dissatisfied. He has reaffirmed her beauty, but he has taken it no further than that. Now that she feels beautiful again she needs more than an unfailing admirer.

* * *

For once Herman wakes early and he is not surprised to find that Selena is missing. She often goes out into the garden and sits amongst the sculptures. He takes his cane, and taps his way down to where the sculptures lie. He picks his way though her dismembered body, and heads straight for the wooden sculpture. She loves to lie next to it. He taps, but can feel only grass. He sits there, bewildered, for what must be hours. When he feels a hand on his shoulder he leaps to his feet.

'Selena sent me.' It is his father's voice.

Herman is too confused to say anything.

'She sent me to fetch you,' his father stammers, 'Said it would be easier that way.'

'What?'

'She's already packed your things.'

Kiwela

Dinis F da Costa

Kibala is a small township, located in the centre of South-Kwanza province, Angola. The physical environment is surrounded by five rivers, all well known, famous for their contribution towards the 1975 independence of this same territory, themselves killing hundreds of foreign troops who tried to force their way to town.

The land is fertile, peaceful and quiet. Calm like the spirit of *Zambi*, the only treasured and venerated god of Kibala's tribe. The land is tranquil like the Longa's river, the killer river, bloody river; unblessed, possessed by the evil spirit of Urubus. Was Kibala quiet, peaceful like the Puimbuije River of miracles?

Was it really the land of Zambi, the life-giver? Or the land of the evil spirit of Urubus, the life-taker? Or yet, the land of the soldiers who came from nowhere, who had no respect for tribes, for humans? No love, no mercy for civilians, no fear for Zambi. Was Kibala a peaceful land, a place to live in?

It was early in the morning, a very hot and uncommon morning, just like the last two days when the inhabitants could not sleep, fearing to be ambushed again by the soldiers.

Everything was strange in the village: the weather, the trees, the flowing of the river, the people, even the birds no longer sang their morning songs.

Kiwela was tired, for almost a week, he had not slept at all, and if he slept, it was just for two hours or less. That morning his mother had gone to the farm before the sun had risen, with a group of five women and two men, vigilantes who were carrying their weapons behind them. They had left before the village was awake. Of his father, he had few memories. He had left the small township of Kissequel – the town where they lived before – a few years after his birth and now the boy was nearly sixteen years old. He knew nothing of his present existence, whether he was alive or dead.

What he knew was that he was the eldest of the three children of his parents; he had to take the responsibility for younger sisters, and the whole family, to protect them, in whatever circumstances and situations, at any price.

Silence reigned over the whole township; everybody was sleeping or just quiet, fearing the ears of the enemies.

He looked at the moon, read it: 11 pm more or less. He went to the toilet outside the house and came back, running like a wild bull, fearing as well as his neighbours to be caught by enemy soldiers. He was still dressed the same as the day before, in red and black shorts of the Angolan flag, of the material that his father had brought the last time he was at home; material that the tailor cut in pieces and made a shirt and shorts for him and a skirt for a younger sister.

As he tried to reach the bed, suddenly he heard soldiers running and shouting: 'The enemies are close!' Afterwards, he rushed to the room where the family were sleeping, and woke his mother who seemed not sleeping at all. Quickly, they packed a few things: food and clothing, and waited for the second orders.

Unexpectedly, they heard the first bomb falling in the neighbourhood not far from their house and that noise broke the silence of the village. Then they heard the second bomb and then the third and so on . . . With each explosion, many houses were destroyed and families killed. Nothing else was heard in the village, only the sound of bombs, shots and the distressed voices of the mourning people. The vigilantes passed from home to home recruiting young people to join their fight against the enemy. Once they got into his home, his mother stared at him waiting to see his response, and started crying inconsolably, and shouting, 'Don't go, my child!'

For a while he listened to her words, but once the vigilantes had gone, he went into the room, stretched his small hands under the bed; he cautiously grabbed the dusty and heavy weapon that had been resting there for a couple of years. His mother was there, behind him, still crying, as if that would stop Kiwela from going to fight. On the other side were sitting two little sisters, frightened, staring at him, at the weapon in the hands. They watched it innocently, wondering what it was for.

He had learnt from Fr Sergio how to shoot, to protect themselves from the frequent attacks. And his mother had known her son could shoot since the day he hunted a rabbit. Firmly, he grabbed the AK 47 – printed made USSR – in his little hands, and after he had wiped off the dust, courageously moved toward outside, like a real soldier. When he closed the door and moved in the direction of the other vigilantes, a bomb hit half of the house and blew away the thatch. Then, he rushed back home, and, sadly, found his family dead. Only his younger sister was alive, half alive. She was bleeding from the neck where a sharp piece of wood had stuck. In spite of much effort to try to stop the bleeding and remove the wood, all attempts failed: his sister had gone, with the saints, to the faraway lands of Urubus, perhaps to the nearby lands of Zambi.

It was nearly morning and soon the sun would appear, but the crying of people, the sound of bombs, and the music of vagabond bullets seeking victims were still being heard.

Outside, he looked at the sky as if wanting to speak to his God, he threw away the weapon on the grass, and slowly walked inside the house, where he sat close to his family's corpses, all resting on the traditional mattress woven by the older women of the village; woven with love, respect and skill, the gift of the most powerful Zambi.

They had all bled: fresh blood, red blood; red as the sunset. He sat listening to the sounds of bombs, waiting for his death; and fearlessly slept on it, until the morning came with the sunshine.

He had not kept his promise to protect his family, his people.

Is he a coward?

No, a coward doesn't wait for the sunshine, to go out and fight. A coward, at least fights for his own life, for the life of his people and of the beloved.

Talking about a beloved, where is his lover, his sweet love?

'Where is Cass . . .,' he couldn't pronounce her name, for the first time since they had made love, meaningless love, in the Puimbuije River, the river of miracles, the river of lovers. 'Where is C-a-s-s-i-n-d-a?' he spelled every letter, cautiously, with all the sweetness that a man could use to capture a lost love. And as soon as he finished, the easily-spelled name of eight letters, he burst into tears.

Is she dead or alive? Is she in need of his help? Possibly to rescue her, like in the legends or long stories, true stories. Legends told, under the moonlight and burning fire, where a man like him, a hero, rescues his lover and they end up together, eternally, forever. Bravo!

Suddenly, he forgets the corpses and manages to escape from the house. He wanders around the village, vigilantly observing his steps, watching for an enemy or a landmine.

While he walks, his small bushman eyes meet bodies, lying on the dry ground, burning at 40 degrees, drying like biltong.

He sympathises with a child of three months, resting next to her mother, a young mother of seventeen, naked. He knows her very well; it is his cousin Samba, the child of aunt Marcela. Further away lies the body of a man, he recognises him also. He is, Lushipa, Samba's husband. A recently married couple, both dead, but he doesn't touch the bodies. He doesn't stop either. He is tired of touching bodies; he is tired of mourning, of crying. By now, his aim is to reach Cassinda's house and, as he gets closer to his destiny, he sees many bodies on the streets, in the broken houses. He has been counting internally but has lost the number: there are too many to count.

Many dead people, not a single person alive. Is she alive? He doesn't know. He knows that the more dead people he sees, the more he loses hope.

Where are the other people of the village? Are they hiding in the bush, and is Cassinda with them? Or are all the village people dead?

No, it can't be. There were always people who escaped when the soldiers attacked the village, but he also realises that the soldiers captured young boys to be trained as fellows, and young girls to satisfy their sexual desire, the desire of a soldier, sweaty, smelly; yet, heavy like those corpses put together.

The more he thinks of Cassinda being dead or being held by the soldiers, the faster he walks. He reaches the house made of red clay; no cement to strengthen the house that is half ruined. He enters, without bothering to unlock the door. He searches for her in every corner but the house is empty, quiet like the whole village. Quiet like the dead bodies that he saw on the streets.

No sign of her parents or of her, beloved wife-to-be. He panics; he calms down; he senses that she is not dead. She is alive in need of his help.

He sees marks of boots and shoes on the reddish sand and is sure that those tracks are not of his people. They are of strange boots, a soldier's boots, and he decides to follow the tracks.

He is very good at tracking spoors, of animals, of men. He follows, walking five hundred metres away from the village and then another eight hundred. He is more patient than before, more confident.

He reaches the savannah bush and loses the tracks, but further away he sees trampled grass and continues his search. He carries no weapon, no food.

Does he need a weapon or food?

I don't think so. He doesn't need food to eat; Kiwela is full, fed up.

He doesn't need a weapon either, because he is not there to fight but to claim what belongs to him, to claim his wife-to-be, Cassinda: a well-made face, long face, goddess of Kibalas with long hair which is uncommon in the tribe. Her nose is flat, flat as her stomach; her breast stiff, alive, sharp, tasty. And the black nipple celebrating virginity could drive any man, any spirit, and any sacrosanct spirit to craziness. Yet, she is 1,70 m tall, taller than Kiwela. She shows no sign of being fat or thin; a body you can classify perfect. She is a woman: you worship the ground she steps on.

He squeezes the bush with confidence. He fears no one. He knows the flora and the flora knows him, he speaks the language of the fauna and the fauna speak his. As he approaches the Puimbuije River, he sniffs like *inja* and crawls like a chameleon. He makes no noise as he draws near Cassinda, surrounded by three black men and a white man. He is not surprised.

Backed by the tall grass, he manages to come closer, five metres away from them, and his eye sees Cassinda, clearly.

Cassinda is naked, and he watches as the white man removes impatiently the multicolour necklace which adorned her chest and hid the pleasant breasts. The two men are holding her hands from the back like a prisoner on the way to jail; she is standing with her legs wide open, tied to two short trees. The third man bends her body over without mercy. The three healthy soldiers are dressed in civvies; all with a white, dirty T-shirt and black pants, their heads are covered with black caps with the golden emblem of the Angolan army in front, and a flag at the back. He can't see what type of shoes they are wearing but he can see the weapons resting at their back.

As he crawls another metre, he notices that the white man is Fr Sergio, the Catholic priest who has lived in the tribe since Kiwela was small. He is loved, admired, worshipped in the tribe. But now he is a bastard, a Portuguese bastard. *Porra.*

Although he had learnt everything about God from him, he has lost all his respect. His first god was Zambi, but now he is worshipping another god, the God of the white man. *Bastardo.*

Like a dog on a chain, he stood there, chewing his anger. If he were a dog would he bark and rip to death the rapists of his lover?

He fantasised himself being a lion or a leopard, attacking, and killing. Bravo!

Unfortunately, he was not a dog or a lion or a leopard. He was a sixteen-year-old boy, a hunter, but in his culture he had been a man since the day he braved the long knife of circumcision, sharpened by the power of his ancestors. He braved the cold, blood ritual: months in the bush hunting for himself, despite being in severe pain.

He braved the cold mornings when he had to go to the river, immerse his penis in the blessed water of Puimbuije River.

Was he really a man? What kind of a man was he, to watch own people dying and now his lover, and fuck off?

As the last man is satisfied, he withdraws from her, pulls up his pants with enthusiasm, 'Hush!' and walks to the river. He drinks four handfuls of water and comes back.

Kiwela is still watching. Is he enjoying?

Bastard, coward. Cassinda or any other person could call him so; laugh at him until the lungs were out, like the lungs of those corpses lying in the village, drying like *bacalhau* fish.

Kiwela is still observing, scrutinising like the UN peace forces.

At last, his eyes see what he never wanted to witness again: Fr Sergio goes for another turn. Within two minutes, his desire is satisfied. The desire of a priest, a man who for many years devoted his life to serve and not be served, to please and not be pleased.

He smiles, exposing his yellowish teeth, rotten with age. He was fifty-nine; thin, no beard, no moustache, hair trimmed; he was Cassinda's height. He was still dressed, neatly, in his black and long-sleeved shirt, handed to men ordained to priesthood. He was wearing brown shoes and navy blue trousers. He looked younger than his age.

He is fulfilled, after many years in the world of celibacy. He never, never knew about pulling down his pants and feeling desire, the sensation of sexual intercourse, the emotion of being in another world. He only pulled down his pants to pull out the dirty water, the urine. He never knew how strong was the reaction of climax, which makes all bones in the body tremble, like a volcano in eruption. This is his first time, he is happy, satisfied. And he thinks it is time to get moving, perhaps, looking for another woman, another virgin.

Fr Sergio looks at the heavens, prays the common prayer 'our Father . . .'. He doesn't finish; he makes the sign of the cross, of the holy trinity and then kisses the wooden crucifix hanging on his neck. Next, he pulls off the weapon from the tallest soldier and dispatches Cassinda's soul to rest. 'Throw the body in the river,' he orders them.

'God bless her,' he adds.

The mission is over, accomplished with satisfaction. They start moving in the direction of the sunset.

Kiwela runs to the river and retrieves the body. She is still alive and as she sees him, she smiles. She wants to say something, but before a word comes out from her mouth, she is dead.

Did she want to say that she loved him or that he was a coward?

He is apprehensive. Desperately, he tries to resuscitate her, in vain.

He thinks the spirit of Urubus or Zambi has taken her away.

From then . . .

He worships God no more, he loves Zambi no more. He decides to sell or offer – as you wish to call it – his soul to the bad spirit, to venerate evil; unblessed spirit, killer spirit.

He waits for the night, for the moonlight; and when the moon emerges he sacrifices a pig, a chicken, to the spirit of Urubus.

For the sacrifice: he lights the fire, and in cold blood, he cuts the throat of the poor animals. Then, as he watches them dying, he catches the blood.

Mentally, he compares the death of the poor animals with the death that he is planning for the four men. Not ordinary men, they are killers, rapists and devils; worse than Urubus. He imagines all of them dying, begging for forgiveness, crying with pain like those animals; dying slowly. He smiles with delight and fury mixed together.

When both small, clay pots are full of blood, he drinks one pot without a break and anoints his weapon with blood. The process is not yet finished: he climbs the mountain and as he reaches the peak, he drops both animal corpses, and cuts off a nail from his right foot, then opens a small cut on his right arm and lets some drops fall on the corpses.

At the fireplace, he strips and dances around it; singing, jumping, and praising the spirit of Urubus. In an unknown language he calls the Urubus, '*eme kamona*'.

Before the moon died at dawn, he was an Urubus, possessed by the most powerful evil spirit. He feels it, he is happy.

He followed the whole process without a minor error; he did it, as his grandmother taught him; grandmother, the most ever respected witch who existed in Kibala. She died at the age of 72, killed by a grenade, a grenade of a soldier.

He dreams of the bad spirit, warning him, instructing him to attack only on a rainy day.

He waits for the rain's day and . . .

Today, Kiwela is wearing his best robe: a piece of lion skin is covering the genitals; the piece is held by two thin strings that meet at the back. His feet rest in the brand-new leather sandals, brown, decorated with red and white beads. His left hand is holding a bow, while the arrows rest inside a light, round container. And three guys who survived the massacre are dressed like him, carrying machine guns. Bravo!

Today, Kiwela is well dressed, and if his mother were alive, she would praise him, sing hymns for him, and dance for him, like the last time when he came home with a lynx. Small boy to kill a lynx, alone: he must be a man, a brave man.

But, today Kiwela is not dressed to kill a lynx, or a rabbit. He is dressed to kill men.

Today is going to hunt men: black men, white man, who had no respect for his people.

Will he forgive Fr Sergio, the man who taught him everything he knows?

Will he forgive him and have mercy on his soul as Jesus did to his persecutors?

Forgive a man who knew him since he was small, taught him the Bible, and yet, raped his beloved, and sent her soul to the grave.

As he studies the direction the soldiers went, he follows the tracks, difficult to read because of the rain. But, he knows the bush and the bush knows him.

Out of the blue, they can see the four men and the four men can see them. 'Do they have the spirit of Urubus, to know that we were coming today?' Kiwela throws a strange question that dies unanswered.

During the battle, they manage to kill one of the soldiers, killed brutally, first by the poisoned arrow followed by stabs, and when they finish with him, the animals party, until no bone is left. And now they are no longer using the machine guns, they are using knives to kill them. Playing monkey games in the trees, they panic their adversaries, who can't stand the heavy rain and the strong thunder. Fr Sergio is afraid of the thunder, of the rain, he is afraid of everything, even of his own shadow. He thinks his and Kiwela's God is punishing him, for his deeds. And when he watches another soldier being killed, he runs under a spreading tree.

Didn't he know that in that land, the land of spirits, when it is raining you can't stand under the tree?

He starts to pray. He prays one Hail Mary in Portuguese, and in the middle of the second one a lightning bolt cuts the tree into two and, sadly, a heavy piece falls on top of him. He cries for help. '*Ajudem-me por favor*,' (Help me please) and he adds again, '*Ajudem-me pelo amor de Deus*' (Help me for God's sake).

Kiwela comes closer to him: he looks at him, disgusted, studying his face with anger as he imagines him making love to Cassinda.

Will he kill him, help him, or leave him there, to feed the Urubus and the rest of animals that he respected?

He doesn't touch him; he leaves him there, stuck on the ground. He knows that soon the animals will notice him, have another party with a strange meat.

The third soldier runs out for the sake of his life, is running without direction like a man possessed by a demon or sheep without a shepherd.

Why is it that sinners fear for their lives, but take other people's lives with pleasure and even with celebrations?

As he runs, Kiwela and his men draw a plan, and out of the blue. Kiwela was in front of him, waiting for him, with a sharpened knife; sharpened with the power of an evil spirit.

As he turns backwards to escape, a knife enters his throat and blood escapes like lava. Instantly, he drops on the floor, fighting for his life. He rolls, but slowly he loses strength until he moves no more.

Mission accomplished. Kiwela wanted to say these words to his friends but instead he held them within and smiled at them, with satisfaction.

On their return, he takes his own route, in the direction of the cemetery where he had built a tomb for his lover, according to his custom. He got inside without difficulty and sat next to the corpse embalmed with palm tree oil. He is talking to her although he gets no answer.

He knows that soon he is going to lose his soul and die. It is the deal he made with Urubus, to give his soul to him once the mission was accomplished.

Early, he recognises that he has sinned against both gods: his and the white man's God. And for the sake of his soul he kneels down, prays for half an hour and rests next to his lover who seems to be looking at him with pride, with satisfaction.

If she were alive, she would have kissed him, praised him, danced for him, made love with him and called him: *my hero.*

Still life in the art room

Liesl Jobson

Ufudu is restless today,' says a boy under his breath. He rinses a sable brush in a jar of water.

'Ufudu indeed!' grumble the scissors on the shelf.

'Silence matrics,' says Miss Dube.

Yesterday the name given affectionately to the art teacher by her students suited her ponderous tread. Today she moves like a plover with jerky steps. She stops statue-like with her head cocked, as if listening to a half-heard sound.

'Go awaaay!' The cry of a loerie outside startles her. She stalks to her desk rapidly.

'She's probably dieting,' says a girl.

'Ufudu needs a man,' says another.

'These children show no respect,' murmurs a charcoal drawing stick.

Sikelela was the first to comment on the teacher's obsessional doodles. Shortly after she had returned from compassionate leave he passed her desk and saw a page half filled with caricature turtles. When he left the class an hour later the page was almost completed. The next day a new one with identical figures had been started.

'You really like tortoises, Ma'am,' he had said.

'Hmmm,' she nodded, flipping the pad closed.

'We should call you Mam'fudu?'

'Hmmm,' she nodded again.

Dalila did not point out that what she drew were turtles, not tortoises. There is no single word in Zulu for the former, only an extension that approximates: ufudu-lwaso-lwandle or the tortoise-of-the-water. The name, which did not bother her particularly, stuck. Dalila was relieved that the boys and girls had noticed only her eccentric drawings and not the hollow yawning that had recently begun to emanate from the collection of empty jars under the sink. The youngsters also appeared not to have heard the rattling complaints of the palette boxes in the cabinet, the restless canvasses and the shuffling sketchboards.

Perhaps these sounds were lost against the scraping chairs and the grinding of the old-fashioned pencil sharpener on her desk. Maybe the stuffiness of polyester blazers worn too long without laundering dulled the children's senses.

Each day for almost a year, while her students have worked, Dalila has doodled to pass the time: serried ranks of the ancient reptiles marching eastward toward an imaginary shoreline beyond the page.

Her compulsion had started a few days before Sikelela's observation, when she presented an easy lesson to the class two weeks in a row.

'Today we're going to do the 'Take-a-line-for-a-walk' exercise. Who knows which artists developed this style?' Dalila spoke like she moved. Grief had dulled her speech. A girl with unruly dreads raised her hand before the teacher had finished asking the question.

'Refiloe?'

'Klee, Ma'am.'

'Good, Refiloe. Another artist?'

'Miro,' answered Salmaan.

'Yes,' she said, switching on the overhead projector.

'There are two ways of accomplishing this exercise. The first allows an abstract line to take shape freely. Allow it to curve, to zigzag, make corners, and so on, wandering all over the paper.'

She demonstrated the technique. In contrast to her plodding diction, her hand whizzed over the screen.

'Now shift the page until you see something that you recognise.'

She swivelled the transparency around.

'Perhaps an eye, a claw, a skeletal tree. Develop it. Add more pattern.'

With rapid gestures she filled in leaves like eyelashes, feathery bones, beaks.

'Keep going until the whole page is covered in detail.'

It was the last time her hand moved swiftly, unselfconsciously for many months.

'The other way of performing this task requires planning to create a specific image. It is more controlled, a bigger challenge.'

She put another transparency on the overhead and drew the tail of a turtle, raised the hump, formed the head, the flippers and lower carapace. Without lifting her pen, she entered the shell cavity interweaving three rows of scutes. Lastly, she created a diminishing spiral to form the eye out of negative white space.

'Try a waterfall, a skyline or a garden. Whatever you do, keep your pen on the paper.'

Most of the class had already begun while she was talking. She had forgotten that they already knew and liked the exercise. She switched off the projector and put away her felt-tipped pens. She drew another turtle and another. On completing a row of turtles, Dalila wandered through the desks to check her students' progress. She stopped a boy who was about to erase his work, 'Keep going, Bhuti,' she said over his shoulder. Pointing to an empty space on the next boy's page she said, 'Keep it loose and free; don't think too hard.'

She returned to her doodles. The bell rang. The students gathered their pencils and sauntered out. After they had left, Dalila completed an entire sheet of inch-long turtles. She put the page in the bottom drawer of her desk, the first page of identical scribbles that would accumulate for a year, until thousands of the miniature beasts crawled around her desk, scraping their flippers, yearning for release. When she first heard them it sounded like the erratic slowing down of the overhead projector fan after being switched off. She opened the drawer and the noise stopped.

Today is the first anniversary of her mother's passing.

'No cartoons today,' hisses a flat pencil.

'Where are the turtles, Ufudu?' taunts a coloured pencil.

Dalila drums her fingers on her desk. She chivvies the daydreaming Refiloe who stares out the window. She complains at Salmaan's dithering. Ten minutes before the final bell, she hurries them along, 'Finish up, Bhuti, don't start another colour.' 'Put your folio away. Now,' she snaps. 'Have a nice weekend.'

As the last one leaves, she flips over an empty bucket. Dalila reads the label stuck to the bottom. Powder Tempera: light green. The colour of hospital walls. Residues of poster paint ingrained in the plastic release a faint odour of sour dust. She places it, upside down, in front of the window. Usually she constructs still life compositions on a plinth in the centre of the room. Today she needs a different perspective.

Dalila removes a faded kikoi from her tog bag. She holds it to her face and inhales deeply. Her mother brought it back from Nairobi, a few weeks before getting ill. Her open suitcase had released the fragrance of grassy plains, Kenyan shillings and Watamu Beach, where Dalila lived as a child.

She had walked beside the water holding her grandmother's hand. They found a strange depression in the sand.

'Look, a green turtle nest,' said Bibi. 'Turtles lay their eggs then leave them to hatch.'

'Does their mother not stay with them?' Dalila asked.

'No. The hatchlings must dash toward the surf before the gulls catch them. Only the lucky ones make it into the sea.'

'To search for their parents?' asked Dalila.

'To continue the cycle of survival.'

'Do they ever find them?'

'Turtles don't really think that way, although they return here throughout their life.'

'Back to Watamu?'

'Yes. Eventually the females will lay their eggs right here when they are 40 years old.'

'They come back looking for their mothers and fathers,' said the girl.

'Hmmm.'

'Bibi?'

'Green turtles live to be 90.'

'Bibi, what happens if the baby never finds her parents?' Dalila tugged on her grandmother's skirt.

'Hmmm.'

Dalila had already learned that when Bibi said, 'Hmmm' in that mournful tone, the old woman had no reply. It served no point to ask again. There were many questions for which Bibi had no answers, including why Dalila's parents were gone so long. Bibi didn't know where they were. Perhaps they attended a congress in Dar es Salaam or a conference in Botswana, or were sneaking in and out of South Africa. They never told her. It was safer not to know too much.

That night Dalila dreamed of the unfortunate turtles, hatched late, flopping in vain against the outgoing tide. They were almost at the shore when hungry gulls plucked them from the sand, their flippers swimming in midair. Dangled low over the water, the babies could see their parents. Then the gulls swooped to the beach where they cracked open the shells and gorged on the rich meat. Dalila woke sobbing for their futile struggle.

Bibi cradled her, rocking her back to sleep, crooning, 'Harambee, Harambee, tuimbe pamoja. Tujenge serikali. Harambee.'

She sang slowly, in the key of blackness, of dark spirits. It sounded like a song for harvesting snakes. The next morning the news arrived that her father had opened a letter bomb in Lusaka.

Dalila pinches her nostrils and blows hard. Her ears pop. Her sinuses feel as if she has been weeping for a week. She wonders if she is becoming allergic to paint. The theme of the lesson is identifying environmental and historical factors that influence visual artists.

Sikelela had brought an mbira, the traditional 'herd boy's piano', Refiloe had brought a bunch of leggy strelitzias. Salmaan provided a flag for the backdrop and Diwali candles. They constructed an eclectic collection of paraphernalia for the project. An exhibition of the work is planned for the Heritage Day celebration and the president is scheduled to visit the school that his grandchildren attended.

'Here we go again,' sighs the bucket.

'Must we endure another plastic snake?' mutters a thin yellow stripe woven into the kikoi.

'Be quiet,' says Dalila, sniffing. She will not tolerate the voices today. Like the matrics, they pay her little attention.

'You should stick to porcelain dolls,' says the bucket. 'You like their gingham frocks and lacy petticoats.'

'We haven't seen dolly for a while,' says a cerise stripe.

Dalila's grandmother had always sewn her party dresses, western style, in pastel shades. Bibi made matching dresses for the dolls from the left-over fabric scraps. Peering through her bifocals she formed delicate stitches. Then she would braid Dalila's hair in satin ribbons of the same shade. Dalila tried to braid her dolls' straight blonde hair.

'White children's hair doesn't braid that way,' said Bibi. She asked Bibi why porcelain never came in shades of brown or black.

'Hmmm,' said Bibi.

Dalila drapes the kikoi over the bucket. It has softened with washing. Once she could still smell traces of her mother's scent in the cotton and a faint whiff of the crisp herbal beer her father had allowed her to sip when she sat on his knee for the last time.

'No, Mandla,' scolded her mother. He laughed at his daughter's lip-smacking enjoyment, and then whisked the bottle away. Dalila tucks the cloth, which possesses only a clean laundry smell now, about the base of the bucket. She arranges the stripes to fall in zigzags.

After her father died her mother would walk along the beach with a kikoi wrapped around her thin hips. She had always been a round and comfortable figure. She stopped eating until clothes hung on her angular form. Her mother sat and stared into the horizon for hours, alone. Dalila would watch her from afar. The next breeding season, a record low number of eggs was documented by Turtlewatch Kenya. Dalila's mother's grief had scared all the females away. They refused to lay.

There is a shushing sound in Dalila's ears, like the sound of waves inside a seashell. She tries to depressurise her nasal chambers again, but there is no relief. The turtles in her drawer are scraping their flippers. She places the pot plant on top of the bucket. Sunlight reflects off the finely demarcated green and white leaves.

Dalila had taken a slip of the hen-and-chickens from her mother's balcony garden when the flat was sold to cover the doctor's bills. She left the cutting in a bottle of water. When it took root, she transplanted it into a large ukhamba, a traditional Zulu beer pot she bought at the Rosebank market.

'Those shocking shades will quite outdo me.' The pot plant glares at the bold kikoi. 'My delicate stripes will be utterly lost.'

'Hen lady, chill your sphincter,' says the bucket.

'How uncouth,' says the plant.

'What a nerve!' says Dalila clucking her tongue.

She runs her fingers over the elaborate patterns of the ukhamba. They are Iron Age motifs that have been incised into the dark clay. She wishes she had a banana frond to frame her composition, but Johannesburg's winter frost burns the tropical plants. There were banana groves around Gogo's kraal.

Dalila has a vague recollection of visiting her paternal grandmother in Gingindlovu before her father fled into exile. Gogo tried to teach her how to twist sticky coils of clay over bunches of grass to make an ukhamba. Dalila must have been about six years old. She never saw her Gogo after that. Her cousin Zodwa terrified her with bedtime stories about green mambas.

As they walked on the muddy path to the long-drop toilet, Zodwa screamed, pointing into the grass beside Dalila's feet, 'Snake! Be careful!' The first time it happened Dalila wet her pants and ran, crying, back to her father. Zodwa disappeared, sniggering, into the long stalks of sugar cane, with the village girls. The second time, her father comforted her saying, 'Gogo has a mean stick. It will talk to that naughty Zodwa.'

This morning as Dalila sipped her first cup of coffee an article in *The Star* grabbed her attention:

GABORONE – The remains of Thami Mnyele were exhumed on Wednesday from Gaborone's New Stands Cemetery for reburial at home. Mnyele, a gifted graphic artist, was one of twelve ANC cadres killed by the South African Defence Force in a cross-border raid on 14 June 1985. His artwork had been deliberately destroyed in the attack. This soft-spoken gentleman with a passion for poetry and music will be buried in Tembisa after a memorial service at the Mehlareng Stadium.

Dalila took the newspaper in shaking hands into her tiny garden to gather herself. On the wooden bench beside the lemon tree, she stared at the shocking words that recalled her indebtedness to Thami Mnyele, the kind uncle she met once at Beitbridge.

She had just fled South Africa in a hot, gritty train with her father. They were both tired and thirsty from the long journey. Her father had an important meeting with a stranger who arrived with two cans of cold Coca-Cola. Her father gave her a pen and an empty envelope to keep her busy.

'Draw me a picture of Mama,' said Mandla.

Dalila stopped interrupting the men. She drew a tiny train snaking around the edge of the envelope. In the centre was a little house. Her mother waved from its window. She had remained behind to keep her father's cover and to sell their few belongings. Uncle Thami noticed the girl's picture, and reached into his briefcase. He brought out a pad of paper and some pencil crayons. At the time she thought he was trying to keep her from disturbing them. But he had taken the drawings she offered him. He admired them, praised her, and remembered.

A few weeks later, Uncle Thami sent her the gift of her first set of paints. She remembers the slip for the parcel arriving. She and Bibi stood in a queue at the post office. She had wanted to open the parcel there and then, beside the counter.

The post office clerk exchanged friendly words with her grand-mother and gave Dalila a toffee. That was the time when brown paper still had a sweet rustle to it, when string and sealing wax bound prom-ises of love, of hope. A package meant then that one had not been forgotten, after all.

A few weeks later her mother appeared unexpectedly and bled into the long drop. When Dalila went to relieve herself she saw clumps of blood that caught the sunlight that shone through the cracks in the tin roof. Dalila stared at the livery chunks in horror.

Dalila tried to understand the whispered fragments she overheard as she pretended to sleep.

'Is this Mandla's child?' asked Bibi.

Dalila couldn't see in the dark whether her mother nodded or shook her head.

'Does he know?'

'He must not,' said her mother.

'How often?'

'Every night for two weeks.'

'And what else?'

Her mother had only stifled sobs for an answer.

'Is Mama very sick?' asked the girl the following morning.

'Don't worry,' said Bibi. 'Your mother will be alright. These are old screams your mother is passing. They will go. When a woman's screams get stuck inside, her sisters have ways to set them free . . .'

An old woman from the village rubbed her mother's belly, pressed cool cloths against her forehead.

In the garden this morning, Dalila clutched the newspaper. The deep purple irises growing beneath the lemon tree reminded her that the previous winter she had been visiting her mother in hospital. That last day she took her mother a bunch of irises in a Heinz bottle. On the previous occasion when she had taken flowers, her mother's favourite vase had been stolen. It had been a wedding present. Perhaps a cleaner or a nurse recognised the fine crystal. Nevertheless the flowers and the vase had disappeared. While driving to the Kenridge, she had sniffed the subtle fragrance, wondering whether it was real or imagined. It was so slight she doubted she could smell anything, yet the tomato sauce smell had vanished.

In the ward she wiped her mother's face with a warm cloth, she brushed her thin grey hair. Her mother whispered in the oxygen mask. Dalila couldn't hear.

'Pardon, Mama, what was that?' she asked, bent close to her mother's mouth. Her breath was rapid. It smelled fruity.

'You are a good girl; you are my blessing,' said her mother.

Dalila picked a single stem with a bud, an unfurling bloom and a fully opened flower. She placed it in a twist of silver foil with a blob of moistened cotton wool. A sudden yearning to paint the filigree fronds of its yellow tongue pecks now at the inside of her heart. She remembers the tiny beak of a green turtle poking through the last egg at the bottom of the nest. An angry gull had hovered overhead as it struggled free. She chased the bird away.

She had urged the baby on. The gull swooped and dived above. Dalila shouted at it flapping her arms.

'Hurry, little one.' She faced her grandmother, 'Why, Bibi?' Tears streamed down her face. Dalila wanted to pick it up, to carry it to the sea.

''If you carry that baby, it cannot develop strong flippers for swimming. It will be too weak for the ocean.'

'It will never get there . . .' Dalila sobbed. She chased the gulls away, over and over again, until the tiny turtle slipped into the waves.

Beyond the curlicued wrought-iron school gates, a queue of children waits at the bus stop. Sikelela and Refiloe disappear into a rickety taxi headed for Soweto. A lemon rolls off the table. Dalila catches it.

'Your roots smell off,' says a stripe.

'Too much water,' replies a clump of leaves suspended over the edge of the ukhamba on a curling runner.

Dalila blows her nose. Through the window, she watches the learners climb aboard.

'Isn't school out?' asks another stripe.

'No peace unto the wicked . . .' says a lemon.

Dalila had shown her mother the striated throat of the iris. The old woman lifted a frail arm to touch its indigo petal, and then removed her oxygen mask.

'Let me smell it one last time . . .'

Dalila wanted to say, 'No! Not one last time. Let me take you to the Kirstenbosch gardens next holiday.' She wanted to ask, 'Will you be my guardian angel?' but they had never talked about death. She would have liked to say, 'I am 40, Mama, but I have laid no eggs . . .'

Dalila had neither words nor tears. No question lingered in the folds of the hospital curtains. Not a tear fell onto the pale green linen. Dalila readjusted her mother's mask in silence.

That evening she had tried to paint her mother's hand holding hers, but all she had to show after empty hours was a blank sheet of paper. That night, and every day since then, her paint box remained still. Nothing else let up: the chatter of desks, the prattle of chairs, the mumbling of the classroom blinds. Even the kiln in the corner of the art room would sigh periodically. In her drawer the pile of turtles waved their flippers in agitation. But neither the pastels nor the oil paints made a murmur. The blues: pthalo, cerulean and sapphire all remained silent. Ultramarine, turquoise and Virgin blue lay like miniature coffins in her paint box. The flat and round sablette brushes lingered soundless; the sablines immobile.

Dalila unclasps the long string of pearls her mother wore and drapes them over the lemons.

'Beats a plastic snake, I guess,' says the yellow stripe.

'Pearls,' says a lemon in an irritable tone. 'Not very good quality.'

'Hush,' says Dalila. The pearls slip and clatter on the tiled floor. Dalila picks them up and curls them around the base of a tomato sauce bottle containing the irises.

'Why can't we be juxtaposed against a simple urn?' asks the plant, glaring at the shabby vase. Dalila chews a hangnail and rearranges a lemon. She plucks a blob of Prestik from her stationery drawer to fix the pearls in place. She removes a little package wrapped in paper towel from her tog bag. She places it, unopened, beside the composition. The pearls glint in the sunlight.

Dalila's mother had pulled the plastic mask off and said, 'Take this away.'

'No!' Dalila tried to slip it back over her mother's face. The mask came apart from the oxygen tube. The bottle on the wall bubbled loudly. The papery skin of her mother's cheeks was greyish against her dark blue lips. 'Not yet . . .'

Her mother turned away from the mask. 'I don't want it any more. It's killing me.'

Dalila opens the package, takes out the oxygen mask and sets it beside the largest lemon. The mask, which is shaped like a ghoulish nostril, has a faint green tinge to it. She tries to identify the exact sheen: copper resinate, viridian, verdigris, cobalt green. As she turns it in the light, she recalls the many-hued shells of the baby turtles.

'What next?' ask the pearls.

'Who can tell?' answers a stripe.

Very softly, the kikoi starts to hum, 'Harambee, harambee . . .'

Dalila's ears are finally clear. A loerie in the tree outside her classroom window calls, 'Go awaaay.'

Her mother had gasped, 'Take me home. I don't want to die here.' The old woman tried to get out of the bed.

'Okay, Mama,' said Dalila as she cradled her mother in her arms. With her free arm, she pressed the button that called the nurse. She wanted to ask her mother whether home meant Watamu Beach, or the little flat in Yeoville. She had no words to discuss the options.

'I want to lie beside Mandla again. It's been too long.'

'Shhh, Mama, shh,' she stroked her mother's hand.

'Where will you bury me?'

'Watamu . . .' she said to soothe her mother, to calm her down. Dalila still believed, even then, that there was a chance her mother would improve enough to be taken back to the village of her ancestors.

The hospital bills precluded that. Her mother lies in alien soil at Westpark Cemetery, where scraggly oleanders drop toxic pink blossoms onto her grave and the grass has been sparse all year long.

Dalila wipes the textured paper with a damp sponge. Her movement across the easel is swift and focused. She blends the underwash in a palette cup with a wide hake brush. At last there is silence in the room. She forms a streak of colour, and another. When she looks up again, the loerie is perched on a branch. Its crown fans out. The large grey bird lifts into the air and flies off. The only sound is the wind in the leaves.

Flowers for her

Pier Myburgh

You should always try to be considerate to others when you try to kill yourself. There are so many things to think of, like who will find you, what you will look like and who will clean up the mess. Then of course you also have to consider what method to use, and if you have the right equipment. I guess you don't really want to think about how it will feel.

Mom made her lamb stew for the last time when she was wearing her special red and white halter-neck dress. I could smell the roasting onion all the way into my bedroom and I knew she would be cutting away the fat, keeping only the best pieces of meat for the stew. When she added red wine to the pot, I almost looked forward to Dad coming home. Mom was a terrible cook, but she could do this one dish really well. She saved it for special occasions.

'How would you feel if we had another baby?' she had said to me that morning. I told her it would be great. I could have told her how scared I was that this baby too would not come home from the hospital. I could have said that there was already not enough of her to go around for the rest of us, and that she should be happy with the two children she already had. 'Maybe it will make Daddy happy,' I said.

As always, Dad came home at six thirty and went straight to the study. He switched on the radio.

'Julia!'

I could hear the buzz and crackle as he flicked from one station to another.

'Yes, Dad,' I said.

'How many times must I tell you, this radio is not a toy. I will not have you listening to your nonsense on my radio or anywhere else in this house.'

He found the classical music station, and after a while I could hear him typing. He always used only two fingers, and the keys beat an odd rhythm against the *Smooth Classics* he so adored. Every night was the same. He would work and listen to his music until just before seven. Then his most favourite programme *Think On These Things* would give him his thought for the day. Only after the news headlines would he switch off the radio and go to the dining room, where we would all be seated at the table, candles lit and food dished up, waiting for him.

But tonight Mom had made the lamb stew, and she had her dress on and she had something to tell him. She wore her hair up, because that's how Dad liked it. She never wore make-up, but tonight I'm sure her lips looked a little shiny.

I could see Jack eyeing the vegetables on his plate. I hoped he would not spoil our evening by trying to hide his peas under his squash again. The last time he did it, Dad got really mad. He did not let us waste food. He made Jack eat it all.

'Put it in your mouth! Now chew. One two, one two. Swallow. Again!'

Jack cried so much that night that he couldn't chew and swallow quickly enough. The spit came out of his mouth like green globs of glue. It was disgusting. We all just sat there with our empty plates in front of us, watching Jack. I remember how the candles made funny shadows on his face. We always had candles. Mom said they created ambience.

Well, we were all sitting ready, with Mom looking pretty, when Dad said, 'I can't eat this, Jane.'

'Are you not hungry?' Mom asked.

'I've decided to become a vegetarian.'

'You've what?'

'I'm a vegetarian. God did not mean for us to kill animals and eat them.'

Then why did God make it smell so good, I thought, and tried to sneak a piece off my plate without Dad noticing. It was strictly forbidden to eat before Dad had said grace and taken his first bite. But he had more to say.

'When God said "Thou shalt not kill" He was not only talking about other people, you know. You have to kill to eat, of course, but you have to choose the lowest form of life.'

'And does your god choose the lowest form of life when he does his killing?' she asked.

He slapped her so quickly, I almost did not see his arm move. She probably should have known better than to talk back to him like that. Dad had found God two years ago and they were now a team. He always said that you can beat anything when God is on your side.

I could see Jack wanted to cry and gave him my meanest 'don't even think about it' look. He was only four, but I was already eight, and understood lots of things. He started to bawl anyway. Mom looked at him as if she was thinking about putting her arms around him, but instead she just walked out the door.

If you have two children, it would not be considerate to shoot your-self. Firstly, you can't put the gun away safely when you're done with it, and everyone knows it's dangerous to leave guns lying around the house. Secondly, it would create a big mess, which would be tricky for children to clean up, unless you do it on a Wednesday when Sanna comes in to do the big cleaning.

The next morning, I found Mom sitting on the top step of the stoep, smoking a cigarette. She was still wearing her pyjamas with just her old sweater with the hole on the left shoulder thrown over them. She drew the smoke in really deeply. She'd given up smoking two years ago, and always said how she was feeling so much better for it. Her lips were not shiny anymore. The car was gone, so Dad must have left for work already. Somewhere inside the house, I could hear Jack shooting some bad guys with the toy gun Dad had given him for his last birthday.

'Hi Mom.'
   She didn't answer, but I sat next to her so that she would see that I was a big girl and that I could be her friend. She just stared down at the step and kept on smoking. We sat there quietly for a while, and then I saw a little black spider crawling past our feet. It was very tiny and not at all something to be scared of. You could almost not see its legs. When it came into my shadow, it curled itself into a tiny ball. I thought of flicking it away, but then my mother took her cigarette and put it out on the spider. 'Let's get dressed,' she said. 'This morning we're going to buy flowers.'
   She strapped Jack into his pram and put on her red coat. I could've sworn she was wearing some light red lipstick. Her hair was loose and it made her face look really pretty. She didn't look like a mom you would want to hit at all.
   I walked really close to her and stuck my hand in the pocket of her coat. I could still smell the cigarette on her, and hoped she would stop smelling like that before Dad got home. He did not approve of smok-ing. I wondered if the butt was still lying on the stoep all squashed up where she had left it. Jack started to sing 'the itsy bitsy spider' song, as if he knew what I was thinking.
   'Shut up,' I said.
   'Don't you speak to your brother like that, young lady,' Mom said. 'In this family we treat each other with respect.'
   Right. It was cold outside, but the sun was shining and I could almost hope that it would turn into a beautiful day. Mom was walking too fast for me, as if she couldn't wait to get to the shop, and I had to

really stretch my legs to keep up.

'Which is your favourite flower, Julia?'

'Roses,' I said, because I couldn't think of any other kind. We did not often have flowers in the house, unless you count the dry arrangement on top of the fireplace. Dad did not like real flowers. He said they were too expensive and died too soon. Since Mom had the last baby, Granny sends us flowers once a year, but they are not happy ones. They always make Mom cry and then Dad gets really cross.

I had never been inside a florist before. It was beautiful. It smelled slightly damp and slightly sweet. 'It smells of life,' Mom said. She must have been talking to herself, because I didn't know that life had a smell. 'Look, Julia, the hydrangeas are the same colour blue as your and Jack's eyes. Let's buy them.'

'I'll have four stems,' she said to the saleslady. She put her hand on her stomach and then she turned to me. 'One for each child.' It was the first time in ages that she mentioned the other baby to me. The one who didn't come home. She looked really pretty with the red coat on and the blue flowers in her hand and her eyes looking at me, like I was her friend. That made me feel very happy.

She asked me to push Jack home. The flowers were wrapped in crisp brown paper, tied together with twine. She cradled them in the crook of her arm and the little blue flowers brushed her cheek as her steps fell into rhythm with mine.

It is very inconsiderate to hang yourself. It is a horrible thing for children to look at. We all once watched a Western on the TV and saw how they hang people from the trees. Mom and Dad tried to close our eyes, but I still saw it and I know Jack did too, because he had some very bad dreams for many nights afterwards.

When we got home, I put the four stems in a vase and carefully cleaned up the water around it. I tried to smell the life in them, but they had no fragrance. Mom sat down on the carpet with Jack, with her shoes off, and built blocks, stacking them, until the tower teetered, hesitated and came crashing down around them. Then she read me my favourite story and I could see she was trying hard not to show how much it bored her.

There were absolutely no smells coming from the kitchen when Dad got home that night. He went to his study all the same and when he came to the dining room, filled with his thought for the day and the news headlines, we were waiting for him with the candles all lit. The four stems of flowers stood neatly in the centre of the table. I got out a box of Chocos and some milk and gave us each some. I thought it was okay, because the box said it showed how much Mom loved us, but I was not sure Dad would see it that way. At least Jack would be happy.

Dad sat down, looked at his plate and then at the flowers. 'Let us say grace,' he said.

'Dear God, we thank You for our food to eat and ask You to forgive us for being wasteful and frivolous.' Then he got up, took the vase with the flowers and threw them in the garbage. The glass shattered as it hit something solid in the bottom of the trash can, and I could just see the little blue flowers stick out from under the lid. The water splashed everywhere. Two of the flower heads had broken off and lay there on the brown linoleum kitchen floor, winking at me. Dad wiped his hands on his shirt, turned around and stepped on the one flower as he walked back to the table. Then he sat down and ate his Chocos as if it were quite a normal thing to eat for supper.

No one said a word. Mom just sat there with her back straight and her eyes seeing nothing. When we left the table she was still sitting like that. I went to give her a hug, but she did not move. She must have eventually gotten up and cleared the table. She must have washed the dishes and set things ready for breakfast. I think she came into my room to say good night, but I was already sleeping and maybe I was just dreaming.

It was cold and grey outside when I woke up. Dad was shaking me saying, 'Julia, where is your mother? Did she tell you where she was going?'

I got straight up and shouted, 'Mommy,' although I already knew it was a stupid thing to do. The house was dead quiet. I went around in my bare feet, opening all the doors as if I was looking for a missing sweater, or a cat that was accidentally locked in. Dad just followed me around. He irritated me, but I let him be. He was still wearing his blue flannel pyjamas and his hair stuck out in all directions. He looked like Jack, but his face was covered in grey stubble, and he suddenly seemed so old. He smelled sour of sleeping. All the time he said, 'Where is she, Julia, where can she be?' I wished he would shut up. Downstairs, the kitchen had been tidied up, and three places were set for breakfast.

When I opened the front door, the cold air hit me like a fist in the face. I saw that the trees were bare and that the leaves on the ground had lost their colour. The stoep felt icy under my bare feet. The windows of our car were all frosted up and I could not see inside. It was not a car of any particular description. Dad had bought it, because it was one of those reliable, economical cars that every family should have. I heard the low, soft humming of the engine and did not need to see the hose that was stuck into the exhaust, to know.

'Sweet Jesus, Julia, what has she done? What have I done?'

My father clung onto me from behind. He was so heavy, I struggled to stay upright. He hung onto the railing of the stoep, and we slowly slid down to sit on the top step. I saw that the cigarette butt still stood all bent where her fingers had squashed it, and thought of the crushed spider. Dad's mouth was wide open and I could see his yellowed teeth. I knew he was screaming, but he did not make a sound. Then he put his arms around me, pressed his head against my chest and I could feel his sobbing. 'Oh, dear God, oh, dear God,' he said over and over. 'I killed her. Julia, did I kill her?'

I instinctively put my arms around him and held him tight. I probably should have said, 'It's okay, Daddy.' I should have stroked his hair and put my face against his rough, wet cheek. I could have told him that we'd be all right. But suddenly I also wanted to crush a spider. I wanted to stamp on a snail, or to squash a bug with my fingers.

I pushed him away. 'Yes,' I screamed. 'And the new baby!'

He did not say anything, but when he looked up at me his face was contorted and ghastly, and I knew then that he had understood.

I went to the car, ripped the hose out of the window and let it flop uselessly at my feet. The blue towel that was neatly pressed into the gap at the top came undone and hung from the window. I opened the door. It did not smell at all like the inside of a florist. I held my breath so that maybe I could one day forget, and turned the ignition off. I left the door open for my father to see and walked passed him up the stairs, to wake up Jack.

Mom knew she could always count on me. Jack's room was still dark, and I left the curtains closed. I kissed him on his cheek, softly, just like she used to do. He opened his eyes and closed them again. I held him tight, so tight. I didn't know that I was crying, but I saw the wet of my tears on his cheek. Jack would be so sad if I cried. So I stopped.

Homing pigeons

Maxine Case

Mr Peterson's body is small and wiry. People say that he looks like an angry, underfed rooster. His house is directly opposite Ma's. Although Ma and Mr Peterson have been neighbours for years, they are not what you'd consider friends. When they see each other, they greet politely enough; exchange the usual pleasantries, but no more than that. Ma says that Mr Peterson is not our class. When I ask her what she means, she just looks at me. But then again, Ma says that most people are not our class.

Mr Peterson had spent most of his working years toiling as a deliveryman for Sunrise Bakery. Every morning he would get up way before dawn, long before Ma's chickens would stir. You could hear him whistling 'Pedro the Fisherman' in the dark as he pulled his old, faded green Datsun out of his driveway. He would drive all the way to Elsies River to collect his huge bread truck laden with basket upon basket of hot loaves of bread.

Whenever I saw a bread truck passing I would crane my neck, hoping to catch sight of him. I never did see Mr Peterson in his truck since his route was far away in 'the townships'. By the time I came home from school in the afternoon, Mr Peterson would be at his usual place on the long, wooden bench on his *stoep*, sucking on his pipe, sipping his tea sweetened with Gold Cross condensed milk from his saucer.

Yes, he knew very well that Gold Cross cost a little more, but it was the one luxury he afforded himself. And so Mr Peterson sat on his *stoep* and watched the world pass by, every afternoon until five o'clock when Mrs Peterson summoned him to the supper table. On weekends Mr Peterson drove brides in their wedding cars. The extra money Mr Peterson made from the weddings he saved separately in a special account at the Post Office. Everyone knew that he was saving this money so that he could go overseas one day.

According to Ma, Mr Peterson didn't have many expenses as he had inherited his house from his late father. 'Now there was a gentleman,' Ma would say, 'so unlike his son!'

'What do you mean Ma?' I'd ask.

'His father fought in the war,' Ma would answer with a faraway look in her eyes. 'In Italy. Some people say that he had a woman there.

A *white* woman, mind you! Some people say that she had a child from him. A little boy.'

'Really Ma?' I'd ask; thrilled every time I was privy to grown up secrets. But she would not tell any more than that.

Maybe Mr Peterson was saving so he could go to Italy to find his little brother, I mused.

Still, I thought it ironic that Mr Peterson would fly all the way to Italy to find a brother when his sister lived right next door and they had not spoken to each other for years. The funny thing about their fall-out is that no one can remember what it was all about in the first place. No one can remember a time when they were on speaking terms, though. Only a low wall separates the two houses, yet it is never breached. Mr Peterson does not allow his wife and children to greet his sister and her family, which is really pathetic, according to Ma as the two families still attend the same church in which their parents married and in which they were both baptised. '. . . and that is not the way of the Lord.'

Mr Peterson lives with his wife Mavis, his daughter Lizzie and his son Patrick. Also living in the house is Mr Peterson's mother-in-law, old Mrs Arendse. Ma says that Mr Peterson spends so much time outside the house because all the women gang up on him. We address Mrs Arendse, Mrs Peterson and Miss Lizzie as such, but Patrick is just Patrick. People say that Patrick is the spitting image of his father because he too is dark and thin and wiry. I think that Patrick can never look like his father since his face is smooth and not flecked with old acne scars like Mr Peterson's is. Also, Patrick is nice. He smiles and calls me by my name whenever he sees me. Sometimes he gives me a Mint Imperial out of the box that he carries in his pocket. Patrick is always sucking peppermints. Ma says that it is to disguise his breath because he smokes behind the bioscope. She says that it serves the Petersons right since they think they are so high and mighty.

By this, I think that she means that they are God-fearing. Very God-fearing. Our family does not attend church. Not since my mother fell pregnant with me and the minister refused to baptise me because my mother was not married to my father.

Mr Peterson's sister is Mrs September. She is a widow. Her husband died many years ago in a car accident. Her daughters May and June live with her. I call them Miss May and Miss June, just as Ma taught me. They used to give me Marie biscuits out of the biscuit barrel in their pantry whenever Ma sent me over with a message. On Sunday mornings before church, Mrs September plays hymns that wake the neighbourhood as the music cascades from her house. Sunday is the only

day of the week that her front door is wide open. She fears that rob-
bers, Moslems or black men will break into her house, so usually the
door is triple-bolted against such threats. Her curtains, too, are never
open, except for a Sunday when the sunlight streams in as the gospel
music streams out.

Once one of our Moslem neighbours complained about the loud-
ness of the hymns, but Mrs September rightly countered that there
was nothing that she could do about it. After all, did she complain
when she was woken every morning by the *bilal* blasting from the
nearby mosque? On this point both of the siblings agreed. Ma told me
so. I thought that maybe Mr Peterson wanted to go overseas to escape
the silent feud with his sister.

There is another sister. A legitimate one. Esther is the youngest
child and the one with the looks, as Ma says. She lives in faraway London. Ma says that she left when she was very young. In those days if you
wanted to go overseas you had to go by ship and Esther left on the last
voyage of the Union Castle. From this I surmise that she can't be that
young after all!

Soon after she arrived in cold, 'it rains all the time' London, Esther
met a nice young man whom she married after a respectable time. 'A
white man, mind you!'

Maybe Mr Peterson wanted to go to London to see his sister. I had
heard that not only was she beautiful, she was kind. Maybe Mr Peterson wanted to enjoy some sisterly kindness.

Not that *he* was a kind person. I'd greet him brightly whenever I saw
him as I had been taught. Sometimes he'd reply with a forced 'good
afternoon girlie'. Most times, however, his reply was more like a snarl,
'hernuff'. The children of the neighbourhood knew better than to
allow our balls to land in Mr Peterson's garden, which was not really a
garden. It was nothing more than a bare patch of sand. Granted, a
neat, meticulous patch of sand, but Ma said that Mr Peterson did not
have the patience to tend a garden.

'When *old* Mr Peterson was alive, that garden had the tallest dahlias
in the whole of Wynberg,' Ma would say. 'He used to give me bulbs to
plant. That son of his,' she said, gesturing in the direction of Mr Peterson sitting on his *stoep*, 'dug up the garden after he died.' With a cyni-
cal smile, she added, 'Maybe he thought that it was a waste of water.'

'Yes Ma,' I agreed wisely.

Ma says that Mr Peterson is so rude because he is a miserable man.
Maybe that is why he wants to go overseas where no one knows him
and his ways.

It seemed that the only things Mr Peterson really had time for were his pigeons. He built a large, wooden pigeon coop at the back of his house. Every evening right after supper he'd go there to feed them.

Everyone knew that Mr Peterson hoped to race his pigeons one day. Some evenings my Uncle Edgar would sit with Mr Peterson on his *stoep* listening to his stories of winning a great pigeon race and, of course, his trip overseas that he would take one day. Through the lace curtain covering Ma's bedroom window, I would watch the two men in animated conversation as they discussed the virtues of the various breeds. And the perils and wonders of overseas travel, of course. We got most of our information about Mr Peterson from Uncle Edgar. When he came home after sitting on the *stoep*, Ma would start asking him questions until she knew all there was to know.

The rest of the neighbourhood was pretty much united against Mr Peterson's pigeons and his pigeon coop. They made the most horrendous cooing cacophony. And the smell if the wind blew in a certain direction, or you happened to venture too close to Mr Peterson's driveway! And pigeons brought rats into the area. Everyone knew that.

The only thing that interested me about the pigeons was how they would unerringly find their way home after Mr Peterson let them fly free to exercise their wings. From our front yard, I would watch Mr Peterson anxiously scanning the sky as he waited for his precious birds to return. I would silently marvel at the precise 'V' formation in which the birds flew as they returned to the roost.

Watching the birds soaring in the darkening sky, I wondered whether they inspired Mr Peterson to fly away.

It took years and years, but eventually Mr Peterson had scraped together enough money for his plane ticket. Our entire neighbourhood was ablaze with the news. It was all everyone spoke about for a long time. The night before Mr Peterson was to fly away, you would have sworn that he was a Moslem man about to go on pilgrimage to Mecca from the amount of visitors he received! Even Ma went over with a plate of *kollewyntjies*.

'How come Mr Peterson is going alone?' I asked Ma. After all, he was still married; his wife was still alive. It was most odd.

'Who knows what that man is up to,' Ma said obliquely, but from the keen look on her face, I could tell that she too was perplexed.

'Maybe you can ask Mrs Peterson,' I suggested.

Ma just rolled her eyes. I should have known better. It was not done to ask such personal questions. Anyway, most people agreed that Mrs Arendse was getting very old and someone had to look after her. That was probably why Mrs Peterson would not be accompanying her husband on his much-anticipated overseas trip.

Mr Peterson's destination was a bit of an anticlimax. It was London after all. The neighbours – Ma included – made unkind comments about this. It had to be that Mr Peterson was too cheap to pay for accommodation in a foreign country. He would be staying with Esther in London. And the gifts that people pressed on him to take to her! Some people say that under the cover of darkness Mrs September left a jar of her famous watermelon *konfyt* on Mr Peterson's *stoep* with Esther's name on it. Other people say that it was jam. I still wonder whether it found its way into his suitcase and arrived at Esther's in London.

The air was still and stuffy the day that Mr Peterson left. A relentless summer's day, but beautiful too. Ma said, 'Trust Mr Peterson to go from the heat of Cape Town to the icy cold of London.' Flowers and people wilted under the burning sun as all the neighbours came out onto their *stoeps* when Patrick drove his father to the airport. We watched as Patrick hefted the heavy suitcase into the old Datsun. Smiled wryly when Mrs Peterson dabbed her ever-present handkerchief to her dry eyes. And of course we all noticed the slight twitch of Mrs September's curtains as she watched the spectacle. None of us could believe that Mr Peterson was finally about to realise his dream. We had to see it to believe it. With a jaunty hoot from Patrick, they were on their way.

As the weeks passed, Mr Peterson in faraway London was soon forgotten. Things were changing fast in our country. PW Botha of the wagging finger had been forced to resign a few months before, to Ma's glee. His position was now occupied by FW de Klerk – not that it meant much to us, Ma pointed out. The 'Nats' were all the same, she pronounced. Yet, now in the new year, there were whispers and rumours that Nelson Mandela, whom Ma said had been in jail for over twenty years, was going to be released from prison. Other people said that our country was on the verge of a civil war.

Then, unexpectedly, it was discovered that there was substance to the rumours after all, when it was announced that several political parties were to be unbanned and that Mr Mandela was truly going to be released. Ma said that it was a pity that Mr Peterson was not here to share the exciting changes. He was a strong supporter of the government. He had gone around to the neighbours to try to convince them to vote in the tricameral elections a few years back, much to Ma's disgust.

Everyone was in a buzz the day that Mr Peterson was due back. Since I was not due back at college yet, I would be able to witness his return. I swept and reswept the *stoep* and Ma kept on delaying watering the front garden until it was quite late. We waited and waited. In those days overseas travel was an occasion and those lucky few who travelled were treated like celebrities.

We all wanted to hear about Buckingham Palace and Big Ben and, of course, whether he had managed to lay his eyes on Princess Diana, whom we all loved. What were the British really like and was it as cold as people said? Of course Mr Peterson was not the kind of man to share such stories with his neighbours, but we knew that eventually all the details of his trip would get around.

I went inside to answer the phone, so I missed it, but Ma said that Mr Peterson barely glanced at his neighbours milling around their front yards. Patrick opened the gates and pulled the car into the driveway, instead of parking it in the street as he usually did.

'Something funny's going on,' Ma intrigued.

'Maybe Mr Peterson's giving himself airs now that he's finally been overseas,' I suggested, disappointed that I had not seen him myself. All I had was Ma's word to go by.

It was Uncle Edgar who told us the story, told to him in dribs and drabs over the weeks following Mr Peterson's return. Apparently the overriding ambition in Mr Peterson's desire to travel was that he longed to sleep with a white woman. Just once, and at any expense. Snowy white was what he wanted. As snowy white as he was pitch black. Actually, not pitch black. He was more blue – navy blue. 'Blue-black' is what Ma thought and she said as much. When he first thought about his desperate need to experience a white woman, it was still illegal to do so. The immorality act was around and was strictly enforced by young, white policemen with flashlights. And there was Mrs Peterson and the church and all that. It had to be overseas!

Mr Peterson had heard stories of women who could be chatted up easily and who did not discriminate against dark, scrawny men with pockmarked skin. Yes, it was easy to get a white woman if you went overseas. The men spoke about it on his bread-route; they spoke about it at the pigeon racing venues; they spoke about it after their tournaments at the darts club. This was the wild yearning that fuelled Mr Peterson through the early mornings as he drove his bread truck. This was what got him through one weekend wedding after another. Visions of creamy white or pale pink pudenda with sparse or prolific blonde or red hair got him through the derision of the neighbourhood, the critical glares of the three women inside his very house and his sister's silent scorn. What man more deserved his ambition to come true than he?

And did it happen? 'Sort of,' Uncle Edgar said with a smile.

'It either did or it didn't!' Ma scoffed.

'Well, the rand is not worth as much as the pound,' Uncle Edgar smiled like the cat that got the cream, 'and when you convert rands to pounds, there is not much and you have to pay for these favours as if they are merchandise displayed in the shop windows.'

'Did he or didn't he?' Ma demanded.

'All he could afford,' Uncle Edgar said wryly and I'm not sure whether he was enjoying this or not, 'was a look at the goods – what after converting rands into pounds.'

'A look?' Ma shrieked indignantly. 'Do you pay to look too?'

'Apparently so,' Uncle Edgar said slowly, twisting his moustache in his fingers. 'Apparently so.'

And so Mr Peterson still goes about his business, ever since he has retired from Sunrise Bakery. He spends his mornings walking to the end of the road and back. He still sits on the *stoep* in the afternoons, sipping his sweet tea from his saucer and sucking on his pipe. He still gets dressed up in his navy-blue suit and white shirt to drive brides around at weekends, although sometimes Patrick does it when the arthritis in his father's knees gets the better of him. And Mr Peterson still has the countenance of an angry rooster, unless of course a plane passes overhead. He rises to his feet and stands to attention as if in the army. He sits only when the plane has passed. People say he is going mad.

The two families, even though they do not talk, still attend the same church in which their parents were married and in which they had both been baptised. Old Mrs Arendse is still going strong if not somewhat forgetful. By the way, Mr Peterson did not vote. He did not allow Mrs Peterson to vote either. He did not vote before 1994, so why should he vote now?

And the pigeons? The pigeons, yes. Some he sold; some he gave away; some died of natural causes. The pigeon coop is empty. These days the door creeks eerily in the late October winds that tease the Cape at this time of the year. The hinges have come undone. The empty pigeon coop is a dismal reminder of a dream that has ceased to be.

Life on the white line

Heinrich J Louw

I once knew a man who was of no consequence, no consequence at all, and consequently, I write you a story.

He stretched out a thin hand towards a closed car window, doors locked. It was a right hand, the wrist supported by the sullied black fingers of a left, and before they came together in this humble position, they were modestly clapped together, twice, rhythmically, in accordance with the traditional approach to fawning. They were attached to a body by the name of Jackson – a nobody by the name of Jackson. A nobody that stood on a white line, in a sea of tar and smoke and cars, indifferent to the flux of the surroundings that defined his existence. His consciousness, for the moment, purely the dim product of alcohol, glue, and the gnawing desire for sustenance.

Attached to the body was a neck, and from it hung his story in vibrant summation: no job, no food, please help, god bless – written with the blackness of coal on the remnants of what was once a cardboard sign in an election campaign, now informing its readers of a different equality, that of a man equated to destitution. Occasionally his advertisement, his new label, would strike a chord of compassion in the god-fearing, a heart and a window would open, a hand extend from the inside and produce profit in the form of change: 'it's all just marketing' says the fat man, artfully.

And yet, in the eyes of many he would stand there as a black hole, a substance emulating empty space, excluded by the selective consciousness of those who do not wish to see, those who blissfully drive, who are briefly vexed by a very faint intimation of conscience, but simply drive on and on and on. They have adapted, evolved, have become accustomed and desensitised, no longer seeing the endless advertisements whilst paging through magazines and newspapers – they are overexposed films, the light, too bright, has blinded them.

Yet there he would stand, in his entirety, waiting for anomalies, man as victim of ideology, or simply, man as victim? The silence between the latter noun and the question mark, the absence of a preposition and its object, miming the cruelty of being. Man in state of nature: life on the white line. And the line between his lips: white-yellow teeth, the skeleton piercing the body, transience shining through. Of that he is a symbol, a symbol unintelligible even to himself, for what he is he cannot understand; he can only bear it through an artificially induced numbness.

So, when sun or rain or life beat down too heavily, he would make his way to a sidewalk or a park where more numbness could be obtained in whichever form feasible. It took him into the night with a degree of strength; it took him to where the fires were made by other insignificants, where there was community, indications of life, but inevitably, no salvation. There he talked and quibbled and slept – there, wherever, he waited for wakefulness to leave him, he waited for the next day, and the next hand, and the next night.

'If you walk over that hill there . . . you see, I once walked over it, you'll see what you've not seen before. I tell you, I've walked there before. There's a big blue dam in which you can bathe, and trees for shade, and at night you can sleep there too. It's not cold. The grass is soft too, there is colour in the flowers, birds (you can eat them), and drink, there is drink if you want. You have not seen such a thing before . . .' he used to tell the insignificants at night. 'Ha, this man, he talks shit,' they would reply.

It was hot, his tongue swollen in his mouth like a dead animal. Speech was undesirable, impossible even, and the mildness of prior intoxication began to wane. Cars sped by as the sun-dulled lights changed colour, and, for the moment, the line was his only sanctuary. He stood precariously, apathetically, a scarecrow in a field, the wakes of moving vehicles pulling at his rags. When most had gone he trudged towards the kerb. A leafless tree cast a thin, stalky shadow onto the concrete; lead-poisoned doves muffled lugubriously in an endless search for nourishment on their baron urban plateau. He slumped down and sat with his calloused feet in the road. Desperately, futilely, he thought: not yet enough to leave for the day, and reality was winning ground over his inebriation. As he looked at his desperate feet, he was nearly sober once more: they ached with such violence – were it only cold, so that they might have gone dead.

His myopic eyes languidly surveyed the area when self-reflection became too burdensome; ennui of mindless lethargy being an equally arduous disposition without synthetic suppressants. Before him was the road, endlessly stretching out to either side, taking the opulent into the city, where they strategically and systematically become more affluent as the sun takes its course across the industrialised African firmament. At the opposite edge of the inbound road arose a long, thin island, a mound, running parallel to this thoroughfare of wealth. And again, parallel to this bank, was the road conveying the significant back to their homes. A magnificent system of input and output, a factory producing subsistence itself, at which a barefooted bystander can but marvel hungrily.

A dull figure emerged from the hedge of dry trees and bushes on the outer edge of the outbound road, yet, a figure of interest, given the tedium of relentless disillusionment. The man came walking across the road and reached the island; traffic had abated slightly. He had a packet in his hand. He was brown. Brown. A white man, browned by life. The hair bleached and the skin, dirty to the flesh, scarred by the sun's persistent rage. Not such an unfamiliar sight nowadays, the barefooted onlooker observed, these brown men, standing on the side of the road, the glorious system, begging for their being. The brown man crossed the inbound road and approached Jackson, the black man, king of the kerb, if then not of his destiny. Such are the privileges of the abject.

A confused 'Ah' was all Jackson could utter when Andries concisely introduced himself and sat down on the kerb, a few feet away. Jackson could not help but stare at the man whose unsolicited arrival undermined his sovereignty as sole observer of this section of the machine. Petulance grew in him; privileges are not prerogatives, it appeared. He resented the complete lack of superiority over anyone, the humiliation with which the complete lack of everything presented him, and the hollow shell that was left – himself. 'Ah' was all he could say – that 'Ah' – an echo imputable to the void inside. He needed drink. But necessity of drink does not precede the availability of money to acquire drink, and accordingly, he could not leave until the late rush-hour on the outbound road afforded him the means.

Silence was the way of the present, as it usually was, but on this occasion it was palpably awkward. He wanted to get up, flee, but there was no destination generous enough to satisfy his wants without charge – simply, no destination. The parks would only fill up with drunken vagrants when the twilight makes way for their revelry – the celebration of successful escape, that escape which is always singular and devoid of the spirit of sharing.

Andries spoke with a broken accent: 'How long have you been here? I've been on the road for two years now . . .' Jackson merely nodded in an attempt at speech. His recollection of life on the street amounted to an eternity, an unthinkable continuation of events not worthy of memory, a quantity not eligible for conversion into years. He could tell that this white man was too amicable to have been homeless for any comparable amount of time. Or, possibly, he was intoxicated. In any event, Andries kept on conversing, in a manner analogous to a soliloquy, recounting the events that brought him to the kerb, at times reminiscing about the contentment that was no more, and at times morosely relating the fateful events of his descent. And indeed, for a wondrous moment, Jackson was distracted from his own predicament – his irritability subsided.

The system spat him out and, consequently, so did his wife and off-spring. Andries was a man with a diminutive house, working hard somewhere in an administration office, breaking even with life. They were commoners, but they had something, a part in the system, and that something was more than nothing. He loved his children but despised his spouse – a position not uncommon for a family man – and the day the system left him to his own devices, so did his wretched wife. His little house was seized owing to payment failure, and the wife moved in with her commoner parents. And that was his life, in summa-tion, a horrendous tale of Western man in his most insipid form, sub-ject to the flux of time in Africa.

Both men sat with feet in the road. Late afternoon was setting in and traffic would soon increase on the outbound road. Andries handed Jackson his packet: 'Have a drink. It will make you better.' He took it and saw a bottle of cheap brandy inside. He took a quaff, and then two more. His eyes lit up. A faint quiver of the lip resembled a smile as the brandy burned him inside, making him feel something akin to alive. His tongue, now moist with liquid, could move once more, like at night, when he tells his stories.

'If you walk there . . . you know, down that road, I once walked there, you'll not believe what you see. I've walked there, and I'm going back there . . . ha . . . soon. You must come and see all the houses there, you can take one for yourself . . . yes . . . take one . . . they have running water, and then you can take a wife. I'm getting one, I must just get everything right. You have not seen such a thing before . . .' he used to tell the insignificants at night. 'Ha, this man, he talks shit,' they would reply.

'You have a family? You don't see your family? Where is your fam-ily?' Jackson asked his companion, with an unexpected interest in the idea of relations. He has no family. Yet, is one not obliged by nature to remain faithful to one's relatives in the case of one having any in such close proximity? Many of his vagabond brothers, if that be an appro-priate term, have families in the rural areas to which they return when circumstances allow it. Indeed, they travel for days to meet their elders and siblings – a journey he has never had occasion for, his lack of kin being the decisive factor. So why does this man not even bother to call on his children? 'Where is your family? Why don't you see them?' Perhaps these brown men think otherwise.

They lived in the poor white suburb beyond the hedge, past the bushes and knolls, where another road took them to the city – the road unseen by the rich. A little house in Genade Street with a green roof and a terrier in the parched garden to keep the outsiders exactly there, outside, is where Andries's family resided. He wished to see his children. He dreamt of arriving there, knocking on the door and showing his children what a worthy man he was, what a redeemed man he was, what a provider he could be. But he wished what he was not, what he could never be, and so, in shame, he walked the streets, like a scavenger, one who picked up the dry bones left by the unrelenting machine of existence. He was the outsider to be kept out by the dog.

The traffic increased as the sun receded for the day, and living became somewhat pleasanter for the kerb-sitters, now less sullen in their endless wait for emancipation, the emancipation that was nothing more than the story of a dream – an eternally deferred freedom that suspended their being. For the moment, forever, they had to beg, brown and black men together, on the white line. They would collect enough money for some meagre nourishment, and perhaps even a bottle of transient refuge. The park would not be cold tonight, and they could drink and sleep and dream, even but for a while. The birds would only come in the morning.

They got up from their seats in the universe, too worn out to stretch, and approached the outbound road in hope of the little money that would realise their wishes for the evening. When the lights turned red they moved into the river of impatient cars, advertising themselves as utterly penury-stricken, pleading with the gesticulation of their trade, and resenting each moment of their desperate act. Brandy will only ever be an imperfect cure for shame, but never one for aversion; it cannot render the dystopic agreeable, only bearable. Thus, they painfully moved from car to car, the hot tar burning Jackson's feet, and the scornful obliviousness of the drivers' denying them being cut their consciousness loose from any sense of self, and smote them into the ever deepening abyss of powerlessness.

But Jackson lived. For Andries, the birds did not come. A car from the right smashed into him and flung his brown body onto the island, metres away. Blood seeped into the dry earth and a severed limb lay still in the road. It would lie there and putrefy, Jackson thought, unless the dogs carried it away. That was his initial thought. There were no unyielding moments of shock and silence, no petrified onlookers, only a damaged vehicle with an incensed driver on the side of the road, by the hedge. Cars drove by undisturbed. Order demands a character of serenity.

Jackson walked up to the mutilated body stretched out across the island. He picked up the packet clutched in Andries's hand. The bottle was shattered; the liquid soaked all other contents and trickled out the sides. His children will not even know he is dead. His body will be incinerated by the state; no place in this earth for his corpse to rest. Perhaps, were his family to know, they would give him a burial. Perhaps, his children will pity their beggar father. If significants could pity him, however few and little, surely his flesh could.

So, when he reached the little house with the green roof in Genade Street, a forgotten sense of power awoke in him, that sense of power derived from nothingness, the utter lack of everything that causes bravery through intrepidity for loss. The dog did not frighten him, as the thought of his body devoured by an animal could not be much worse than the incessant struggle for survival he unwillingly participates in each wakeful moment. Having no life necessarily implies that one cannot lose one's life. And so, he ventured to open the wire-mesh gate, with the intent of knocking on the front door, and informing the family of their loss.

'Go away, rubbish . . . we don't have anything for you!' came a voice from inside. The dog barked furiously and jumped up against the fence as if to jump through it and grab the black man by his throat, tearing it out and satisfying its desire for blood.

Jackson froze, ossified; his road only ever leads to the cul-de-sac, the bottom of the bag. The bottom. He thawed, liquefied, and took to the street.

'I once knew a man who was of no consequence, no consequence at all . . .' he used to tell the insignificants at night.

The silver thread

Melanie Wright

The Taliban took Herat in September 1995, the week after my sixteenth birthday. The last time I danced was the night of my party. My home life was very different to most Herati's; I am half-Afghan and half-English and the only daughter in my family, so my father used to spoil me. He is a writer and was in London attending a series of lectures when he met my mother. He says he loved her from the first moment he saw her but it took a lot of persuasion before she would agree to have dinner with him. Their romance sounded like a Hollywood fairytale to me. My father used to tell me how he wrote poetry to her in Persian and how they danced to *Strangers in the Night*. He laughed when he spoke about the day she taught him to ice skate and how she held his hand to keep him from falling. He said he couldn't help falling in love with her.

I wish I had known her. Her name was Abigail and she died giving birth to me. Consequently, my birthday is a bittersweet anniversary for my father. I'm named for my mother, but everyone calls me by my Persian name, Leyla.

The occasion of my sixteenth birthday, then, was extraordinarily special as my Aunt Anne was visiting from London. She'd kept in constant contact with my family but this was her first trip to Afghanistan. She burst into tears when she saw me, saying that I had my mother's eyes and her smile.

There was music that night. Persian music and Western music, both a big part of my life until then. I danced with my father to Frank Sinatra and dreamed I was Ginger Rogers. All I've ever wanted to do is dance like Ginger.

My father, as I've said before, has always indulged me. He allowed me to watch old American films, smiled as I taught myself the dance routines and, on occasion, let himself play Fred to my Ginger.

Aunt Anne brought me a red dress and matching heels from London. When I tried them on, I felt like a film star. My father told me I was beautiful and he spun me around and around until I was dizzy with laughter.

I don't remember what it feels like to laugh. I can't imagine what it is like to be that happy any more. When we first heard the rules, we didn't see how they could possibly be enforced. But the Taliban found ways, though we got away with a lot more in Herat than people in other cities.

It's funny how you begin to die inside, a little at a time, and you don't even realise what's happening until one day you wake up and everything's grey. Even the flowers are afraid to bloom, as if they think the Taliban will destroy them for daring to do so.

They killed my brother's bird. He kept a nightingale in a bamboo cage. We woke up each day to the bird's sweet song – nature's own melody, a blessing just for us. All Hamid has left is an empty cage, the bamboo bars spattered with drops of dry blood and a few feathers littering the bottom. He loved that nightingale.

It's the little things I miss the most. The nightingale's lullaby. Flying a kite with my brothers. The different-coloured flowers. Being allowed to paint my fingernails. I had a friend, Zena, who lived on my street. For as long as I knew her, she painted her nails with pink polish. To make an example of her, the Taliban chopped off the fingers of her left hand.

I miss Zena. She survived a whole year before she drowned herself in the Hari-Rud. I'll never know how she made it to the river without being stopped by the Taliban. In the weeks after that, I wondered who was stronger: Zena, for setting herself free or myself, for enduring?

I didn't think it would ever end, but there was a part of me that refused to give up. The part that tried on the red dress in the privacy of my bedroom. The part that wouldn't forget what it was like to twirl around in my father's arms as Sinatra sang of Lady Luck.

I didn't have to remain in Herat – I had a British passport and I could have gone back to London with Aunt Anne. Yet staying was not a conscious choice. I'd been to London for holidays, but Herat was my home. It was as much a part of my soul as singing was to a nightingale's.

My rebellion was small at first. Looking back, it wasn't really much of a rebellion. No one knew about it, and I didn't change anything. But it was a sign to myself that I would not be broken by a bunch of ridiculous rules put in place by a group of men.

I wore lipstick under my burka; a pale pink Aunt Anne had left behind. It was safe, for no man outside the family would ever see my naked face. I used to sit in front of my bedroom mirror and stare at my reflection. My skin is fairer than most other people's here and after a few months under a burka, it was even paler than usual. I could have passed for an English girl.

I tried to smile at the face staring back at me but it looked more like a grimace. When I realised that I'd forgotten how to smile, I cried. The tears were silent at first, burning hot paths down my cheeks. Then I began to sob; deep, noiseless cries from the very depths of my soul. Was this my life? Would I never again feel the sun on my face or laugh with my friends? Would I never dance again? I thought of Zena walking into the river with stones in her pockets and I understood.

There are a thousand different ways to break a person's spirit. I wasn't as strong as I'd thought.

Still, I couldn't leave. I can't explain how I was bound to Herat. I knew I was here for a reason but I didn't yet know what that was. It would be another year before I began to feel alive again.

My family is not Muslim and my father struggled with the Taliban law more than most Herati men. My grandfather came to Herat in 1945 as a missionary doctor. He wanted to help a land forgotten by the West in the wake of World War Two. He met my grandmother in the market one spring day. A few months after that, she converted to Christianity and returned with him to America. But there is something about this land that seeps into your spirit and claims it as its own. After three months, my grandparents came home to Herat.

When I was younger, a girl in my class at school – when we were still allowed to attend school – told me I wasn't Afghani. She said because my skin wasn't dark enough and, since I wasn't a Muslim, I should go back to where I came from. I was six years old and I didn't understand; I was born here, my mother was buried here, and I didn't want to leave. The world outside Herat was as foreign to me as the stars. When I told my father about it, he explained that people were afraid of what was different and he assured me that I was as Afghani as anyone else who lived here.

Maybe that's why the Taliban were so harsh. Women were foreign creatures and they were afraid.

Understanding something doesn't necessarily mean you can accept it. There comes a point where it's easy to give up and just let things happen.

When you're that deep in depression, the days blur together until you can't tell where one ends and the next begins. I couldn't even bring myself to make my bed in the mornings. The red dress was banished to the back of my cupboard and the tube of lipstick stuffed in the far corner of the drawer. My father and brothers were worried about me. They offered to take me for walks around the city – a woman was not allowed out unless accompanied by a *maharam* – but what was the point? At least if I stayed indoors, I didn't have to wear the hated burqa.

Then, when I thought I couldn't take it anymore, when I was ready to give in to my father's request to go to London, my neighbour, Fatema, invited me to attend a sewing class with her. I didn't want to learn to sew and I don't know why I agreed. I just couldn't be a prisoner in my own home for another day.

I put on my burqa and followed Fatema down the street. My brother Ahmed was our escort for the afternoon. I envied him the freedom of being able to go where he pleased. As a woman, I could not even buy from a male shopkeeper.

We arrived at a house with a sign proclaiming it to be *The Silver Thread*. On the outside, it looked like countless other houses in Herat. Inside, however, were two women who were to change my life forever.

Najema and Ramahna had been teachers before the Taliban took over. Under the new law, women were not allowed to go to school or university. I'd never been passionate about school because all I'd wanted to do was dance, but I could still relate to the hundreds of intelligent, ambitious women who'd had their dreams squashed just like mine.

Within minutes of meeting Najema and Ramahna, I learned that this was not a sewing class. They told me they were tired of being submissive. They wanted to change things. They wanted to give the Taliban something to be afraid of. They wanted to teach.

And they wanted my help.

At last, a reason for my presence in Herat! They explained that it would be dangerous, but I didn't care. I thought of Zena sobbing in my arms, unwrapping the bloody bandage and saying, 'Look! Look what they've done!'

When I returned home, my father noticed the change in me. I told him that I was going to teach English to a few women, almost daring him to forbid me, but he smiled and wrapped his arms around me. 'It's good to have you back,' he said, and then asked, 'how can I help?'

Herat had once been renowned as a centre of culture. Poets, artists and writers had found a place here to express themselves. When the Taliban came, they took all the books from the libraries and burned them in huge pyres outside the city. They left us with books on religion and the Qur'an, all written in Arabic which no one here spoke. A few brave librarians managed to preserve some books, but they could never be openly read.

With my father's help, I planned my first English lesson. When it came time for me to return to *The Silver Thread*, I was nervous enough to wonder about whether I was doing the right thing.

'Your mother would be so proud of you,' my father said, and my courage returned. No compliment could have been greater. 'If your mother were still alive, she would have done the same thing.'

In the weeks after that, I discovered two things. The first was that *The Silver Thread* was not the only establishment offering female education. The second was that I really enjoyed teaching. While it would never replace my desire to dance, I loved it for giving my life back to me. I was making a difference; I was taking a stand.

Fatema, Najema and Ramahna were incredibly smart and it wasn't long before they had a basic grasp of the English language. When Najema asked for a book to read, I turned to my father for advice. He contacted Aunt Anne and made arrangements to smuggle books into the country. In the meantime he told me to use the one English book I had in my possession: my Bible.

I was reluctant at first, unwilling to jeopardise my friendship with the women even if it meant sharing the gospel. I discussed it with them and, to my surprise, they told me to bring the Bible to our next meeting. Apparently their hunger to learn overruled their doubts about Christianity.

I started with Old Testament stories: Ruth, Esther and Hannah, strong women who rose above what life dealt them. Our discussions got so intense that my father had to come and answer the questions I couldn't. I saw a different side to him, and began to realise that my decision to teach had enabled him to come to terms with living under the Taliban law. In talking about God, he found his reason for being here.

Though we were always careful, it was easy to become lulled into a false sense of security. We kept the ruse of sewing classes by concealing our notebooks under half-complete dresses in our bags. Ramahna kept a dressmaker's dummy in her living room, ready for any surprise inspection. In January 2000, we were almost caught.

We were discussing the resurrection of Lazarus and how someone could possibly be brought back from the dead when there was a knock at the door. My father disappeared into another room and we quickly put our burqas on. While Ramahna went to answer the door, the rest of us hid the Bible and notebooks, and made it look like we'd been sewing.

I was convinced the stranger could hear my heart; it was beating so loud. He said nothing but carefully studied the room. My father came in and began speaking. He explained how Ramahna was teaching us how to sew. I didn't dare look up, not that I would have been able to see much through the veil anyway. It seemed that an eternity had passed before the stranger left the room with my father. Fatema later told me that that was the first time she prayed to 'that God your Bible talks about'.

I shouldn't have been all that surprised when she came to me shortly after that and asked me to tell her how she could meet this Jesus person we'd been discussing. I called my father into the room and we knelt in a circle and prayed. I wish I could put into words the expression on Fatema's face when we stood. Her eyes shone with an almost unnatural light and I could see the joy radiating from her.

The strength of her faith amazed me. She was so eager to learn more about Jesus and there were moments when I felt guilty that she was more passionate than I was. She started spending more time at my house and soon became good friends with Hamid. There was enough of the romantic child left in me to think about playing matchmaker and I secretly hoped they would fall in love.

They did, but it was nothing like a fairytale.

Fatema came to me in tears, saying that her parents had arranged a marriage to a man she'd never met. We'd both decided months before that there wasn't a point in getting married when the bride couldn't wear a wedding dress or dance with her husband. Fatema's concerns had nothing to do with dresses and everything to do with the fact that her heart belonged to my brother.

Her husband-to-be was twenty years older than she was and a devout Muslim. Fatema didn't want to disobey her parents but she couldn't spend the rest of her life with a man who didn't share her beliefs.

I didn't know what to say to her. We prayed and then she went home.

A few hours later, she arrived back at my house. When I opened the door, she fell forward. Hamid carried her inside and I removed her veil. When I saw how badly she'd been beaten, I had to struggle to contain my nausea. Hamid was livid. He wanted to punish whoever had done this, but Fatema clutched the edge of his shirt and begged him not to.

While I tended to her injuries, she explained what had happened. When she got home, her parents had announced that her husband-to-be was coming to dinner. Fatema told them she had no intention of marrying him. When they asked why, she said she'd recently become a Christian. Her mother reacted by crying, her father lashed out. She didn't know how long he spent hitting her before he tossed her into the street.

'Please, Leyla,' she said. 'I can't stay here. You have to help me.'

The three of us stayed up talking late into the night. Hamid outlined his idea and once Fatema agreed to it, he slipped out. I don't know where he went or how he even knew where to go, but he returned shortly before dawn with a false passport for Fatema. He said it wasn't safe for her at our house and took her to stay with Najema. That was the last time I saw her.

A week later, Hamid said goodbye to me. For months after that I had no idea if they'd made it across the border into Iran or if they'd been captured and killed. Then I received a letter from Aunt Anne, telling me they'd arrived safely in London and were making plans to be married. I was happy; Fatema would get to wear the wedding dress she'd dreamed about.

Here, life carried on as usual. I continued to meet with Najema and Ramahna. When I excitedly showed them the copy of *Pride and Prejudice* my father had smuggled in, they smiled at each other and said they would rather continue with the Bible. I was able to think of Zena without wanting to cry and my father started telling me about my mother again.

We kept praying for change. Don't ever tell me God doesn't answer prayers. Today's date is 12 November, 2001. The Taliban has fallen. I'm standing in my red dress and heels, looking in my bedroom mirror. In my hand is a letter from Hamid; Fatema is pregnant with their first child. I dance around the room to the music in my head. After all this time, I still remember how to dance!

I know it isn't over yet. It will be a while still before we are truly free but at least now there is hope. Besides, my soul has been free for a long time already.

There is a different kind of music filling the air and I don't immediately realise what it is.

I'm laughing.

The light at the end of the tunnel

Silke Heiss

Kuki plodded beneath the wire-pyramid of the pylon in the newly-electrified squatter camp. The wires had drawn birds into the area, which now perched above the shacks with their brick-topped, plastic-encased roofs, where before the same birds had once or twice sat on the concrete fence that was supposed to control the camp. Several concrete slats had been removed for cows and young men to wander through, which they did, crossing the highway at their peril.

It was marvellous and strange to have electric light, and Kuki was unable to sleep soundly now, due to the fact that darkness had been banished. It was therefore difficult in some respects to adapt to the new situation. Her daughters, their babies, and the babies' fathers were delighted. No, the babies did not mind. They were of the light. But the birds disappeared when evening fell.

Kuki walked from beneath one extreme of the spidery pyramid to the other, till she reached a recently levelled section of the develop-ing, that is to say, ever-expanding settlement. There were new houses here: square, rather than crooked, with angled, rather than flat, roofs. The birds sat on those angled roofs too, on the roofs' very peaks. They were only common pigeons and starlings. But still. Kuki had never seen a pigeon or a starling on the plastic mess, nor on the corrugated iron glare, of her own, or her neighbours', shacks.

Her heart hung huge and heavy in her breast. Her mouth tightened and straightened.

She did not know what to feel in response to the situation. The new houses had had their eyes torn out: windows were smashed, and win-dow frames had been removed. They had had their lips unhinged, such that they could no longer open and close to speak: no doors were left in this section of the township. Inside the houses, all that was moveable had been moved; the inner organs had all been extracted. Human urine and faeces had been deposited in some of them.

Kuki was the owner of one of these Reconstruction and Develop-ment Project houses. Number 94 was hers, to move into with her daughter and granddaughter (who had no father). But it was not pos-sible now.

Upon the gable of number 92 was a large white bird with black head and sabre-bill. He opened his wings at her approach, lifted up briefly, settled again, then kicked the roof with thin, black legs and propelled himself into the solid air that held him, his breastbone flatly extended, as if on an outstretched hand. Kuki's not-very-good eyes followed the ibis into the sky and beyond, as far as she could imagine. He'd go down maybe eventually at the sewerage farm. Kuki looked around her. Nobody else seemed to have noticed either the bird or its flight.

This heart, this head, this heart and this head of hers. At a time when connections for light and power are made everywhere, even here in this dump. At such a time she is made owner of a house with-out any hope. Well, the councillor had said they would move in under the protection of the army and police. Kuki stopped in her weary homeward plod and turned, and lifted her head again to grin at the vanished ibis. Or perhaps it was only the sun in her face.

'Good day, Mama. How are we today?'

The shopkeeper's friendly eyes twinkled. Kuki sighed noisily.

'Good day, young man. Pity me – winter is coming.'

The shopkeeper looked down at her from his gaunt height and waited. Kuki's face pursed up.

'My youngest grandchild – you have seen her, yes you have, she will not survive. She is so weak, my son.'

'Mama,' said Simon, 'must not lose hope. This fear can be evil. I understand. She is a strong sister – little yet, but strong like Mama. She will not die, she will not. Look at your brother.'

She did. He was a man late in his youth, perhaps 35 – thin, tough, with soft, confident eyes. She sighed again. She wanted him to bear her melancholy, or her fear. She felt he might resist or even save her. She said, 'To have hope in this place a person must be a fool, Simon. I know what you are thinking – that is why the old woman is ill.'

Simon shook his head gently, but let her go on.

'I tell you, listen now. My spirit will still fly out of here. When I go, I go. I will haunt no one, that I promise you! You tell everyone. Tell them.'

She gestured vaguely, broadly, behind, beside and even above her. She was promising herself. And expected him to bear her.

'All right. I am glad to hear that, Mama. One ghost less – it's a good thing. Very considerate of you.'

He smirked conspiratorially and she cackled softly, hoarsely, and looked over her shoulder. They both knew the other had no god, that their ancestors were less presences to be relied on than questions that curled around the doubting consciousness occasionally, like smoke. Their shadows came and went at random, offering no protection that either of them had seen. It was up to oneself they both knew. But who dares to say these things?

Simon slapped a packet of instant noodles and some powdered milk onto the unpainted hardboard counter. Kuki stared at him through cataracted eyes.

'Yes, Simon,' she said.

Simon was silent. Then he pointed gently at himself, and said: 'This man, me, I can say "God be with you, Mama". Can I? I cannot. In this here, now, the two of us and everything around – what words can a person find? I am looking. This life is too hard. It is too hard. Even me as well, I must become soft like water not to fight.'

He gazed at the small, top-heavy woman. Then suddenly grinned – 'Mama will always haunt me.'

'No, you are impertinent! Have you no respect? I am not dead, but soon I will be, and your conscience will be flooded by regret!'

She shivered with joyful fury. Looked again over her shoulder, noticed the bright light witness outside.

Simon turned swiftly round and took some infant formula from a shelf in the murky interior of the spaza shop.

'A gift,' he said, 'for the little one.'

Kuki scrabbled in her bag. She took the items. Then she looked up at Simon and lifted a finger.

'I am close enough to the end, boy, to say this: God will bless you,' she declared, frowning and wagging the finger, 'whether or not He exists!'

'Go well, Mama,' said Simon, adding 'and exactly follow the instructions on the tin. It tells you step by step how to administer.'

Outside again the nexus of lines, centred, calling out: 'We are here. Time has arrived.'

If Kuki could have spoken to God, she might have said, 'I am your child, I have no brain. Fetch me. Please.'

But the woman did not speak to God. The woman worried about rain. She thought about mud on the floor. She imagined cold blankets of cloud. She wondered how much longer. She felt the weight of the formula like love and her heart hung huge and heavy in her huge and heavy breast.

It was shame. Kuki was shamed. She was a sinner whose dark thoughts tainted her environment and those in it. Only the birds, and now these wires, were above it. If her granddaughter was ill, then it was Kuki's fault. Kuki had thought: 'She will get sick,' and Maudie fell ill. Kuki had thought for years, over and over, 'I am not well.' And thus it was now. And yet, on the other hand, 'The world is a dark place,' she had thought, with equal frequency as those other thoughts, often wondering why so much fuss was made in the brief interval between birth and death. And now, the world was lit. 'How heavy is my heart,' Kuki had told herself (unknowingly then receiving the virulent growth). Yet now, here was an ibis right next door to her broken, new, empty home, or house, or shell without a future. Kuki felt well, she felt happy when she thought of the ibis. She felt young. Sort of eternal, even.

Well, one must remain active and positive. It has never helped any-body to give in to dubiousness. But as she sat, knitting together the sections of a pink cap, she did wonder, again, why the soul bothers to clothe itself so mortally. Life might be truly exciting if it were touch and go – if a person had a choice in this. But no. One had to go. That made it so predictable, where was the fun in that? That she *must* go, and take poor Maudie with her.

Electric horror struck Kuki at this notion. Where, why must she be a vessel for such unbidden evil? It coursed through her, seeming to come from outside of her more often than not. She knew, even, from where this one derived. Or, at least, she suspected. Her daughter, Emelina, had not after all made a secret of the fact that Maudie had been an unwel-come burden in her mother's body. Nor was Kuki altogether unsympa-thetic towards the daughter's situation. 'We are vessels of others' desire. They deposit themselves in us and move on. We must stay and bear,' she had said, and would say again. 'We carry all the world while they fly.' And her heart hung not so much heavy as it cooked, and the steam rose to her head and scalded.

On her last day in Claremont, where she had been employed as a char for thirty-two years, Kuki had shed not a single tear, although her employer did, along with the details of her pension. If there was water in Kuki, it was that hot steam in her brain, distilled and empty of min-eral wealth. And as everybody knows, electricity and water are not friends. And her brain was sparking; there *was* light up there, for a moment. Then utter pitch-black darkness, through which, however, her hands groped tightly to hold the pink cap, which must not ever, ever go on Maudie's head, for fear of contamination, because she must still grow up and make her own decision.

'Because –' said Kuki to Emelina, who was dutifully tending the deteriorating patient, 'because, Emmy, it is a choice. You ask God for forgiveness, if you have one. Except, Emmy, this mother has no God. So a woman must ask herself. A woman is not in heaven. A woman is on earth, remember that, that's where she stays, we stay. And I say no. Emmy, do you hear me? You must listen, girl. I do not forgive myself.'

'Ja, Ma,' said Emelina. Who also did not cry. But she slung, or rather flung, the baby on her hard, black back, and fastened her with a blanket. And did a hobbling sort of dance to quieten the distressed child, that living rucksack on the journey through life. Maudie quietened. She had no choice what with her head bobbing so violently, and she subsided into hiccups. Then did the mothers smile at one another, or at the tiny chirping noise within the fluffy blanket? But they smiled.

* * *

Kuki and her family lived in Ward 36 of Crossroads. But her new, broken house stood in Ward 39. It had come to pass, a few weeks after the houses were completed, that homeless people, or rather people living in overcrowded conditions in Ward 39, had attacked (shot) one or two of the new homeowners, who came, happily carrying their keys, from Ward 36. The Ward 39 residents were outraged by the possibility that Ward 36 residents should move into luxury in what was not their home-ward, as it were. A person is not a person. A person is either from this ward or that, that is obvious. All the prospective homeowners from Ward 36 became afraid of occupying their houses, which thus remained vacant, and were soon vandalised to their current state. The city mayor said it was impossible, and the responsible councillors from various political parties blamed one another for inadequate communication and insufficient information, though one or two blamed the residents for being violent, greedy and ungrateful people, during meetings with them. They were shouted down, which was when Kuki's intense sporadic headaches first began. The residents (Kuki was among them) blamed the gangsters – the unsupervised children with guns, who were unfortunately almost always invisible.

Several months later, the houses were repaired using further government funds. They were occupied by people from Ward 39, which was in order. It was at that stage – around the time of the pink cap and the occupation of her restored house – that Kuki became bedridden in her never-quite-dark-enough shack. The rains were late that year, the warm, windless autumn carried on and on, but Kuki was helplessly cold. So Emmy bought a blanket with roses on it, soft, so soft without any thorns.

'They say,' said Emmy, giving Maudie to Kuki to hold, 'that they have set aside land in Nimmersat, for us where they will build.'

Kuki smiled at Maudie. She smiled at Nimmersat. Maudie smiled at her grandmother. She could sit now, was starting to crawl, and had become much fatter. Simon kept donating formula. So much that Kuki had developed a hope. For Emmy. Hope. In such an old woman.

Kuki's weakness forced Emelina to take Maudie. The grandmother sank back onto her cushion.

'I am happy,' she said, although Emmy could hardly hear her. Her voice had turned into a rasp. Whether it was the chlorine in the drinking water, or the daily doses of carbon from the smoke of coal-fires, or, indeed, whether it was the weight of the woman's thoughts, the soil of them through the years, who could say, and what did it matter? The air in her lungs seemed to have solidified, and would not flow easily in and out anymore. There was fermentation in her breast, a hot, painful compost. At any rate, her body was being radically altered for the departure.

So she had to rasp and struggle under Emmy's supervision, while the other children worked, or looked for work, and overhead buzzed incessantly the power of the new dispensation. Kuki did not lose awareness of that.

Then Juwena, her third-born, got a job as a shift-worker for a cleaning company that did shopping malls. The compost felt slightly aerated then, and Kuki succeeded in grating a sigh. Then, on the Wednesday, she whispered, 'I want to see the plot.'

As with a child, the adults – Emmy and Juwena – ignored Kuki in the first instance. Kuki repeated: 'I want to see my plot.'

Maudie crawled over and pulled herself up by the rose-blanket. Maudie would live. And she, Kuki, would live in Maudie. With the months passing, and the cancer spreading, Kuki had given up on rebelliousness, and on berating herself for her every thought. She had become quite plain, in fact. Scrubbed clean as a pot with the steel-wool touch of pain. Perhaps that is how God would want it, if He existed. But above all, it is how oneself wants it, as an old char, Kuki realised, and felt readier than ever. To meet the others in the realm over the rooftops, above the web of power that had enmeshed her final months, to startle everyone now with this sudden bulb of desire.

'I want to see,' she panted hoarsely, 'where you are going to live – without me.'

Somebody noticed the mother. Somehow, together in the shack that had suddenly become crowded, they discerned her last wish. Though they could not figure out how to grant it.

Juwena and Emelina with the Maudie-rucksack directed the fathers and husbands and Simon, who was neither a father (as far as he knew), nor a husband (although Kuki had a hope). The women watched as the men lifted the Mama onto Simon's wheelbarrow, at the broader end of which he had bolted on an old car-seat. She had not, Simon saw, the strength to wince with the pain he saw contained in the half-dead body. They wheeled her very slowly, very carefully, at midday in the winter sun, with grave-faced Emelina holding a black umbrella over her mother's scarved, bald head. On the road to Nimmersat, along the five-lane highway. Then taking the off-ramp onto the R411.

There were cows, and Arum lilies, and Kuki's procession passed them all, noticing. They hoped she would survive the journey, if not necessarily the trip back.

Nimmersat was not far from Crossroads, except if a person walked. So it took them three and a half hours. Feeding of the young ones, and re-adjustments of the mother's position, swaddled in her blanket in the travelling cradle, needed to take place several times.

Nimmersat was brown and flat and deserted. Perhaps the builder had been intimidated again. There were Econo-loos, a digger, and a corrugated iron shack without a door and windows. Masts stuck out at intervals on the expanse. Kuki took off her scarf, by herself. She sort of rubbed it off weakly and it fell into the dust. The men took off their caps. Emelina was still holding the umbrella. She seemed to wear a snarl upon her face, Kuki saw Simon see. He could sense it was the snarl in front of a bag of tears or something. Yes, he must see that. Could he see? Kuki leaned against the car seat, which creaked and jolted gently. She rasped something to Emelina, and lifted her weak hand. The daughter interpreted the mother and directed the men.

Another father and husband took his turn at the wheelbarrow. He wheeled it into the hot shade of the corrugated iron shack, and as many of them as could sat down on the wooden bench. Overalls hung round their faces as they stared at the brown masts, and the grid of wires holding down as it seemed, though there was no need, the brown, deserted ground.

Kuki felt, rather than saw, her family with Simon in her land of promise. She felt her own husband stir in his casket of memory. She felt that everything was as it should be. She was aware of how quiet they all were, how tired. And how tired she was. Almost without pain already, as if, on this unbearable trip, the pain had somersaulted right out of itself, anaesthetising her by its audacious vault, or was that voltage? Because was she already brimming there?

Then she became conscious of one of the husbands and fathers speaking in Afrikaans (he came from the wine farm), pointing at something for a grandchild, 'the fifth, I think, my Isabel,' thought Kuki.

'Kyk die skoorsteenveërs,' he said, 'kyk die skoorsteenveërs,' with the excitement of an adult showing a child. Look at the chimney sweeps.

They all looked at the chimney sweeps, the ibises in the sky. It was the best thing they could do. Kuki watched them look, through her own blinking, thick-skinned eyes. The drama was all her own on the threshold.

Then Simon appeared close by. He manoeuvred her neck. It was sore, but that was unavoidable. He laid her head, her face, back, shielding her bad eyes from the glare in the sky, his dry hand pale with dust. She saw the dusty dust on the hands. Then also sort of saw, saw the black and white arrows. Knew more than saw, knew their sickle-shaped bills and the planes of their clean wings.

But then there was Juwena, or the fifth grandchild. Or was it Maudie now? They all melted into one, Kuki could no longer tell the difference. Those lungs of hers were fighting, or was it something hot in her head seeping down? There was a war, most certainly, somewhere it was taking place, but where here in Nimmersat, with that echoless, sacred squadron gone?

The pain, it seemed, was suddenly concentrated all into one, unfulfillable wish – yes, Kuki still had wishes, sinner, lover of life that she was –

But the wish was inarticulable on every level.

The pain relented somewhat.

'Let go, Ma,' she heard Emmy saying.

Kuki managed very cautiously to turn her own neck, by herself, and to look at her last-born.

'Take me home,' she croaked serenely.

Then she watched, milkily, Emmy's burst bag of tears, and found that she was capable of marvelling at all that rain in her own blood.

And everyone stood up to go from empty Nimmersat – the promised land – back to their shacks, or houses, in Crossroads. To prepare for the next day, which was the Thursday, which was the day that Mama Kuki did pass on.

The trucker and the trucker's wife

Huw Morris

'From Thailand to Timbuktu, I've attended "the University of Life" – and I've paid for my degree in scars!'

A drunk at a wedding once said that to me and it had impressed me enough to remember it. I'd used it now to impress the Trucker and the Trucker's Wife during a conversation that had continued from Johannesburg to Ventersdorp.

I'd met the couple on the afternoon of my return to South Africa from London. That morning upon landing, Johannesburg International Airport had welcomed me with a shrug, a smile and a 'next please'. That's what you get for asking for a free flight to Cape Town. So now, a few hours later, my lack of funds has put me in the cab with this trucking couple. I had to find the highway first though, in order to hitchhike back to Cape Town, and then I planned on leaving it to Africa to send me some ubuntu, some goodwill from her orange earth.

As I walk along the N1 I imagine I'm an actor in a movie. I even manage to convince myself that every car that drives past me sees me as Redford or Duvall or Fonda. Two teenage girls in the back of a Honda Civic look at me for longer than a moment and I look back at them trying to look like Travolta. Naughty stares come from the safety of their back seat, I hold their gaze for a few seconds before they sink into the highway, giggling at me no doubt. I must look like faecal matter. I know I smell like faecal matter. My only companions up to now (the two flies) ignore last night's road kill in favour of my mouth fumes. I turn my gaze from horizon to feet where the hard orange Transvaal soil is stark in contrast to the green of England. A few metres ahead of me on the ground lies a huge locust that must have flown into the window of a passing car. It moves its legs really slowly in a t'ai chi protest to the ants that are breaking it apart in order to carry it back to where it will serve its last purpose. Ants always throw mind glue at me, ants and fire. I watch each one touch and then move on – their communication eludes me . . . it's probably Africa's oldest language. The ant trance has me again for the first time in two years, that's how long I've been in England for, that's how long since I've seen ants . . .

and I get the urge to shrink down and join them. The locust has stopped its slow rebellion to the inevitable, in a few weeks it will be part of the humus giving life to new life. I want to be part of this continent too. I want to be new life. I think that's why I've come back here.

* * *

You know the guy with the ping-pong bats who waves the planes into position on a runway? That's who I felt like when the truck pulled up behind me – shaken to my boots. We're not talking small veggie truck here, it's the real deal, probably got a Boeing engine in there or something. The ants went subterranean, it must have been Armageddon for them, they left me with their locust. I looked up in wonder from the beast at my feet, to the beast above me.

'It's a Peterbilt, this truck – American import,' said the Trucker. (But only much later on, because right now I'm still on my haunches, as if I'm taking a kak, but I swear I was only looking at the ants.)

He's in proportion to his vehicle, the man who gets out the cab – he looks like part of the machinery, steel and bolts and oil. Smooth as the Queen's toilet seat. He's a big Dutchman, in his mid fifties and he's busy lecturing me on the dangers of this particular stretch of road and the hijacking that occurred only last month.

'I don't like hitchhikers boy, and I don't like the hippies, the only reason we've stopped is to save your life because a hijacking happened on this road only last month – and why you sitting like that? Looked like you were taking a kak!' He throws his head back and laughs.

The 'we' in 'we've stopped' is his wife. She gives me that kindly airhostess look when I climb into the cab. It works on me every time even though I know it's fake, I know airhostesses have got to be happy all the time, but I don't know why the Trucker's Wife has got to be happy all the time. I decide to give her an Al Pacino. I think I've got his smile down pretty well and, besides, it makes you look in control – and her husband has just made me feel like a three-year-old. So I slip her a Pacino while she slips into the driver's seat and the Trucker follows her placing himself in between us, and I get the window. They agree to take me as far as Bloemfontein.

* * *

The Trucker is talking (we're discussing journeys home): 'I'll tell you what happened to me once, boy, and it's one of my saddest stories. I grew up in a house in Kalk Bay, in Cape Town. Me and my boets had a hell of a time in that neighbourhood, you know what I mean. My happiest memories are from then. So anyway, the other day I had to make a delivery to Stellenbosch and I thought, maybe I'll go in and take a look at the old neighbourhood. So I took a trip there and walked down my old street. Boy, it was just like pulling out a photo album and remembering beautiful things. I got to my house, and I felt like I was ten years old again. I felt like I was in love . . . you know what I mean?' he laughs. 'So I knocked on the door to see if I could have a look around the garden, just to see how things had changed. The maid answered and looked at me like I'm the devil! I asked her if the madam was in . . . you know what she says to me!

She says: 'Do I look like a maid you fool, I own this house!'

I tune her, 'Hey, I used to live here too! I just wanted to come in and take a look at the old house.'

She says to me, 'Go bother someone else, I already have someone to do the garden . . .' Someone to do the GARDEN! Who does she think she is?!' He sighs and taps on the roof of his truck, as if it would qualify his next statement: 'In Africa, if you think you know, beware because you probably don't.'

Now there's a quote, don't you think? And I'm thinking he came up with that himself, and there's silence after it – and I feel like I can capitalise on the moment, so I throw in my line that a drunk at a wedding once said to me . . . something about the University of Life. It reverberated around the steel Peterbilt walls, my comment bounced like a golf ball in a squash court. It did me some damage. I should have kept quiet. You see, I don't qualify for that statement. Making a statement about having attended the University of Life is like having a framed parchment on your wall behind your desk in your office. The Trucker has one but I don't. Not yet, they know it too, but what they don't know, and neither do I at this point in time, is that very soon I will have one. A Bachelor of the Road degree – you wait and see.

* * *

A small child's toy hangs down from the rear-view mirror and laughs at the Trucker's Wife every chance it gets. It dances with every pothole we hit.

'I've been driving from Kenya to Bloemfontein for the last fifteen years, boet, I've seen some things . . . you know what I'm saying?'

I'm trying to ignore the guy but it's not easy. He has a 45 percent share in the cab space. I'm staring out the window, directly down at the road. The broken white lines stand out in contrast against the mass of black tarmac. If you stare at them long enough they become one singular strong line – but it's only illusion.

'You know what I'm saying?' continues the Trucker, 'I own this company buck, and I know one thing for sure and that's that there's still money to be made out of Africa.'

He's not expecting a reply so I'm staring again at the white lines on the road. They remind me of how I used to draw bullets as a child. Straight lines coming out of a gun, stick men firing into anything I chose: bad guys and good guys; houses and cars; even firing into crowds.

'For okes like you it's tricky. You can't fool me, your accent – you only speak English, hey? You can't speak a word of Afrikaans . . . you maybe know a few commands in Xhosa?' The Trucker's laughing again, it's becoming more and more difficult to shut this guy out. 'English okes are better off in England.'

Hoowaah, that hurt me, but only because he may be right. That's my big question . . . am I better off in Africa or somewhere else?

At least the Trucker's Wife isn't amused by her husband. She hasn't buried little reserves of prejudice to make herself feel more Afrikaans.

She's looking at the farmlands. They're beautifully worked. She's not in the cab with us really, this woman. She'd love to be in the fields, happy to be even a scarecrow, just so long as she could watch the cars go by instead of watching the lands go by. As I follow her gaze, the symmetry of the rows of corn I see out the corner of my eye cause an illusion that warps my point of view. I think it's from trying to keep my eyes on the road and trying to watch the corn rows at the same time. It's corn row mind glue, like ants and fire. They whip past with such precision that I'm surprised there is no sound to them. The phenomenon begins to mesmerise me. The straight road suddenly bends in illusion so that I'm afraid because the Trucker's Wife is not turning the wheel. It feels like too much birthday cake, or dodgy Chinese food – nausea threatens – I snap my eyes back onto the road and it becomes straight again.

* * *

The Trucker begins to speak, picking up the conversation from a point already so elapsed that I'm trying to remember what we were talking about.

'It's the same now for you kids in the New South Africa, you white kids, you reckon you can lean on a traditional education and expect things to run well for you, HA! those days are over buckballs! And you've just spent two years in England too, by the looks of things you can't afford a bloody Translux bus home let alone using your pounds

to buy a car . . . you're buggered pilgrim! It's only very clever, hard-
working white men who will make it in this country now, the mediocre
spoilt kids need to pull finger or they are dead in the water! Is that you,
boy? Are you a mediocre spoilt kid?'

* * *

For the last two years, my cultural identity seems as if it has been written in fridge poetry, or as if I'd painted my self-portrait from a 'paint-
by-numbers' pack. I'm not sure where I belong. I'm returning home
now but I'm not sure if I'll be welcome on my street. I have incredible
memories of South Africa . . . this landscape around me, the air and
the sky, is like a photo album for me. When I return to collect my
nostalgia from my old house, I'm not sure if the woman at the door
will look kindly on me and let me in and accept that I too have reason
to be an African.

* * *

'I'm telling you my friend,' the Trucker continues . . . 'I'm telling you,
you okes are stuffed now, it's because the scales are no longer tipped
in your favour. There was a time when a whitey from the suburbs had
his way paved in gold. But now you okes have got to be resourceful,
like me.'
    The Trucker slaps his wife hard on the thigh and laughs. She snaps
quickly out of her dream world and looks coldly at us, obviously angry
at her husband's action but aware she has to stifle her response. She
begins to say something but thinks better of it and looks away again.
    'My wife cries every time we drive through Harare, boy,' says the
Trucker, 'The whites in the nation of Zimbabwe are like a dead elephant. Every bloody animal in the bushveld is keen for a piece of them,
but they don't realise the sadness of that once majestic creature that now
lies dead on its side with flies crawling in and out of its eyes . . .'
    The Trucker trails off about the woes of the white man in Africa and
I've stopped listening long ago. After a while there is silence in the
cab. We pass some rural men and woman walking along the road in
what seems to be the middle of nowhere. I look back at them but they
are already tiny, in this cab you float above reality.

* * *

The Trucker has his arms folded, and the peak of his cap over his face.
He's asleep and his 'larger than life' character is diffused by the kind
of harmless snoring your grandfather might produce as he doses off
after Sunday lunch.

He has a large silver belt buckle that says 'Texas' on it. He is wearing cowboy boots. It makes me think of a photograph I once saw at the Gold Reef City theme park in Johannesburg. There was a stall there where you could buy a sepia-tinted photograph of yourself in cowboy regalia, with boots and a hat and an inscription that said 'Billy the Kid' or 'Wild Bill Hicock'. This guy's a real cowboy, this Trucker man. He's losing his culture faster than he knows. He's like some Wild West hybrid that's been imperialised by the Hollywood ideal of the frontier, the kind that used to exist in South Africa in his great-grandfather's time.

I reckon I've got my own frontier to face, my New South Africa frontier. I'm coming in as the unimposing sensitive kid, there's no other way I know how to fight.

* * *

She has been speaking to me. She isn't looking at me but she has been speaking to me very softly, I haven't heard a word of it though, her hushed voice has been lost in the drone of the engine. She finishes with what I guess is a question because she looks across at me now, expecting an answer.

'Did you say something just now?' I ask her.

She summarises her dialogue into one point for me, undeterred that I've missed her commentary: 'We will always have a voice in Africa, no matter how bad it gets for us.'

It's my blank look that makes her smile and explain herself: 'I've been driving this route for fifteen years now. In fifteen years you get to recognise the families who work in the stores along the road, the beggars at the border posts, the faces of your stretch of Africa. I see it every week. But nobody else will ever see what I have seen, and that's the difference . . . in Africa the plight of the white man will always be heard loudly, in newspapers and on televisions all over the world. There is an empathy for us, isn't there? But for the simple people along the road . . . they're like ants to the rest of the world. No one cares about them. If you care, if you want to be really effective as an African, if you want to be part of this continent then you need to help your people.'

'But who are my people?' I ask her.

The Trucker's Wife looks across at me and smiles sadly.

On the horizon, the white lines have become like thin ellipses, like a pause in a sentence, before something interesting happens . . .

The Trucker's Wife is looking at the traveller who has fallen asleep. He has not slept since leaving his room in Earl's Court two days ago. The truck hits a pothole and she is surprised the two men do not wake up because their bodies jolt in unison along with the doll hanging on the rear-view mirror – all three of them in a strange dance together to the music of a stretched Creedance tape.

The traveller's head vibrates as it rests on the truck window and it causes his nose to itch. The Trucker's Wife laughs as the boy grunts in his sleep every time he has to scratch it. Her husband and the traveller are dreaming and she wishes she could join them. To amuse herself she carefully aims the vehicle at larger potholes in order to make the two men nod in unknowing approval to the doll's silly movement, she is a strange choreographer to a strange dance on this strange road. It grows even stranger though, because it begins to slowly warp and bend. The Trucker's Wife has once again taken to looking at the rows of corn flash by while keeping the road in view out of the corner of her eye. She is surprised at the way the road changes shape and contorts. She begins to grow afraid and turns the truck's wheel ever so slightly to compensate for the bend in the road and as she does so she snaps her eyes back on the road again to reveal a straight highway. The doll, for the first time in fifteen years, becomes dead still. By now two of the truck's wheels are already on the verge. She panics and turns the wheel hard to compensate and veers once again into the middle of the road. The Trucker jolts awake and, trying to control the vehicle, grabs the wheel and pulls it towards him. For a split second they look at each other in horror. The truck begins to swerve uncontrollably now, the Trucker knows it is too late and leaves the steering completely in the hope that it will compensate itself. The vehicle sways once to the left, once to the right, and then hard to the left again.

The truck is on its side in the space between a field and the side of the road. There is a trail of debris 50 meters behind it. The red tarpaulin that covers its spilt guts of cargo flaps slowly in the breeze as if in a ribbon dance protest to the men that move towards it in order to pick it apart and carry it off to the place where it will serve its last purpose, to communities where it will give life to new life.

I have woken up. She is stiff. Her head is resting on my thigh and her legs are bent strangely over my stomach. Her husband is lying beneath me. I decide it is better not to move. I decide to lie there and try to make sense of everything.

The seat behind my back is hot against my skin. The spot of sun that had warmed it up has caused the blood on the seat to congeal and bits of glass hang happily to it. As I disturb them they bounce lightly down against the far side of the cab and make a soft sound, like little bells in the symphony of destruction that lies around me. It's sore like when you stub your toe. I thought it would be worse. My left arm is useless like if you've slept on it all night. Except there's something a lot more sinister about the pain . . . like it's the danger sign on a live electrical wire. I need to leave the aloofness of the truck, it is no longer refuge. I wedge my foot onto something hard and point my arm upwards to find a grip. I begin to float upwards. I am a beleaguered superman. I am a sentinel to the animals that smell blood on the wind. I begin to drift slowly out of the wreckage. I aim for the driver's window above me which is open. The Trucker's Wife falls off me. She has soiled herself and I gag and wince with pain as her glass encrusted jeans grate past my face.

A large arm has reached through the window and has been pulling me by the shirt collar. I have not needed to put in any effort myself such is the strength of the arm helping me. This is Africa's goodwill. I rise up out of the window and float down on a mattress of hands which delicately try not to hurt my wounded arm. I am covered in afterbirth.

The men around me share a confused look: perhaps having witnessed the accident they are at pains to believe that anyone could crawl out of the truck alive? Someone strokes my blood-matted hair away from my eyes and I see a group of African farm labourers. A smile from my dizzy haze – it is the only effort of communication that I can make. A few of the men begin to pick up the large wooden beams that lie strewn alongside the road – part of the truck's cargo. They pick up as much as they can bear and carry it off. A few of them go around to the front of the cab to try and help the Trucker and Trucker's Wife but return with saddened expressions. These men are African, as much part of the land as the soil. I wish I could understand what they are saying, they sound beautiful, as if they are speaking the oldest language in Africa. I want to be one of them. I bend down to try to pick up a plank but cannot stand up again, some of the men move forward and lie me down on my back. One of them sits next to me and asks in English, 'Your drivers have left, it is a very bad accident, why are you not gone too, my friend?'

'I did go,' I say, 'But I've come back now.'

Leopard man

Jonathan Cumming

Man, though phylogenetically a primate, has lived ecologically as a social carnivore for some two million years, and possibly more can be learned about the evolution of his social system by studying the lion, hyena and wild dog than by examining some vegetarian monkey.

George B. Schaller, 1972

When Saracen woke, he was in Lily's bed. Or rather, Lily and Dudley's bed. Lily was beside him, asleep, shoulders golden and hair blueblack in that afternoon light. The curtains were open; sun fell directly on the foot of the bed. Saracen sat up groggily. There must have been some soporific in the herbal tea Lily had brought after they . . .

He would normally have thought to draw those curtains. Perhaps Lily had woken earlier and opened them.

He sat up, shifted down the bed and looked out. Dudley's Land Cruiser was outside, parked under the usual tree. Saracen darted to the floor to retrieve his shorts and shirt. Crouching, he pulled them on, stepped into his sandals and moved to the bedroom door, which was open. He slid his head around the doorpost. No sign of Dudley. Saracen sprang on tiptoes down the corridor, into the kitchen, past the scullery and out the back door. His mountain bike was still leaning against Lily's rabbit hutch. There was a path out the back of the property, leading past the old servants' quarters and on, surely, to where the servants would have accessed the main road. He mounted and pedalled away, hunching his neck and shoulders as the only disguise he could give his retreating form.

Leopard Ridge School was about two kilometres down the gravel road from Dudley and Lily Shale's house. On either side of the road was farmland that had been allowed to return to bush, in keeping with the trend for turning pastures over to wild game. A herd of zebra was meandering across the rightward field, but Saracen did not slow down to admire it as he ordinarily would. Nor, when he arrived at the school's colonial-style gatehouse, did he acknowledge the security guard with his usual courtesy. The gate swung open before him and he braced himself against his handlebars and slammed his feet into the pedals to race for his cottage.

It was the new young teacher's cottage; its curtains faded, its garden flowerless. Saracen had come to understand that there was always a new young teacher at Leopard Ridge; few would last more than a year, he reckoned. He leaned his bike against the front wall and went in. The cottage had a kitchen section, a shower and toilet unit and a central space that served as bedroom, living room and study. He had not bothered to put any posters on the walls.

He sat on the narrow bed, dug his calves into the metal edge of the frame below the mattress, and gazed at the blankness around him. 'Many of the boys think of themselves as prisoners of this place. They do not realise that actually it is a prison for the masters,' he had written in his diary three weeks after arriving at Leopard Ridge to teach English and Biology. Yet here he was, stuck in the school grounds over the long, dry-season holiday, when he could have gone to stay with his parents in the city. Lily had kept him, of course, with the forbidden promise that had flitted between their eyes since their first meeting. She had been worth it, more than worth it, but he had to try to think clearly now about her and Dudley.

His telephone began to ring. He did not pick it up. The answering machine clicked on and his own voice issued through the speakerphone: 'Hello, you've reached Saracen Hammond, I'm sorry . . .'

Dudley's voice followed, larger than Saracen's: 'Saracen! Dudley here. Yah, I'm back – workshop was okay but they cancelled the last two sessions. Anyway, erm – I thought maybe we could do an evening walk on the Ridge. Hope you're up for it. Either way, call me back, won't you, please.'

Dudley was the lone warden of Leopard Ridge National Park. He was almost twice Saracen's age. Dudley had met Lily through an Internet matchmaking site where both had typed 'leopard' under the hobbies section. Lily travelled to Shenzhen Zoo almost every weekend and could spend hours in front of the leopard cage. She had also typed 'rabbit' under hobbies, but that did not bother Dudley, who ascribed it to some Chinese association between rabbits and good luck.

Dudley was writing a masters thesis on patterns of predation among the leopards in his park.

Mr Stanhope, the senior biology teacher, had once told Saracen – with a glint in his eye – that Dudley had begun the thesis several years ago. Whatever institution he was writing it for would long ago have given up hope of seeing a finished manuscript. Besides, it was so long since anyone had seen a leopard at Leopard Ridge that a saner man would surely have begun to doubt their existence. Saracen had wondered then whether Mr Stanhope saw Dudley as something of a rival.

Dudley often guided the boys on nature walks through the park; they seemed to like him and behaved more enthusiastically than they did with Mr Stanhope.

As Dudley's message ended, Saracen put his palms on his temples and his elbows on his knees. He sat like this for a long while. Eventually he got up and stepped into his kitchen section to make tea. He found he was out of teabags – recalled, now, throwing the last one away yesterday, having used it thrice. He would have to cycle to town. In any case, he needed to do something, anything, to dispel the sense of being steeped in adrenaline by what was happening between himself and the Shales.

Town was a general store, a filling station, and a bottle store adjoining a small motel-cum-brothel. Local farm and municipal workers and their families would sit on the concrete verges of these buildings to wait for the minibus taxis that came by at long, random-seeming intervals. There was also a sprinkling of permanent loiterers and the occasional vagrant.

Saracen, on his mountain bike, was about three hundred metres from the store when he noticed a bundle lying on the near edge of the road. Oily, mould-eaten rags spread over . . . The bundle stirred; it was a man's body, a vagrant. The vagrant rose and lurched into Saracen's path. Saracen swerved. His front wheel hit a rut in the gravel and he had to brake and put his feet down.

The vagrant was crouched now, watching him through the eyeholes of a mask. Saracen's first thought was that the vagrant wanted to sell the mask. It was a crude representation of a leopard's face, hewn from softwood and branded repeatedly with the end of a heated metal pipe. Circular black 'leopard spots' were imprinted where the pipe had singed the wood. The mouth hole was a grinning gash, and thick white acacia thorns had been inserted behind it to represent teeth.

The mask was attached to the vagrant's head by loops of bark. He raised his hands. Saracen expected him to lift off the mask and hold it out as any curio seller would. He did not. His hands hovered in the air. His fingernails were yellow-grey; each was at least an inch long. He angled his head and Saracen saw foam and spittle clinging between the acacia thorn teeth. From behind the teeth came a mewling sound . . .

Saracen straightened his wheel and rode forward, pedalling hard for the store. The loiterers around the store's verandah seemed not to have noticed either the leopard man or Saracen's panic. Saracen looked back over his shoulder. The leopard man was gone. He must have scampered down into the dip on the other side of the road.

Saracen slowed as he neared the store and told himself to breathe deeply. By the time he had chained his bike and entered, he was almost calm. He bought teabags, long-life milk and a packet of coconut-flavoured biscuits. He did nothing unusual, but as he came out of the store and onto the verandah, he felt someone staring at him. He turned his head and saw a young woman standing, slightly hunched, with a baby secured to her back by a blanket. She dropped her eyes and touched the fastenings of the blanket. It was as if his glance had threatened her child.

While he rode home he kept alert for any sign of the leopard man. But the man did not reappear, and Saracen reached the school gate without incident.

Back in the new young teacher's cottage he put extra milk in his tea and ate enough of the coconut flavoured biscuits to make himself mildly nauseous. He found his eyes straying continually to the telephone. Eventually he replayed Dudley's message. He listened for anger or malice, but could hear none. Curiosity began to grip him. He had to find out what Dudley knew. He dialled the Shales' number, wondering what he should say if Lily answered.

'Hell-low,' said Dudley.

'Hi! It's me.'

Saracen had not meant to say 'Hi!' so brightly. Dudley seemed, though, not to feel the oddness of it.

'So you got my message?' Dudley asked.

'Yes.'

'And you're up for it?'

'Yes . . . Thank you.'

'Pick you up in half an hour, then . . .'

While waiting for Dudley, Saracen tried to read a portion of the thriller he'd set aside for the holiday. He found he could barely keep his eyes on the page. When Dudley arrived in his Land Cruiser, Saracen was simply standing in the driveway.

Dudley opened the passenger door and Saracen climbed in.

'How was your workshop?' Saracen asked.

'Not bad,' said Dudley. 'Just, the facilitator for the last two sessions went down with malaria, poor girl. Anyway . . . glad to get home early. I've got a surprise for you, but I hope it's still there.'

'What is it?'

'No. If I told you, it wouldn't be a surprise.'

Leopard Ridge was an elongated hill crested by sandstone boulder formations. Many of the formations were dramatic: here, the head of a prehistoric rhinoceros extending back to a vast, encrusted turtle shell;

there, a flying saucer perched atop a conical pillar; and beyond that a pondering angel with a stegosaur's spine . . .

There were two streams at the Ridge. One was swift and shallow, with its source in the seeps of the Ridge itself. The other gathered in the tribal lands beyond and cut a deep gorge along the western border of the National Park. Dudley took the turn-off for the gorge and parked in the restricted access area. The authorities (both Dudley and the powers beyond) did not encourage sightseeing at the gorge. People had gone missing there, in the not-too-distant colonial past, and expensive searches had had to be undertaken.

It was around five-thirty. The late afternoon sun extracted rich colours from the sandstone, and the shadows extending under the ledges and wrinkles of the rock formations made them seem all the more sculpted.

'Shall I lock?' Saracen asked as they got out of the Land Cruiser.

'No need,' said Dudley. 'Isn't it glorious? I love being here, these evenings.'

Dudley led Saracen up the main track, then off along a side path that had seen more duiker and baboon than human feet. It led through a thicket of low, scrubby trees, and Saracen found himself unable to walk more than a few paces without having to push aggressive-seeming branches away from his face.

The path came out at a less overgrown area near the edge of the gorge. A flattish, table-like rock hung above the descent. Dudley was perched on this and surveying the view. He gestured to Saracen to join him. Saracen hauled himself onto the rock and sat at what seemed a respectful distance from Dudley, not too close and not too far.

They sat in silence for a while. The trees that grew from the depths of the gorge were far taller than those on the ridge; indeed, some were so tall that they threatened to rise above the gorge's walls. Their canopies obscured any view of the stream.

Saracen hoped they would see baboons, particularly the huge males for which the area was known. Though there was no hard evidence that this strain of baboons had ever harmed a human, the males' size and surliness gave a fine tingle of menace to walking at Leopard Ridge. In their presence the scrub was transformed into big-game country. This evening, however, there was none of the usual barking, chattering and swaying of branches within the gorge. There would be no distractions to stand between himself and Dudley.

They sat in silence. At last, Dudley spoke. 'You know, Saracen,' he said, 'I've always thought this place would make an amazing set for a film about primeval man. *Australopithecus* and old what's-its-name would've loved it here. Good rocks, water, no telephone poles . . .'

'Absolutely,' said Saracen.

'Ah, yah,' Dudley continued. 'It's quite a thing, this business of being human. We need each other, you know, just like we did when we lived in little hunter-gatherer bands. We weren't blessed with fangs, claws, speed. When the great cats came along, all we had was our brains and hands. Ability to improvise weapons and tactics. But you know what the key was?'

'No,' said Saracen.

'Sociability. Every man in the hunter-gatherer band has to more or less get on with every other man. That way, you can share knowledge about defence and getting food. You can look after the pregnant women and infants. God, our young are helpless for years after they're born. Sociability is our strength, our tooth and claw.'

'You're saying, basically we're good to each other – ?' Saracen mumbled.

'Of course. The flip side is, loneliness is a killer. You make a man lonely, outcast, his humanity starts to die. To survive, he has to become something else.'

'How do you mean?'

'Ah, maybe I'm just rambling. But I was thinking – look at a leopard. Superbly equipped. Incredible teeth, jaws, claws, night-vision, weight-for-weight enough speed and strength to make any human athlete look puny . . . But then, it's the loneliest creature on earth, and happy that way. You hardly ever see them together, except when they're mating and that's just lust of course. Your normal leopard likes to be at least fifteen kilometres from its nearest neighbour.'

'I don't mean to contradict you,' said Saracen, 'but I remember reading somewhere, there are more leopards around than we think. They're so shy of us and good at concealing themselves.'

'You're not contradicting me. What d'you reckon the chances are that there's one watching us?'

'Right now?'

'Right now.'

'Slim.'

'Fat,' said Dudley. 'Come on, I want to show you my surprise.'

They eased themselves off the rock. Saracen had been wondering if Dudley's surprise was a new route down into the gorge, but instead, Dudley was making for another patch of thicket. Saracen followed. Soon he found himself entangled in a maze of chest-high branches. Dudley had been crashing on ahead, but now Saracen became aware that he could no longer hear him. He listened. Somewhere, a bird chattered. The silence was otherwise complete.

'Dudley?' he called, raising his voice slightly. He could not quite bring himself to shout.

There was no answer.

Something nearby smelled unpleasant. A dead bird rotting, that was the smell. His father's cat sometimes killed pigeons and then did not eat them. He tried to keep his breathing shallow.

As he ducked under the next branch, something twitched at his shoulder. Or seemed to twitch. Actually, it was just dangling there. He must have made it stir when he scraped the branch. It wore an inverted smile because its head was upside down, teeth grinning above where the eyes had been. Some hair still tufted the scalp – an inverted goatee to go with the inverted smile. Pale motes scurried across the remaining crusts of hide, no doubt feeding and laying eggs within. On the other side of the branch, a foot or so of the vertebral column counterbalanced the head. The lower part of the body had been torn away entirely.

There was a noise in the overgrowth. Saracen turned. Dudley was crouching opposite him, holding a club.

Saracen began to raise his hands –

'Sorry,' said Dudley. 'Bit scary, isn't he?' He prodded his club towards the carcass.

Saracen saw now that the club was a knotted root; bush driftwood that Dudley might have found only moments ago. 'The surprise,' Saracen asked. 'Is it – ?'

'Yup. I wanted you to walk into it like I did. Experience the drama, sort of thing. Didn't mean to, er – are you alright?'

'Yes. Thank you.'

A pause hung between the two men. 'One of those big stroppy males,' said Dudley, switching his attention back to the baboon. 'Quite a devil-may-care leopard, to take him on. There was one time, I watched three of these guys see off a leopard. All for one and one for all. I sort of felt for the leopard.'

'Sure,' said Saracen. He paused. 'Can you use this for your thesis?'

'My thesis? Maybe.'

'How long d'you think it's been dead?'

'Nine days, maybe ten. Could've got killed the day I left for the workshop.'

'It looks . . . ancient.'

Dudley gazed at Saracen then, and his eyes seemed shrewd and very blue. 'Things go fast in this environment,' he said. He looked as if he would say more, but instead shifted his driftwood from right hand to left and back.

'Dudley –' Saracen began.

Dudley spoke over him: 'What killed this big bugger, really, was loss of love.'

'Loss of love?' Saracen echoed in query, and gave up on what he had been steeling himself to say.

'Something happened. It lost its energy, the younger males out-gunned it, whatever; the love was gone and it took itself away from the troop. Loneliness has its own scent. Leopards, being lonely bastards themselves, can pick it up immediately. The leopard came and killed and consumed and the two became one. And then the baboon's spirit could rest, because a leopard makes a proper home for loneliness . . . But how can you write that in an academic thesis? They'd laugh you off the course.'

'It's – I like it, though,' said Saracen. 'I mean, what you said about the leopard – that it makes a home for loneliness.'

'Actually, won't you do me a favour and forget I said it?' Dudley's tone was tetchy now. 'I'm supposed to be a biologist. Shall we go back? I thought maybe we could go down into the gorge, but you don't want to be here when it starts getting dark.'

It was still light, however, when Dudley dropped Saracen back at the cottage.

'Thank you,' said Saracen, 'for –'

'Goodbye, Saracen,' said Dudley.

Saracen slept badly that night. He woke three or four times feeling he had suffered nightmares that he could not now remember. At seven the next morning he lay hating his own listlessness but unable to rouse himself. The telephone rang. He let it be. It kept on ringing. On what must have been about the thirtieth ring, he sat up and answered. It was Lily.

'You come, must come,' she was saying. He could hear she was on the brink of hysteria.

'Is it Dudley?' he asked.

She said something in Cantonese. Saracen felt how fiercely she was willing the words to make sense to him, but all he understood was her fear.

'Lily,' he said. 'Hush. Sh-sh-shhhh. It's okay – it'll be okay. Try your English, please. Is it Dudley?'

'He . . . has gone. Go away.'

'Where, Lily? Where has he gone?'

'You come now.'

It took perhaps fifteen minutes for Saracen to pull his clothes on, mount his bike and pedal at a sprint to Dudley and Lily's.

Lily was waiting at the front door. She had a shoebox in her hands. Her makeup, always thick, was marbled with the patterns of weeping. Saracen's mind threw up a snapshot of how she had smiled the last time he came riding to her, and he felt now what it might be like to drown.

Saracen dismounted and flung his bike against the wall.

Her face was too numb for speech. Silently, she led him around to the back of the house, to her rabbit hutch. Something had ripped the wire netting off the frame of the hutch. Lily kept five rabbits, Saracen recalled. None were to be seen.

Lily was clasping the shoebox to her stomach. She saw Saracen glance at it and lifted the lid. Inside was a mess of white fur and blood.

'Dog,' said Saracen. 'It must have been one of the farm dogs got loose.'

Dudley's Land Cruiser was gone. Saracen stayed with Lily, waiting. They were not able to make conversation. The act of waiting fed off itself; having waited an hour, Saracen felt he might as well wait a little longer. Besides, he could not abandon Lily to the unpleasantness.

Morning turned to afternoon and evening. Midnight came and passed and Lily went to her room and Saracen lay on Lily and Dudley's couch and could not sleep. At dawn he telephoned the police. Around mid-morning, three policemen arrived in an old patrol van. Saracen squeezed in beside the driver and guided them to the restricted access area at the gorge. Dudley's Land Cruiser was parked there exactly as it had been when he took Saracen to see the slain baboon.

By late afternoon, the police had called in an aerial search and the mountain rescue service. The mountaineers flew out from the city in a large helicopter. If Dudley had fallen into one of the deeper chasms of the gorge, they would be able to get down to him and stretcher him to safety. The helicopter made a tremendous roar as it swept repeatedly over Leopard Ridge.

Dudley Shale was never found. Three weeks after his disappearance, Lily Shale returned to her family in the Shenzhen Special Economic Zone. Saracen Hammond remained at Leopard Ridge School for another four months, thus completing the contractual requirements of his first real job.

A few days before Saracen left Leopard Ridge for good, he rode out to the store to buy the usual teabags and milk. As he pedalled along, he found himself reflecting on Lily. Since that final happy afternoon

with her, those hours before Dudley had shown him the surprise, neither she nor any other woman had touched him – unless you counted
the boarding house nurse, nearing her retirement, who had stitched
his forehead after an unfortunate collision during cricket practice . . .

He saw the vagrant at the last second, and had to brake hard. The
leopard face weaved in front of him, snarling and spitting through the
acacia thorn teeth.

'No!' Saracen barked.

The vagrant backed away. He was wearing grime-blackened overalls
and shredded gloves and socks.

'No-ho!' Saracen barked again. It was a bark he had once cultivated
by mimicking the baboons on the ridge and trying to draw them into
the game of call-and-response.

The vagrant turned and ran towards the patch of thicket bordering
the far side of the road. Something about his shoulders, his gait . . .

'Dudley!' Saracen was shouting now. 'Dudley! Dudley! Come back!'
He began to pedal after the vagrant, but the gearing of his bike was not
set for a quick start. While he fumbled at the gear levers, the vagrant
reached the thicket, dived into it and was gone. Saracen leapt from the
saddle, ran with the bike to the side of the road, dropped it there and
scrambled down to the point where the vagrant had disappeared. It
was impenetrably thorny.

'Dudley! Dudleeeeee . . .' But he knew, even as he called, that there
would be no answer, and that he would soon begin to doubt it had
been Dudley after all.

Black stone

Thishiwe Ziqubu

My grandmother always said I was a stone. A water stone. A black stone. A rich, dark, smooth stone – the kind you find in the shallows of a river.

'*Uyindoni yamanzi*,' she would whisper in my ear as she ran her fingers through my coarse, black hair.

'This stone, my child, *indoni yamanzi*, it is not like all the other stones on the riverbed, no. This stone is black. It is so beautiful and fine, for it is kissed by the flow of waters pure. Waters so pure, you see right through them to the glorious shine of this precious stone. *Indoni yamanzi*, it is the eye of God. You are *indoni yamanzi*.'

But I had bleached my soul white. I had forsaken Gogo's words. I had turned away from my dark reflection. My father's black skeleton was locked up in the white closets of Laverna Girls' Academy. All my life, I had refused to embrace my black. This black haunted me. Like the jagged, sharp rocks of the roof of a cave, this black overshadowed me. I tried to creep away from it, but when I slept at night, it crawled before me, demanding my acknowledgement. Like the night and its dark clouds, like the black sky, my own blackness hovered above me. I did not understand it. I did not want it.

But this summer is different. I think it is because it rains harder every night. And every morning, I am greeted by the fresh smell of rain-soaked soils. The sun shines brighter this summer, placing sweet kisses on my black skin. As I look out the train window, I see the rains come down on KwaZulu's hills that are shaped like the buttocks of African women. Maybe this belief I hold is a romantic illusion, but I feel the rains come down for me. For it is these rains which anoint me. They fall on the seed of my true identity, growing me into a real being. These rains wash away the white dust of false existence. These rains give birth to my inner revolution.

I love rain. I love it so much because I was born in it. That is why my mother and father named me Zanezulu, which means 'she that comes with the rains'. Gogo told me that a bout of heavy rains started on the day I was born, drowning away a long period of drought in the village of EmaThondwane. Livestock died, fields were left parched and the people were sucked into poverty's bottomless, hollow stomach. Every morning, Gogo woke up and cursed the skies and their infertilities.

Life was barren. Baba had no work and Mama was terribly sick. Silence became the bread they dined upon. They even stopped making love. But the dawn of Mama's labour pains came with drops and drops of rain! Close to midnight, the region was drenched. And close to midnight, Mama gave birth to this dark child of the waters: Zanezulu, me.

I spent the first eleven years of my life in EmaThondwane with Gogo. I was a happy child, even though I knew I was an orphan. Gogo had raised me telling me that both my parents had died in the State of Emergency unrest of the late Eighties. The only knowledge I had of them was a classic, black-and-white photograph. I still have it.

I sleep with it every night, and feel that these two people in it are holding me. It is the three of us in this train cubicle. The man in it, my father, wears a brown suit with a matching bowtie and two-tone shoes. The hat perched on his head is adorned with a feather on the side. His big, black eyes look so fire-filled. He smiles beamingly with his nose flaring. I always wonder what it is that excites him so. Perhaps it is the woman he has his arm around, my mother. On the contrary, she does not look so full of euphoric ardour and zeal. She is plain but very beautiful. Her eyes tell no story. She looks like a pure angel.

All my life, this photo was the only glimpse into the souls of my parents. Gogo always told me that when it rained, it was their spirits blessing me, their tears kissing me. Raindrops are their tears of happiness, because they are so proud and so glad to have such a beautiful daughter who is a precious river stone.

The day I turned eleven, Gogo told me I was going to live in some boarding school called Laverna in Pietermaritzburg. I knew the chickens and vegetables she sold could not possibly pay private school tuition, so she told me the truth. She started being very honest with me that day. She started speaking to me like I was an adult. Before then, she had always tried to protect me from facts that might have hurt me, but I was now old enough to know the truth.

My father was not dead, but alive and living in Johannesburg. He had left Mama and me when I was a few months old to go and fight for freedom with Umkhonto WeSizwe, the ANC's armed resistance. Gogo told me of the last conversation they had had before he had left.

'I am a man. I have a duty towards my community. If I sit down and fold my arms like I can't see what is going on, I am not fulfilling my duties as the head of this house!'

'As the head of this house, you should be protecting your family! Maybe I am stupid, Vusimuzi, but I just do not see how going around planting bombs, carrying AK–47s and gunning down the police is protecting us!'

Even though Gogo painted such vivid pictures of these people, I could see only their black shadows in my mind. I saw only their ghost-like form.

'Why can't you just accept the situation? People are dying, Vusimuzi! Nothing is going to change. You cannot fight *amaBhunu*.'

I could not see the angel in the picture shouting like this. Her blank, innocent eyes could not possibly hold anger. The only disquiet I could imagine her having was about when the next rains would come.

'Do you know how it is for me giving your crying baby my breast while I look out the window, wondering if the police won't perhaps find you and kill you? Do you think it is nice for me when they come in here with their big guns, demanding I hand you over to them? These are my daily concerns. When other women worry about what they will cook for supper at night, I must worry about whether Zanezulu will have a father tomorrow.'

Gogo said Baba had been too caught up in this conquest. He had been fanatically intent on shedding white blood to perhaps give rise to a tall tree of liberation to give shade to his scorched nation.

I did not want to know the man who had made Mama cry. I did not want to know the man who had not come back for me after hearing Mama had died of leukaemia two years later. I did not even want his money, or his private school. But Gogo insisted I go. A good education was a luxury she and my parents before me had not had. By sending me there, he was giving me a wonderful gift, this father of mine. So I went.

Laverna was nothing like EmaThondwane. Laverna was cold. Laverna had cruel winds that thinned the soul. Laverna was a white, empty cloud. It never rained like EmaThondwane.

My friends at school did not know I was a farm girl, or the daughter of an anti-apartheid pioneer. I made up many stories about a rich businessman father and his white lawyer wife, my stepmother. I told them of imaginary mansions in Umhlanga Rocks, stories of many blonde-haired Barbie dolls, many staircases and many servants. I resented the mudhouses and grass huts I really came from. I despised the freedom fighter whose seed I really was. I would even scrub extra hard when I showered, praying the black might wash off. I refused to accept my dark realities.

Every holiday for the next seven years, I went back to EmaThondwane. I began to hate it there. As I sit in this train looking at my parents in the picture, I remember last December and how my blackness came back to me.

During the five-hour taxi ride from Pietermaritzburg to Ema-Thondwane, I thought only about January, when I would be back in Laverna, back in civilisation. When I could speak English again. For the next month, I would be confined to Zulu, the only language the uneducated villagers know. I knew the girls I grew up with would gossip about me behind my back. They were envious because I went to a rich private school only their imaginations could ever take them to. I went to school with white people. I did not wear the old, torn Pep Stores takkies they call *ogogongiholile*, meaning, 'my granny has just received pension'. And the skin on my knees was not hard and ashy from smearing cowdung on hut floors. I could never talk to them long, how could I relate to their stone-throwing, river-courting, mud-slinging talk? They talked very loud, and laughed like hyenas. They would even scream at each other from a donga apart! Etiquette was obviously a concept unknown to them. When would these six weeks end so I could be with Mary-Jane and Antoinette from school? I thought of them as I got off the taxi that had been torturing me with the sounds of *Soul Brothers*.

The sun danced in the sky as if to the same concertina tune I had heard in the taxi. It made the horizon before me glisten water-like mirages which almost metaphored the surreal world I had created in my head. The surreal identity I had forged, forsaking who I really was.

'*Hawu!* Is that you, Zanezulu?!', this woman shouted very loud even though I was standing right next to her. She was probably a distant relative I could not remember. She threw her hands on my shoulders like she was a Zionist pastor exorcising demons from my soul.

'But my, you have grown! The last time I saw you, you were half this size. I can't believe you are so tall! You can't even tell my Khanyo and you are the same age. It is because you eat white people's food. That is why you are so skinny! How are you? When did you get here? Is it nice going to school with white people?'

She gave me no time to answer her endless string of questions before she offerd to help me with my bags.

'No thank you Ma, I am fine. They are not heavy.'

I put on a smile for her before walking away and discarding the shallow grin.

As soon as Gogo saw me, her eyes lit up like her pupils were a full moon. She looked older, her eyes tired and her skin more wrinkled. She wore a dirty, brown Seshoeshoe skirt and her pockets were heavy with *umnhlonhlo* fruit. She had obviously just come from the fields. Her breasts were shaped like *izivovo*, the cylinder-shaped sieve made of dry grass used to sift traditional Zulu *umnqombothi* beer. She wore no bra

under her old T-shirt with the 'VOTE ANC' slogan almost faded out.
Her bare feet were cracked underneath like the face of the mudhouse
she stood in front of. I walked faster to her. I was glad to see her but
she made me sad. Mary-Jane's grandmother looked nothing like this.
She went to gym and wore foundation which kept her looking forty.

'Child of my child!' She embraced me and held me tight. She
smiled so wide I could see the brown teeth scattered in her mouth like
an overhead view of the village's clustered huts. Her eyes filled with
tears as she kissed me all over my face. She lifted me up, not caring
about straining her weak back.

'I swear you get thinner every year.'

I would not tell her I had been dieting for the past five months. She
would not understand there was no space for my swollen rear end in
my life.

'What have you done to your beautiful hair?'

She touched the blonde highlights on the extensions that adorned
my head with her nose in the air in disgust as if she were touching cow
insides as she prepared tripe.

'*Ewu, Nkosi yami.* Lord help this child.'

It was as if she was crying above the grave of my lost identity. As she
took me inside, she started telling me stories of a good harvest
throughout the year, and of my young cousins that had come to stay
with her. She was too old to be raising seven-year-olds but there was no
other option. Aunt Gertrude had died a few months ago because
'Satan was in her', as Gogo called the devouring animal that was AIDS.
She had gotten 'Satan' from her husband who worked in the mines in
Johannesburg and only came home twice a year. Gogo gave me a plate
of mielie potbread and bones stew. Her cooking was still good. And
the house looked neat. As we ate, she updated me on everything that
was going on in every villager's life, from Skofolo up the hill stealing
MaKhumalo's fattest cow to my peer Nomadlozi getting pregnant
again! She cut herself midsentence and I looked up to see why she had
stopped so abruptly. Her eyes were fixed on my naked wrist.

'What do you think you are doing?'

The light in her eyes died away and an anger, a disappointment, a
fear entered them.

'You cannot disrespect the ancestors, Zanezulu. That is foolish.'

I had taken off my *isiphandla* the day I had gone back to Laverna the
previous holidays and forgotten to put it back on. How stupid of me!
That winter, Gogo had held a traditional *umsebenzi* ritual under the
special request of our ancestors. A goat had been slaughtered and the
village called for a feast. A strip of goathide had been put around the

wrists of every family member to ensure the eyes of the elders stayed
with us, guided and protected us. Or so Gogo said.

'The school will not allow me to wear it.'

I lied, looking down at the dry, white bones on my enamel plate.

I understand this summer's rains so well. As they fall, leaving their
kisses on the train window, I know it is my mother's spirit calling me.
These tears are no longer of happiness. She is mourning the loss of my
pride. That is why I must listen to her and take my father's skeleton out
of the closet.

'I understand, child of my child, but I am so scared for you. I am
afraid you will get hurt. Vusimuzi was a wonderful man, but he had so
much fire in him, maybe too much. It ended up burning people that
loved him. I am afraid you will get burnt.'

But she let me go. Gogo knows why I have to find him and she is
behind me. And so is the army of the spirits of my ancestors. Gogo
slaughtered another goat and held another *umsebenzi* for my going. I
need the elders now more than ever. This *isiphandla*, this goathide
bracelet, I will not rip off, I swear to myself as the train nears Johannesburg. In my pocket, I have the address Gogo scribbled for me, and the
black-and-white photo I have grown so close to. I have been staring at
that picture the entire eleven hours. I look at him. I look into his eyes,
at this raging fire that is in the furnace of his pupils. I have to find him.
I am not looking for explanations, nor have I gone searching for
apologies. I do not expect him to justify his absence in my life. All I
want is my own redemption. And I know I can only find it through
him. I have to find this fire for it will solder my identity. It will refine
me. It will make me the black ore I was ordained to be.

Gogo always described him as a mighty warrior. And all my life, I have
known him as a burning beast. But there is no fire here now. He sits in
front of a shack built out of old pieces of corrugated iron, slates of
rotting wood and even a green board of direction signs that reads:

Durban 60
Port Nolloth 130

I wonder for a second how he got his hands on a road sign, but I
quickly come back to this jarring image before me. He does not look
like the flame in the picture. He sits on a black SAB crate in front of
the shack with an oval zinc basin at his feet. He is washing a pair of old,
torn white All Star takkies with a scrubbing brush and a bar of green
Sunlight soap. He is totally absorbed in this activity. He grits his teeth,
his face sweats and his eyes have drawn closer together under the deep

frown on his forehead. Dirty foam splashes on his cheeks and he wipes it off with his elbow. He wears a pair of brown Brentwood pants which look like they have seen the turns of many centuries. His ribs stick out painfully under a leopard-print vest. His feet are ugly and his toenails long and dirty. They even look rotten in those *izimbadada*, traditional Zulu shoes made out of car tyres. He finally feels my presence, looks up and sees me staring at him. He does not know I am his daughter. I looked nothing like this eighteen years ago.

'*Sawubona*, my child.'

If he only knew the truth of that statement.

'Can I help you?'

I cannot talk now. I have rehearsed my speech well in the train but now I remember no words.

'Are you selling something? Or has someone sent you?'

I seem to be making him uneasy. Without thinking, I reach into the pocket of my denim jacket and take out the picture and hand it to him with both hands. Strangely, I do not feel nervous. He looks at the picture and his face muscles tense up. He does not understand what is going on.

'Where did you get this?'

He touches it as if the woman in it were real and he was caressing her. He is no longer here. He seems to have travelled far away. He is in some deep trance, lost in the picture. I interrupt him.

'My grandmother, Basithile Ndlovu.'

He looks up so fast I think his neck might snap.

'Yes. MaNdlovu, Lindiwe, she was my mother. Gogo says that you are my father. My name is Zanezulu. If that is you in that picture, you are my father.'

I am very calm about all this, unlike him. He is sweating harder. I am afraid he will have a heart attack. But I see a smile find home on his face. I don't think he knows it is there. His mouth is wide open. And his eyes, his eyes! This fire I dreamed of, I start to see it in his eyes. So I smile too.

'Zanezulu! *Ngane yami!* My child!'

He jumps up at me and holds me tight. His fire-filled eyes are filled with tears. I have never seen him happy before but I am sure he has never been this happy.

'The struggle consumed my youth, my time, my very life. And now it is all over and I feel it has all been somewhat in vain. Like I was pregnant and gave birth to wind.'

There is a sadness in his voice that stabs me inside. I cannot believe this stinking shack has housed him for almost two decades while he spent thousands so I could sleep in white ammonia-reeking sheets and walk in white ammonia-reeking halls. I do not respond to anything he says. I am still taken aback by being here. I let him kidnap me with his stories.

'We made so many sacrifices. Zambia, Tanzania, Mozambique . . . The MK made us fearless beasts armed to fight, to destroy, to kill the white man and his system. But this is not the vision we had as comrades. Us, the frontline fighters of the struggle, remain unrewarded. Meanwhile those that were living lavishly in exile returned to comfy parliament seats.'

He stops and looks at me.

'You look so beautiful. You look just like your mother, but I think you have my eyes. I had nothing to give to you.'

I do not want his excuses. I only want him to talk about our eyes.

'I killed your mother. She would not have gotten leukaemia if I had not given her so much heartache. All I wanted was for you to go to school so you won't end up like me. I could not come back. I failed you.'

I take his hand in both of mine and I kiss it, sparking vigorous flames in his eyes and in mine.

The dark, pregnant cloud above us bursts open and the rains come down on us.

A story about Sam

Pier Myburgh

She fetched her son's ashes on a Friday. When she opened her diary that day, she read on the page that had no other appointments: *Fetch Sam's Ashes.*

'Can I help you?' the man behind the counter said. He smiled at her so she had to smile back.

'I've come to collect some ashes,' she said.

'And the name?'

'Sam Conrad.'

He nodded and walked to the adjacent room, still politely smiling, as if he were a dry-cleaner and she had just come to collect her coat. On the polished black marble floor his reflection followed him upside down, feet connecting with feet each time his steps echoed in the empty space.

It was not a cold day, but her hands felt chilly, so she put them in her pockets. She felt a tissue there, crumpled up and hard. She squeezed it in her fist when she took her hands out again and folded them into tight balls on the large counter in front of her. The huge arrangement of red and white carnations smelt of pepper and scratched her throat. She closed her eyes and, with the thumb and forefinger of her right hand, squeezed the bridge of her nose.

When the man returned, he put a little box, about the shape and size of a toddler's shoebox, on the counter between them. It was wrapped in brown paper; the kind she might have one day used to cover a boy's schoolbooks.

'Please sign here.' With narrow hands and long, neat fingers, he slid a release form over the empty counter. And so she signed her name, wrote 'mother' next to 'relation to the deceased' and carried her son to the car for the first time.

It was not easy to carry something so small and so light. Important things should be heavier, she thought. One should strain and sweat under the burden of them. She held Sam with two hands in front of her as if he were an offering. At the car, she grasped him tightly in one hand, while she fumbled in her handbag for the keys with the other. Her fingers grabbed at lipstick, more used tissues, a small plastic hospital nametag that had been cut off and given to her at the last moment, a bottle of Aspirin. But she could not find her keys. So, she put Sam on the roof of the car to free up her other hand. All the while she kept her eyes fixed on the box, worrying that she would forget he was there and drive off. She had already lost her cellphone that way two days before.

She put Sam on the passenger seat, turned the key in the ignition, but did not drive off. Instead, she listened to the hum of the car's motor and looked at her baby on the seat next to her. He seemed so unprotected there; he could so easily slide to the floor. So, she put him on her lap, snug against her stomach, and only then did she carefully pull away.

With both hands on the steering wheel and staring straight ahead at the road, she thought of the things she could do with her son's ashes. She could throw him into the sea with a great flourish and squint against the glare of the water for hours as he drifted away to places she had never been to. She could bury him in her garden and plant a tree and watch the birds as they sat on the branches and picked at the ripe berries. She could have him plastered into a wall next to the ashes of others she didn't know on the property of a church she never attended. She could put him in a beautiful Chinese urn on a shelf in her bedroom and dust it off carefully every day and light candles next to it at night. All those things she could do.

When she arrived home, she found her husband sitting on the bedroom floor, even though it was not yet noon. The smell of gun oil stung her nose. His head was bent over one of the two new shotguns that he had bought the month before. The other one, smaller than usual, just right for a boy, lay on a newspaper next to him. It was a bargain, he had said when he had brought it home. He would teach his son himself. They could go shooting together. Their son could learn to be a good shot with that gun.

'You're home early,' she said.

'Oh, hi. Yes. Some guys from work are going wing shooting this weekend. Said I should join them. I'm just cleaning these and then I'll be off. You don't mind, do you? I couldn't get hold of you with your cellphone gone and all.'

She stood there with the small brown box in her hands and said nothing. In his hands he held an oily rag. The fringe that flopped over his forehead was smeared and he again tried to push it away with his dirty hand. He had taken his wedding ring off and it lay in some spilt oil on the newspaper in front of him. He peered down the barrel of the gun, holding it up to the light with one eye closed.

As there was nothing more to say, she walked past him, stepping over the smaller gun, and went to her bedroom where she opened a drawer. It was a tidy drawer with panties and bras at the back, vests and socks in the front. She tucked the box snugly between her underwear and carefully closed the drawer. She did not tell him that she had fetched the ashes. He did not ask.

The next morning a grey cloud blanketed her house, but like the final sheet that covered Sam, it gave no warmth. Still, she wanted to pull it closer and feel its weight on her head. She pushed her duvet off and went outside in her pyjamas. She looked at her lush garden that had become overgrown; shrubs greedily jostled for position with roots sucking at the dank soil. She felt them closing in on her and pushing her down.

She went back inside, took her sports bra from the drawer where Sam lay and put on her old tracksuit. Then she fetched an axe, a saw and some shears. She had no gloves.

She started chopping down the bignonia that darkened her bedroom window. The branches that supported the creeper were thick and tough and gnarled and twisted, but she lifted the axe high over her head and brought it down on the plant. The wood splintered away. Some orange-red trumpet flowers popped from their little stems and lay uselessly at her feet. She stepped on the spliced branch and heard the crack as it snapped under her weight. Then she bent over it and pulled with her bare hands until it finally broke off. The bark of the plant was rough and her hands bled on the inside of her thumbs. While she sucked at the cuts, she noticed how the creeper's upper limbs had curled themselves around a drainpipe. Some flowers waved from the gutter like witches' fingers. With heels dug deep into the soil, she pulled it away from the gutter. It cracked and screeched, and when it finally gave way she fell backwards, collapsing on the grass under the weight of it.

The house looked naked and broken without the bignonia. Scars of grey cement showed where paint and plaster had been ripped away from the wall. The drainpipe hung loosely in its brackets. Her ears hummed and it took a while before she heard the phone ringing.

'Hi,' her sister from New York said, so cheerfully. 'I'm just calling to see how you're doing?'

'Oh, I'm fine. I'm doing some gardening.'

'That's good. Gardening is good. Um, I was wondering if you felt like visiting me? Why don't you fly out next week and we'll do some girl things. I thought it might be good for you to get away for a while.'

'Oh, I don't know. There's so much to do here. Maybe . . .' she said.

Then she went back outside and cut back a eugenia with its red berries. She pulled out and divided a clump of clivia, even though they were in bloom. She cut away a huge jasmine so that she did not have to

smell its nauseatingly sweet flowers. Finally, she pulled out the ridiculous impatiens she had planted two months before and that had
already become lanky in the shade.

When she was done, she piled all the plants on top of some old dead
wood in the middle of her lawn. She fetched some newspapers, stuck it
in amongst the branches and the wood, and set the whole lot alight.
The grey, ghostly smoke swirled up and disappeared into the clouds.
The fire struggled with the green wood and the plants hissed and
sighed. So, she fetched a half-empty bottle of paraffin and, with an
outstretched arm, poured it on the cuttings. The flame that had
moved slowly along the moaning branches licked at the paraffin and
at once exploded, engulfing them in its hot, orange embrace.

Her husband came home the next day covered in dust. Like a
migrant worker, tired after weeks of hard labour away from home, he
dropped his duffel bag from his shoulders. He kissed her lightly on
her cheek.

'Good weekend?' he said.

'Not too bad. I did some gardening. How was yours?'

'Okay. Gardening's good, isn't it?'

She nodded. 'My sister invited me to visit her next week. I'm not
sure though . . .'

'Go. Really, you should go. Travelling will be good for you.'

He went back to the car and fetched their old polystyrene cooler
box. He wearily put it down on the kitchen floor.

'Here are the birds,' he said. 'I think there are about seven. We just
shared them out evenly between us. We should have them cleaned
tomorrow.' Then he turned and went for a bath.

She opened the lid and looked at the small pile of guinea fowl
inside. Unplucked, their beautiful dark-grey feathers with white speck-
les looked soft and warm, but when she touched them they felt cold.
They lay in the box haphazardly; heads crooked awkwardly, eyes
half-open.

She went to the bathroom where her husband lay in the steaming
water, eyes closed. She took off her clothes. Without a word she
climbed in and sat, knees held tightly against her breasts, facing him.
He did not open his eyes, but he turned his palms up and she took his
hands. She pulled him up until their knees met. With bent backs they
leant forward, towards each other, until their foreheads softly
touched. Then she put her face in his neck and held his shaking shoulders tightly, rocking him gently from side to side.

A week later she packed three pairs of pants (one of them black),
three skirts, six shirts (two of them white) and two pairs of shoes (one

black, one tan). She packed six sets of underwear, three pairs of socks and three pairs of stockings. Her black mohair coat.

In her hand luggage she put her sponge bag, a warm sweater, a blow-up neck rest and a book-club novel she knew she would never read. 'Take this one,' her friends had said, pressing it into her hands. 'It's a fun holiday read.' Every girl needed a fun holiday read. Then she packed a change of underwear. It was an eighteen-hour flight from Johannesburg to New York; a girl would need a change of under-wear. She took the last pair of panties, bra and socks from the drawer where Sam lay.

When she closed the empty drawer, she could hear the box slide around inside and hit the back of it with a soft, accusing thud. She tried to ignore him, but could not. So, she took Sam out and put him in her hand luggage, on top of the novel and under her sweater.

She loved being at the airport; to her it could be a final destination. There were so many other people to watch, other lives to imagine, to trade. A boy of about three with blond hair stopped swinging on the rope that herded them to the check-in counter, turned to her and said with big eyes: 'You know, tonight I'm going on a big aeroplane!' He spread his arms wide open to show just how very big the plane would be. 'Mommy says I can watch TV and even sleep there, do you know, do you know?'

After she cleared passport control, she went straight to the departure lounge. She would have a coffee there, perhaps even read her book. She carried her cabin luggage over her shoulder, and the strap bit into her back. So, she took it by the handle instead and it banged against her legs every time she took a step. Other people passed her, pulling their bags behind them on wheels.

But then, at the entrance to the New York flight's departure lounge everyone, fast and slow, came to a stop. With irritated frowns, strangers pushed against her, stretching their necks awkwardly to see what was causing the delay. Ahead of them, tables were set up in two rows, and on them the luggage was being checked by officials wearing latex gloves. Bags were zipped and unclipped and, with jutting elbows and knees, shoes and jackets were removed, laptops unpacked. Cell-phones and keys were thrown carelessly into plastic trays.

When she reached the tables, she watched how an Indian-looking man ahead of her stood motionless while his case was being inspected. He stood very upright, hands folded lightly behind his back, the thumb of his right hand slowly stroking the palm of his left hand. His turban remained absolutely still, like a huge, sleeping snake coiled around his head. He did not move while they unzipped every zip and stuck hands in every pocket of his luggage. It seemed that they spent much more time on his bag than any of those of other people. Thank goodness I'm blonde, she thought as she shifted her weight to her other foot. She needed the bathroom. *Come on, come on!* She did not think of the little box wrapped in brown paper inside her bag.

When it was her turn, she smiled at the man with the latex gloves, but he did not smile back. He's probably somewhere in his thirties, she thought. Fat cheeks bulged softly at his ears. Such small ears for such a big head. His nose was thin and sharp and he kept his head low over her suitcase as the hadedas did when they pecked at her lawn.

He unzipped her bag and some of her stuff fell onto the table. He picked up the box with Sam in it and shook it.

'What's this?'

Her mouth felt dry. 'Oh hell, yes. It's my son's ashes.'

'We need to open this,' he said, louder now and already motioning to the official working at the neighbouring table.

'Please don't. We can't open it here. It's nothing, really. It's just some ashes.'

Already he had started to pick at the tape that kept the brown paper closed. His knuckles bulged and she could see the black hairs on his fingers squashed against the inside of the thin, opaque gloves. When the other official joined him, he had already opened a little pocket-knife, and with one quick flick, he cut open the brown paper, immediately below the lid of the box.

'No!' Her arms shot forward as she tried to grab the box from him. A hard shoulder pushed her aside and she felt fingers wrap around her upper arm. She saw hands and a knife and watched the little box do a jig in the air. It tumbled with small quick turns and when it landed on the floor, it barely made a sound. It rolled over only once before it lay there quite still. But then a passing woman's foot accidentally kicked it, spraying Sam all over the grey floor. The woman stopped briefly and bent down as if to pick up the box. But then she saw her little boy run ahead of her shouting: 'Come Mommy. They are waiting just for us!'

'Wait there,' she called, and ran to catch up with her son.

Sam's mother stood dead still, even though there was no longer a hand around her arm, and looked at the prints the other woman's sneakers had made in Sam's ashes. Zigzags lay etched in the fine powder.

'You need to come this way for some questions,' she vaguely heard someone say.

She nodded at the voice whose words had become warped. She knew that they were leading her away, but she could not feel her legs move. As she walked off she looked around once more. She saw other feet carrying Sam away from her, towards the aeroplane. Then a short man with a little broom started sweeping what was left of him back into the box. She did not look back at Sam again.

Even the rains are warm there

Carel Alberts

The sun is over the eucalyptus on the west wall of the dam, the bark coming off the tree in strips. The water lies darkened and still and laps soundlessly at the edges. The house is to the left.

The man finishes his work. In 1975 his grandfather built the dam on the entry point of the river to their land. It is uphill from the house; the water it gives the family augmented in winter from a small reservoir round the back, where the servants' quarters were.

In the front of the house as one pushes open the lower half of the kitchen door – the upper half always open – and the outer door with the fly gauze bangs shut, a water pail stands. Its chipped enamel sides are white, and it is filled with pristine, cold water from the reservoir, as it was in the time when his grandmother filled it every day at an unseen hour and ladled it into mugs for lunch in the year they came to live there.

Then it was he and his mother and sister, and he remembers: stubbing a big toe on the cobbled courtyard; a broken great-aunt saying 'Morning, my sweetheart' at dawn; eating a lemon on a bet.

He squints against the sweat and lets out a long breath. The cutter goes on the back of the truck, next to the roll of wire on top of the pile of petrified-looking thorn wood slats.

The great-aunt is now dead, as are his absent father and his grandfather and grandmother. His mother lives with his sister in the town. It was he and his wife now – twice pregnant, twice disappointed. The two of them, Biggles the cat, and the two dogs.

His wife named the animals. The cat gets its name from a comic strip she had been fond of as a child, and answers to no one. Zelda buys it soft toys and tinned food, as well as a sweet-smelling paste that does away with the need for the cat to heave up fur balls. Biggles is seven years old and was neutered when he made mechanical complaints of a festering sore in his cheek one night, the result of a fight with another cat.

The dogs are named for dogs his wife's family had owned. They are both Rottweilers, but, as the saying goes, couldn't be more different. The male is an indomitable and distant specimen, at best insouciant, at worst sullen or challenging. The bitch suffers from the nightly cold, and shows signs of advanced hip dysplasia. She was their first animal (his wife calls them companions) nine years ago, but Leya's emotional dependence soon necessitated the purchase of a mate, and Bruno arrived on the farm.

The man opens the driver's door and gets in. He puts his hat next to him on the seat and leans over to his left, opens the compartment on the dashboard and takes out a pair of glasses for night driving. His forehead is pale and swollen on one side, with dried blood caked to a cut from a wire that snapped during the day's mending of the fence. He will tell Zelda he'd been wearing the goggles.

The dam is looking fuller than it has been all summer. The northern wall may need reinforcing. Samuel will have to bring the earth-moving equipment out tomorrow; that can be done first. He will need supervision. Long before that– tonight – there is the chicken coop to be seen to, at eight o' clock, maybe. It won't be too late if everything goes to plan.

He reflects on the latest in the series of small headaches that have kept him busy, busy enough to imagine that he is happy. (And who is to say he and Zelda are not happy? It's not something they have talked about.) The chickens are being murdered with the last of the jackals on the loose. But there is time for the jackal tonight.

He drives the truck a little way onto the low first gradient of the dam wall and turns it around to face homeward – fifteen minutes in the dark on the uneven road. Zelda will be home with dinner, probably lamb chops and potatoes or a stew.

Unexpectedly then, and wholly incongruously, like an attack, it occurs to him that he has never so much as considered the possibility of her leaving him. Although this eventuality seems completely unlikely, he reasons, as no signs have been forthcoming, he continues to stew on the thought, and it seems to him that this very male assured-ness is a monstrous failure on his part. Also, the fact that he had long ago stopped thinking about them – together – much, and his failure to notice what now appears to him to be a lifetime of service she gave him, suddenly looms large in his brain as breathtakingly unjust. His chest fills up with remorse; then anxiety about their respective fates, should such a thing happen. But the deluge of feeling and different possibilities overwhelms him, and his mind again closes to the thought.

Soon, all he is aware of by way of disturbance to his formerly placid mood is a dim underlying nervousness, the cause of which altogether escapes him after a while. All he can think of when his mind returns to its own discomfort is his earlier admonition to himself when putting the matter aside: 'There is no reason to worry.' And, trusting his own ability to judge whether there is reason to worry or not, he ignores the voice of anxiety within himself, and forgets the matter completely.

The moon settles over the fields on the right of the modest-sized house. The dogs, he knows, will greet him in their individual ways – Bruno with insolent nonchalance, the bitch behind, waiting her turn, uncertain and progressively more fawning as the years wear on.

He can't stand the thought of the dog not coping with the weather. Her bones are giving in. She cannot get up in the mornings, and whines pitifully twice a day, once at daybreak, the longest, and again when she goes to sleep.

Zelda hates the way Bruno bullies Leya into submission, beats her to the food, hogs all the attention, with the comical pretence of indifference now wearing thin. But what is a dog if not a political animal? Why should it not vie for dominance? The female is a bloody nuisance, and if it weren't for the fact that nine years is a long time . . .

He should have sent her away long ago. His wife has pleaded for years for her to be sent to a warmer climate. It would be more humane, she says. But it always seemed excessive and almost . . . unnatural. And Zelda has stopped asking, he realises, a small fragment of grief moving through his heart.

For years, he ignored the more fundamental and unreasoning motivation behind his failure to get rid of Leya. He loves her. He loves the way she loves him, and hates it at the same time. He loves her companionship at night when he cannot sleep, sitting silently next to him for hours on the old car seat outside the kitchen door, the only remaining fixture of his grandfather's Valiant. She always sits next to him long enough to begin whimpering with her aches until he can't take it any longer and hugs her head and slaps her on the rump, gets up and goes to bed.

And the truth is that now it is far too late to do what his wife asks. He has not broached this particular topic with her yet, as it is, after all, his fault. Now it is too late.

Leya is a good hunter, he'll say that much for her. At least, she always was, and has been until recently. Her instincts are still sharp, as are her senses, but she's just not as mobile as she was. He remembers getting her as a puppy, and being amazed at the prodigious number of rats she would weed out from the storeroom. Rats being vicious devils, a good ratting dog, one that doesn't get ripped to ribbons in the contest, is a true find. Although a large ginger, Biggles was not suited to the task.

The going levels out and settles, coming from the last of the hills, with the house lying ahead at the end of the whitish road. It is exactly as his grandfather had built it, only the thatched roof made way some years ago for, first, corrugated metal, then tiling. Zelda had insisted. But she'd been right. It made little sense to have thatch in an area fraught with lightning.

The south has the strangest of climates, he reflects – winter rain, normally associated with profuse downpour, but in this case barely enough to sustain the tobacco crops, and those waning. And to complete this climatic failing, it has electric disturbance in summer. The dogs, especially Leya, have suffered through countless thunder storms.

As he enters the house and extends an arm behind himself to check the swing of the sieve door, he sees his wife in the kitchen, in front of the coal stove. The only change in here from the days of his grandmother is the incongruous-looking monstrosity of the Thermofan oven next to the stove, for Zelda's cakes. Zelda bakes more or less constantly, for bazaars and her friend Susan's shop in town. She makes nothing out of it, but seems happier, perhaps enjoying the social aspect.

When, years ago, he cut his university career short on the death of his grandfather, suddenly free from the pretensions of theological studies, which had long before ceased to occupy his mind even while in lecture halls, Zelda followed him to the farm of his childhood days. At twenty-two, she seemed happy, and this strikes him as inexplicable for the first time, to settle, fall pregnant and give up her own studies (psychology). Since the miscarriages, they stopped trying (it always seemed to him to be *her* wish). The only concession she'd made to defeat was to order the modern oven and start baking. That and the comfortably small band of ''companions'' they have in their animals.

She greets him with only half a lilt in her voice, her face seeming strained tonight, and she doesn't quite meet his gaze, he registers for the first time, with the sadness he felt earlier back again. But the strain he sees in her, he realises, is the very same stiffness he feels in his cheeks when he tries to smile at her. Conscious for the first time of how they must seem together, or he to her, and aghast at this state of affairs, a smile tries to break the years of unacknowledged love. The effect is total atrophy.

They're still intimate, he and Zelda. They have to be. Nothing would make any sense if they weren't. And they speak. They speak more than most couples. The understanding between them that had been bitterly fought for in the early years is now easily and minimally achieved, with careful avoidance of estrangement. Having someone is a life-giving well. Who dares divide the indivisible history of matrimony? Who would page through the photo album of what might have been? A husband does not fear these thoughts. He is grateful for them. They are proof of his salvation.

'I'm going for the jackal tonight,' he says, to which Zelda doesn't reply. 'It is time. The fences are up, the dam will be fixed tomorrow and there is time for it now.' He repeats it as it occurred to him earlier. She remains quiet. A moment passes.

'I'm taking Leya with me.' At this, his wife looks around, but still doesn't speak. Eventually, she sits down at the table with him. Biggles jumps on, and for once, she lets him.

'Are you sure?' she asks. 'Why?'

'I think it will be fine. She's still a good hunter. She can find him.' Bruno, though far clumsier than Leya, because of his size, already does an adequate job of hunting rats and other pests, so it makes sense to use him, but out of respect for Leya's abilities he will take her this one last time. Let Bruno guard the house, he thinks.

Zelda nods. 'Would you like to eat now, or is there paperwork first? I got the tax forms today.'

He watches her closely, looking for something, not knowing what. There is little knowledge to be gleaned from her general demeanour, though. She is as adept as he at smoothing out appearances. He has no reason to suspect anything, but hopelessly wishes that this heaviness, this politeness of years, could be shifted with just one gesture. A touch to her cheek, an arm around her waist. He doesn't try – knowing she will move away, pretending to get the salt off the shelf. We are out of practice, he thinks. And to get back into shape seems a big obstacle to clear. A shard of his theoretical studies crosses his mind momentarily: 'It is in the nature of things to be undone in the same way as they were assembled,' the theory goes.

'It will take too long. I can do it anytime,' he answers her about the paperwork. 'Just a small helping, please.' They eat.

Then: 'I'm glad it's the last time,' she says. 'I know you hate it when she cries. When she hurts.'

She doesn't say it, but he knows Zelda is scheduling a time for the conversation in her mind once more. Tomorrow, she will remind him of her brother in Natal. 'Even the rains are warm there,' she will say. 'I can drive her up there just before Easter.' But that is tomorrow. Tonight is tonight.

When they finish, he gets up and stands against the sink while she makes coffee. She lets him be silent while he drinks, and busies herself cleaning the table. When he goes to the toilet, she thinks to ask him about the dog, but decides against it.

He finishes, brushes past her in the kitchen and they talk about the time when he will return. Then he goes out, his hat on.

'Leya!' he commands. Nearby, her sacking stirs. Bruno stays down, recognising, for once, Leya's role. She yelps small and low, once. 'Come on!' he says, softly. The dog saunters with stiff hindquarters behind him towards the truck.

The coops are within walking distance, but the idea is to be below the night wind, so he half-lifts the dog to put her on the back, then checks himself and lets her into the front. She needs a push from behind and, once in, she turns just once and half-leans against the seat with a shoulder, looking past him and staring into nothing. When she feels his gaze on her, she looks quickly in his direction, but avoids his stare again almost immediately. His heart is bursting with sorrow. Dogs are so polite, he thinks.

He stops the truck a hundred metres on the other side of the pens, and they wait. Half an hour before midnight he gets out, leaving the door open. He lifts the dog out and leads her slowly to the roosting chickens until they are within hearing distance. The air has chilled, and there is a dry breath of wind from the cages.

Wait.

He closes his eyes, sits down carefully and holds her against him for warmth. Then she lies down and they sleep.

At a quarter to twelve, he wakes up. The chickens are drowsy but upset, sounding the discord of independently broken sleep. The jackal is in. Using the immediate noise, he gets up and treads evenly to the cages, the dog silent and held by a collar. Ten metres away he lets her go and she bounds towards the enclosure, making haste to cover all corners and barking loudly, to cut off all escape.

Now. He shines his torch in the cage. The animal blinks. The man lifts his Beretta .22 and shoots twice, hitting it in the hindquarters the second time. He lets the dog in and she finishes him. Leya snakes her head around to avoid the flashing teeth, and once inside the self-protective circle, simply closes her jaws on the flailing, then shivering body and lets go after a time. Then she licks a torn shoulder and comes as he calls her.

'Thank you, Leya,' he says, hugging her stocky body from behind. 'Thank you, my sweet girl.' Then he shoots her in the ear, three times, to make sure the small calibre gun does what no trip to warmer climes can, anymore.

The broom plant

Jessica Druker

The Negev is too dry for greenery: colour clashes with the landscape. The reds and burned-out oranges, the dry brown all exist as a vast, rusty kaleidoscope on the desert landscape. Green looks out of place.

The Broom Plant wears a tired colour of sun-scorched olive. This is not a youthful green and it does not belong on a youthful plant. It is possible to believe that, perhaps in youth and in shade, the Broom Plant dressed itself in fresh tones, wearing the promise of a new season.

On the sand-hardened plains, the Broom Plant sits like a hunched old woman wearing a dry riverbed of wrinkles in her exposed skin.

The plant splashes over itself. Long, tough reeds tangle themselves like knotted curls as the plant tumbles over its own thin, sun-toughened leaves. It is a mass of long strands; tough dry fingers that occasionally splatter horizons and pathways of the rocky Negev desert.

He arrived when the sun was at its closest to the red earth and hung flushed against the sky like a warm bronzed coin. He had followed a trail of goat prints and scattered pebbles of dung until he heard the sound of conversation and occasional bursts of laughter coming from a number of large dark tents that had been pitched in the shaded valley between two rocky slopes.

The Bedouin tent stood waiting with open flaps, a promise of hospitality and shelter. Generations ago Avraham's tent had stood in a similar position; a four-sided dark house of a tent, with all four flaps kept open as a statement of welcome to an approaching traveller in need of rest. Regardless of direction, the stranger was met by an open front door, and no unnecessary ceremonies of 'may I enter' were required.

It was common knowledge that Bedouin culture had inherited Avraham's sense of hospitality.

Sayid stood by the entrance of the large tent, across the threshold where the red sand met the material home, head bowed as a sign of respect, waiting for the head of the family to greet him. His robes were warm; his camel scratched the hot earth behind him. Next to him a clump of strands of the Broom Plant that had been bound together was perched by the entrance, available to sweep out the sand and pebbles the desert ushered into the tent.

Upon seeing Sayid, the head of the family, Assaf, moved quickly to the younger man, his thick arms spread out, offering an eager embrace to the stranger. Assaf was a stocky man, squat, with a muscular, rounded belly that seemed to propel him forward. His dark, woolly beard was streaked with a number of frizzy grey strands, and when he smiled his cracked lips opened wide in genuine pleasure to reveal dark pink gums and a white-gapped smile.

Assaf greeted the traveller with warm enthusiasm, guiding Sayid into a cool corner of the tent, and seated him on large embroidered cushions.

Behind the men a young woman, Assaf's daughter, heavily robed, her face concealed by a burka, waited for her father and his new guest to be seated before taking Sayid's camel to the well to rest and feed. Naama was Assaf's eldest daughter who always enjoyed tending to her father's guests' animals far more than she enjoyed tending to her father's guests themselves. As she guided the camel to the animal trough, she heard her father's loud voice boom out his pleasantries and welcome, while the camel lowered its head in lumbering grace to snort, quietly, above her head.

Inside the tent Assaf immediately poured two cups of the sweet juices, a honey and nectar cocktail, and handed a cup to his new guest. When a traveller arrives this is the first item to be served. The sweetness is designed to rejuvenate a tired, sun-drained body. Sayid drank his cup with one enthusiastic swallow, his mouth suddenly desperate with a need for flavour, thanking his host and wiping his lips and short beard with his long and heavy sleeve.

The host and guest smiled at one another. Sayid knew that it was impolite to give the impression of unease, and Assaf and Sayid each sank comfortably into their cushions, ready for an exchange of information and small talk. As the conversation between the two men slowly swelled into a natural and easy banter, Sayid spread himself out more comfortably over the cushions, feeling the tensions of his journey gently trickle out of his muscles like warm sand.

Sayid told the story of his two-day travel from Jerusalem. He was headed for Petra. His father specialised in tapestries and they intended to extend their market. Hence the reason for his journey. He told of the recent politics in Jerusalem; the Jordanian emigrants were accusing the Syrians of bringing leprosy into the land, and the Hebrews were celebrating the festival of the new fruits and seasons, Tu Bishvat. There were many pilgrimages being made to the temple ruins with sacrifices of the first crops and the first livestock. Jerusalem was, at present, flooded with visitors.

While the two men were talking Naama quietly entered the room carrying two half-full cups of coffee. When his cup was placed before him Sayid thanked her and her father for their generosity and kindness. He knew that coffee was a rare delicacy to acquire. He knew that he was a valued guest because of this gesture; being offered to drink this rarity with his host was an honour. Sayid smiled at his half-empty cup, knowing that this was an invitation to stay as a guest in Assaf's home and drink the other half at a later time. If his cup had been full it would have been a polite indication made on Assaf's part that he was not invited to stay at all. The coffee was mud black and thick. Sayid sipped at the murky drink slowly. The taste was dry and bitter, but left delicious flavoured wisps of roasted nuts hovering like a ghost at the back of his throat. He handed his empty cup to Naama, thanking her for his refreshment as well as for tending to his animal. Naama cast her eyes down, and murmured a polite statement of welcome through the veil that covered her mouth.

Sayid was astounded by her voice. Her sound tickled his skin like a light layer of honey.

Sayid was invited to stay in Assaf's home for two weeks, having an opportunity to rest his camel as well as himself before continuing his journey. He assisted the family harnessing and roping a new tent, and mended the worn and broken cloth in the cushions and tapestries within the home. He learnt the family's routine with relative ease. He joined the men for early-morning prayers; he learnt quickly when meal times were and arrived punctually at all gatherings; he quickly found a comfortable place for himself amongst everyone else's daily responsibilities.

Every day Sayid watched Naama and her two sisters, heavily robed so that only their hands and eyes were not concealed by the thick cloth, herd the goats out of their pen and up into the rocky slopes of the Negev to graze on the tough leaves and bushes that protruded out of the difficult earth. He would have offered his assistance in the herding – in Jerusalem he knew that that would have been a sign of politeness – but in Bedouin households it is considered extremely rude and brazen to approach the women of the house without the permission of the head of the family. Even when contact between a man and the woman of a household was granted, whatever conversation or activity ensued was generally chaperoned. Sayid knew better than to think it would be considered appropriate to be left alone with the women while they were herding away from the house.

But Sayid had been watching Naama from a distance. A respectable distance. He saw how she tended to his camel with a tenderness he would have reserved for a human; how she cared for her herd with a gentle authority; never allowing one of her goats to stray too far from her sight. She had a kindness that moved about her like a refreshing breeze, making all comfortable in her presence.

A few afternoons ago, while she was rinsing out garments by the well, a gust of desert wind had blown, and raised by a few inches the veil that covered her face. Sayid saw, for a brief instant, the most beautiful features he could recall ever having seen. All he had ever seen of her skin was a pair of small, sun-stained, gentle yet strong hands and a pair of dark eyes, shaped like those of a cat, that seemed to observe everything they saw with a silent clarity and acuteness. But it was the shape of those slanted eyes, and the heavy curtain of lashes, that made her concealed face fascinating to look at and wonder about. Now he had a clear picture of how those eyes looked in relation to her face. That brief glance that he stole when she was sitting by the well seemed to quench a curiosity, but the imagination he had used in guessing her features started to dance over the possibility of looking into that face on a more personal basis. He tucked the memory of her slanted eyes, her mouth, the round smoothness of her cheeks, into a private, lavish corner of his memory, which he allowed his imagination to decorate with hopes and emotional glory. At night, when alone in his sleeping compartment, he would return to this throne room inside his head with anticipated pleasure, like a man who steals off to marvel at and count a recently discovered treasure. And he would remember how the slight sound of her voice had dripped honey over his skin . . .

Sayid began to find arbitrary excuses to pass where Naama was working. He was constantly searching for ways to snatch patches of glances of her to add to his limited collection. Late one night he ripped a cushion in the tent, knowing that she would approach him the next day asking him to repair the sudden damage. During meal times he would hold his breath as he watched Naama enter the room to serve the food. He offered to help her and her sisters make goat's cheese. He began to dream about her face, her voice . . . One night, after drinking in her features from the goblet within his mental throne room, he made a decision.

The next morning Sayid left the tent early to climb the slopes of the Negev desert. He followed the same route he knew Naama took every morning with her herd to their limited grazing spot. The air was chilly at that time of morning, when the sun's fingertips were just beginning to tickle the tips of the horizon with pinks and oranges.

He knew where he was going.

After having put a kilometre behind him he stood in front of the Broom Plant that rooted itself in a massive slump on the path to the grazing ground. He sighed heavily, breathing in the cool air as he took a number of the long strands of the plant and tied them into a knot. He stepped back and looked at the obvious sign that he had left for her. He decided that it was noticeable enough, that it was not some-thing that she could walk past and ignore. He turned and began to follow the path back towards the tent, covering footprints of goats with markings of his sandals. Halfway down the slope Sayid passed the herd and Naama. He smiled politely at her, offering a word of greeting, knowing not to stop and attempt a conversation. She made no gesture in return, but Sayid thought he saw her cat's eyes crinkle in a slight smile she could have been making beneath her veil.

Hours later, when Naama and the goats had returned and the sun was beginning to darken as it scratched at the western side of the hori-zon, Sayid returned to the pathway that led into the desert. He moved quickly through the path and up the rocks, eager to reach the plant. As he raced and stumbled through the darkening desert he hoped, prayed, that another knot had been tied next to the one that he had made. If she had returned his gesture it meant that he had her per-mission to pursue her; that he had her permission to approach her father over the possibility of a courtship and marriage; that he had her permission to desire her and that she had a mutual interest in him. He had left his wedding proposal, an offering of himself, in the leaves of the Broom Plant, and now he needed to know if she had accepted him.

He arrived at the plant, his quick breath making small puddles of steam in the chilling desert night air . . .

Hours before, Naama had stood in front of the plant, staring, unmoving, at the clump of strands. As the goats bleated around her, she thought of the stranger who had been living amongst her isolated family. She thought of his voice; of his skin; of his smile; she thought of his conversation and routine-politeness. She thought of his tapestries; of his eventual destination; of his camel. She thought of his hands. She sighed into the red Negev heat, and lifted her arms to make her reply within the leaves of the plant.

Sayid adjusted his eyes to the swelling darkness. He focussed, and breathed heavily.

His knot had been untied.

All that was left was a slight dent in the leaves. He had been rejected.

He turned away, moving slowly down the rocky pathway towards the tent, his pulse sluggish, his legs heavy with disappointment.

He would pack his belongings, close up her throne room, and leave in the morning.

There was no reason to stay longer.

As Sayid walked back to Assaf's tents the Broom Plant waved at him softly from behind. A wedding proposal had been made in the nothingness of the desert. An arid space had become a container of young hopes and dreams, a place that could have grown a fresh green love. As night time tucked the Negev into a blanket of blackness, a wind skimmed over the surface of the earth, scattering pebbles and sand, and ruffling the leaves of the Broom Plant, smoothing out the remaining kinks of Sayid's proposal.

White boy

Kirsten Miller

It was summer when Richard awoke. Morning light poured through the suburban window of his parent's home; the chill in the air would fade as the day wore on. He moved his arm around the pillow and shifted his head into it, examining the close-up vision of his skin that was white and close to the blue-tinged flesh of a fish.

'The wrong colour,' he muttered into the pillow. 'Trust me.'

In a moment of bracing himself he shut his eyes, opened them again and made the move from the bed to the floor.

Two guitars leaned against the wall near the window, a single string snapped on the Gibson. In the corner stood a pile of music, a short lifetime's collection of his songs and the songs of other people, a small tower waiting to be sung.

Twenty-six years he had inhabited this room, the only respite and sanctuary from the family activity of religious fervor that happened around him. An enlarged image of Jimmy Hendricks looked down from the white space of wall above his bed, and on the opposite side was a Free Mandela poster left over from the struggle days. Richard had just caught the tail end of the march for liberation as he emerged into adulthood. He had tried to leave often enough, to go and create his own way in the world, but somehow when bad things happened, when his girlfriends left him or when he lost his job, he always ended up back here because this space always remained for him, consistent and unchanged.

He pulled on jeans and a sweatshirt from a pile of washing on the floor and moved his hands through the hair that was still soft and blond as a child's but thinning steadily now. Sitting on the side of the bed he pulled on his boots, threaded the laces all the way up to the top and then tied a bow and pulled the legs of his jeans down over them. He glanced out at the sun and the unforgiving trees that peered in at him through the window.

All this time he thought of the phone call that came the previous night. The way it rang three times before his father answered it, the way his father called him to the phone as if it were any one of his friends at the end of the line. The way his father sat down to the television again and he himself got up to hear words spoken that he never would have imagined possible before. And now; now the sun was too bright for this day.

'*This is the day that the lord has made,*' he muttered aloud as he rose from the bed. 'Yup, this is the goddam day.'

It was already gone eight-thirty. His mother was at work but his father sat in front of the television, retired from everything in his life apart from his faith in his god and his addiction to the media.

While Richard was making coffee he glanced at the cheap poster stuck with Prestik on the white tiles above the kettle. It was faded now and it had been there since he was a boy, but today, unlike every other day, the words jumped out at him. *Ask and you shall receive, seek and you shall find, knock and the door will be opened unto you.* The picture showed an old wooden door set into a stone wall that was partially covered by leafy green foliage. Richard hated the way the cardboard curled at the corners; he winced when he saw visitors noticing it. Stealing his eyes back from the wall he focussed on spooning the sugar into the mug and stirring. Today for the first time since he was a very small boy, Richard felt the urge to pray.

'Everything alright, son?' his father asked from his chair.

Richard took the mug from the counter and turned towards his genetic prototype. 'Yes Dad.'

'Your mother and I prayed for you last night. She had a vision. You're not in trouble, are you?' The older man lowered his head and looked at his son over the top of his glasses and without waiting for an answer he said, 'Are you going to look for a job today?'

'I suppose so.' Richard took a sip of the coffee and scalded his tongue, but kept the pain to himself. He swallowed and narrowed his eyes, waiting for the heat in his mouth to subside.

'That band of yours – you've broken up then?'

'We're taking a break,' Richard said and scraped his burned tongue on his teeth as though he could scrape the pain away. 'Magic's guitar was stolen and Sandile's gone to play with a group in Cape Town for a while.'

'And the woman? That singer?'

'Dudu? She left months ago, Dad. She found a job in town so she couldn't do nights anymore.'

Months ago. He thought about the night she told him she wanted to pack it in, the night in the car after a gig at a hotel in town. She had stared out of the window as she spoke and he drove knowing there was something in her words he could or would not believe. She wasn't the type to give up singing for anything, let alone a day job. But she'd made up her mind and closed the subject and he had been left to wonder out at the rain and the streetlights while he drove her home in silence.

Why did she wait until now to call him? And if he had been out when she'd phoned, would she have phoned again? Or she might have lost her nerve long enough for him to find a job and move away; she could always get his number from his parents if she wanted to.

'Well, probably a good thing,' his father said as he got to his feet and moved towards the kettle to make a cup of coffee for himself. 'You can get some early nights and concentrate on getting a job.' He flipped the switch on the kettle although it had just boiled and there was steam still rising from the spout. 'Your mother and I don't like you hanging about like that with those people anyway.'

'We don't hang about, Dad. We play music.' But Richard knew it was just another way for his father to say what he could not admit. It wasn't so much the music, but that the other band members were black. 'It's not a colour thing, it's a class thing,' his father liked to say. His mother said nothing at all. But this was a timeless game his parents played. Even as a child when his father had beaten him with a leather belt over the bath he had paused between strokes to talk to Richard and make sure the child understood. 'It's because your mother and I love you, son,' he would say with sweat on his shiny head while Richard's bare backside burned. 'And the Lord loves you. We only want to teach you to do what is right.'

Now the man poured water from the kettle into a mug and spooned the instant coffee in afterwards. 'Your mother and I only want you to do the right thing, Rich,' he said. 'That's why we pray so hard for you.'

* * *

Johannesburg was bright with summer sun as Richard's yellow car pulled away from the house to find an uneasy path through the suburbs. He stopped at his girlfriend's house where she was readying herself to go out to have her hair done. He sprawled on the couch in the lounge from where he could still watch her carefully applying lipstick in front of a rectangular mirror in the passage. Just looking at her like that made him lonely.

'There's a new band playing in town tonight,' he said. 'Want to come?'

She wound the stick of red back into the tube and blotted her lips in a dabbing motion with a pink tissue.

'I don't know why you even ask me. You know I hate those seedy clubs.'

'The music's great and I want you to come with me. Just once. Come on Tracy.'

She turned towards him, momentarily distracted from her own image, and put one hand on a bony hip.

'Do any white people go there?'

He laughed, a chortle from deep in his throat. '*I'm* white.'

'I'm serious. It's dangerous, you know. You've got to be careful, Rich.' She shook her head and turned back to the mirror.

At the door on the way out he tried to kiss her but she averted her head and gave him her cheek instead to avoid smudging her lips. He looked hurt and made no attempt to conceal it, and in response she turned her doe eyes upon him and gripped the sides of his sweatshirt with her long fingers. 'I do miss you,' she said. 'We can have dinner tomorrow night, if you're not playing or anything. I know this great Thai restaurant. I'll pay.'

He took a step back, pulled away from her. 'I'll give you a call,' he said, looking at her eyes. 'We're giving the band a rest for a while. I don't know why you spend so much time at the hairdresser. Your hair looks fine to me.'

She stood on the steps of the house and watched Richard reverse his car down the driveway. She thought that he looked a bit down today, sad even, and maybe she should give him more encouragement to find a decent job.

Before the sprawling inner city of Johannesburg he veered off onto the highway to bypass the metropolitan area and emerge on the other side where poverty began. There was a soft pack of cigarettes on the dashboard and he took one and lit it without taking his eyes off the road. He felt the nicotine coursing through him, firing him up to jumpstart the day. He knew this road. He had taken Dudu home enough times late at night after gigs when there was no traffic at all. Those nights they would sing all the way to her house, working out harmonies for their songs or talking about her old life in Mozambique. Sometimes they drove in silence after a night of music and revelry. And then for months there was no word from her. Slowly they had become used to the band without her rich and powerful voice, without her huge hips swaying to the languid rhythm of the blues they created together. Gradually they had substituted the sensual, smoky image she brought to it with their boyish and upbeat hipness, and they had watched their target audience become younger, more transient, less committed. Eventually they learnt to do without her.

'Do you think she'll come back?' he'd asked Magic. The older musician only shrugged, turned his back and muttered 'Women! You can't tell what they'll be doing,' as he put away his guitar.

Dudu. They'd had their nights, the four of them. Sandile on drums, Magic's bass, Richard on the Gibson and Dudu's voice. It was Magic and Richard who'd found her, two years ago in a late-night club on Rocky Street, singing her heart out for the country she'd left behind, tears streaming down her round black face and eyes closed in the ecstatic indulgence of memory. Afterwards they sought her out backstage where she was drunk on cheap whiskey and clinging to the bottle, swaying to the sound of the blues that had died in the club as the people drifted away, but had not died inside her. 'Come and sing with us,' Magic told her. And she smiled a mystery at the black man and reached out a hand to brush Richard's cheek.

'Sing with a pretty white boy,' she said. 'And why the hell not!'

* * *

An off-ramp from the highway led onto a road that rattled and shook the car. Small children and old people littered the pavements, some aimlessly but most with some kind of mission as they carried parcels and bundles and buckets of water on their heads. Richard noticed there were streetlights now where there had been none the last time he drove this way. He went carefully, watching for the side road that would take him to her. It came upon him suddenly and he put his foot down on the breaks hard and turned into it, throwing the cigarette out the open window and putting his hand to his head in one motion. 'Shit.' Her voice on the phone had been so quiet that he could do nothing but believe her. There could be no discussion as his parents were in the next room and although the television might have drowned out his own voice he could not speak knowing they were there. 'I'll come tomorrow,' was all he'd said. And then he went straight to bed and slept so deeply and with nothing in his dreams to suggest that his life would alter in any way in the morning.

He pulled up in front of the tiny brick house and as he knocked on the front door he noticed that the windowpane of the front room that had been broken for months had been repaired. The door opened and a shriveled old woman stood there with a red blanket around her shoulders.

'Hello,' Richard said swallowing hard. Something in him shifted in the meeting of his own eyes with the eyes of this woman, something that he could not name. Only his voice spoke now, nothing else that was a part of him. 'I've come to see Dudu.'

'Richard,' the old woman replied, softening the 'ch' sound with her accent and she stepped aside. He went into the two-roomed house and felt that he was being swallowed whole by the darkness. A radio was on and water boiled above the stove in the part of the front room that served as the makeshift kitchen. The old woman motioned for him to sit and there was silence between them as she made him tea and presented it to him steaming and hot in a red enamel mug.

'Dudu she's out,' she finally said in English as broken as her teeth. 'She coming now. Jus' now.' He nodded and she went back to her seat beside the radio. He sipped at the tea and was grateful for the electronic voice that smoothed over the silence between them that otherwise might have frozen his heart, or made him leave.

Twenty minutes later his cup was empty and she walked through the front door, twice the size of her mother, half the size that he remembered.

'White Boy,' she said when she saw him but she did not smile. It was her name for him. It was the name she uttered that night in the car after a gig forty kilometers out of the city, the night they had not driven home but instead chose to wait for sobriety and the morning light. White Boy. The night Magic and Sandile stayed up to gamble and drink and he and Dudu chose to go back to the car together to get some sleep. White Boy. That time she'd had a smile on her face when she said it. A smile that was turned upon him where he lay squashed between the leather of the back seat and her soft nutty skin that smelled of soap. She'd smiled at him then, before she closed her eyes.

Now he stood when he saw her against the light of the doorway and she moved to kiss his cheek. She turned and said something to her mother in their language and the older woman gathered her blanket around herself and scuttled out into the street without looking at him again.

'How have you been?' she asked Richard.

'Okay. We've missed you in the band. We've kind of split for a while.'

'Those times have gone for me.'

'So there's no day job, is there, Dudu?' He couldn't keep the irony from his voice.

'There's a day job alright. It's the hardest work I've ever done, it just doesn't bring in any money.' She was looking at him hard and he did not sit down again, but she made no sign that she wished him to. She had not invited him here on a social visit.

'I don't understand why you didn't tell me then,' he said to her. 'When something could still be done.'

She looked at him. 'Done?' He loved the way her mouth rounded the edge of words to make them smooth, like the sea does to a stone.

'We could have fixed it. You could still be singing.'

She weakened visibly before him and sunk into the chair that her mother had recently vacated. She covered her face with her hands and then looked up at him and he saw something in her that spoke of her loss and her fear. 'I'm thirty-one,' she said. 'I am lonely, Richard. This is not my country, and I have an old, sick mother to look after. In our culture a child is some sort of comfort, some sort of hope that there will be a future.'

He nodded then, understanding more than she could know.

'Why did you only phone me last night? Why not before?'

'I need money,' she replied.

He laughed.

'I don't have a job. I still live with my parents. I'm not even playing at the moment.'

'You have rich parents, they have a nice house. If you can't help me, maybe they can.'

He nodded again, lips pressed together, not looking at her anymore. He understood the threat though it was spoken so gently. Now there was only one thing left to say and he could not speak it, but instead she formed the words for him in her own way.

'Come and see her,' she said.

In the next room the child lay like a tiny coffee bean nestled into the cream of the blankets. He had no thought as he looked at her, he was lost in how small she was, how small and vulnerable in sleep. Her eyelashes were black against her cheeks and her mouth puckered in a half-formed kiss. 'What is her name?'

'Hannah,' Dudu said from where she leaned against the doorframe.

Later, when he was leaving, he told her he was sorry.

'Sorry?' she replied. 'Sorry for what?'

He nodded and lowered his head while he started the car. 'Hannah is a white name,' he finally said before he looked up.

'She has a white father,' Dudu replied, stepping back from him to let him go.

On the way home Richard thought about Tracy and her new hair-do but there was nothing in him that could make him turn towards the direction of her house.

He walked into the house of his parents and his mother was home. She sat with his father watching the television, safely cocooned by the couch and their middle-class comfort, and he could smell the dinner cooking in the oven. Roast lamb.

'Hello, Richard,' his mother said as he walked towards his bedroom.

'Everything all right, son?' his father asked. 'Find any jobs today?'

'Nope,' he replied, and went to his bedroom without pausing.

Later when dinner was over and his parents were seated in front of the television again, Richard made coffee and looked at the poster above the kettle for the second time that day, and then he took two steaming cups to his mother and father. He fetched his own cup and went to the television and switched it off. He placed his coffee on top of the set before he turned to face them. They stared back at him, trying to fathom his behaviour. If it was a joke, they didn't get it. *Ask, and you will receive . . .*

They seemed so small, these two people; more vulnerable even than the child he had seen today. He thought of a life without music and the sickness in his stomach that came with the thought made him banish it instantly from his mind. He would deal with that later. But they had their god to protect them, even from him, their own son, and they waited. *Seek and you shall find . . .* 'Dear Jesus,' his mother said. She was watching his face. Richard had never known such terror, and he swallowed hard as though he could banish it.

'I've got something to ask you,' Richard said. His life was on the cusp of change; so was theirs and they did not yet know it. 'How would you cope with being grandparents?'

'Tracy's pregnant?' his father said. He heard his mother draw in a single sharp breath.

'No, Tracy's not pregnant.' There was a silence as deep as his heart. *Knock, and the door will be opened unto you . . .*

'I have a daughter,' he began. 'And her name is Hannah.'

We're never in such a hurry that speed is more important than safety

Gill Schierhout

When Lydia was a child, her grandfather lived hand-to-mouth in an old green house on a one-and-a-half-acre plot in an outlying working-class (so the papers called it) suburb called Waterfalls, where there were no waterfalls, or none that Lydia ever heard of. His plot was scattered all about with old Dauphines, green, they spawned themselves, and he was never short of parts. There were old fridges no longer working filled with metal bits and screws. No lawn at all.

Lydia is his eldest granddaughter. Now grown with children and a life of her own. She lives 500 km away. She visits too seldom. One day, on impulse, Lydia squeezes two days off after a meeting in a nearby town, and she looks him up.

His embrace is as hard as the rock once mined below the surface. They harvest some sweet potatoes from his garden. She must not forget to take them with her when she leaves. Then they settle down to talk. Talking is her idea, they have been corresponding for several years, for she says he has had a remarkable life. She wants to document the story of his life.

It was years ago outside his old green house that Lydia had first met her cousin Zot. All the relatives crowded inside for tea after Great-uncle Bob's funeral. He'd been killed repairing pylons after a storm – some helpful Harry turned on the power. Lydia and Zot were eight or nine. They had played together on an empty five-gallon drum lying about the yard. It took the two of them, standing arm over arm at the shoulders and walking in unison, to get the drum to move, and on this giant rolling stilt the world wavered all about. Zot wore overalls, like the service station boys, red, a Caltex badge on the front chest pocket. A songololo stuck helpless in their print, held there by the heavy line left in the dust by the drum's rim, its glossy black body and thousand patient legs pasted against the dry dust earth.

It is a very fertile family, children born every year, most out of wed-lock. Like Lydia, her cousin Zot has always been a little different from the rest of them. For Zot, as she grew older, this meant routinely shaving her head to a bald egg, borrowing the old man's army boots and never returning them, cutting up every photograph taken of herself that she did not like; a person determined to reinvent herself. For Lydia, what was written in books could be read, and criticised. No one else in the family knew this like she did. Lydia was the only one to go to University, she went to Medical School, then specialised in Immunology, a specialist in how the body alternately defends and attacks itself. The old man and Lydia share this special bond; his knowledge of the human body is from the inside out.

The lifespan of a miner is seven years, he once told her. He was not ready to die yet, so after thirty years underground he gave it up. Before his luck ran out, he found other things to do.

Lydia has not seen him for three years now, each time she sees him his body is grown more weightless, as if preparing to be blown away. As they sit in the afternoon light, he seems firmly anchored in his chair; his time is not yet come. Yet his frame blends into the shadows so that you can't properly tell whether the shadow you see jutting across the wicker seat is a piece of a limb or a piece of darkness, a rafter or pot plant or tree, blocking out the cast light. His face is half in shadow too, but the face with its stubborn morning stubble and pursed pink lips and eyes so cloudy, yet with the sun still behind them, leaves no room for doubt; no mirage has ever aped the human face. And the glare of the sun that moves behind those cloudy eyes, the heat, the way it has given them all life, is inescapable, warm and cold by turns.

A thread hangs down from beneath the cushion. He sits back in the chair and his form shifts on the hard round ends of his bones.

He was classified as a Demolition's Expert in the War; coming from the mines he knows where to place explosives to do the most damage. Words too, he can destroy in a single breath. Lydia's mother attended seventeen different schools as a child, always moving on. Often he was jacked in the job, couldn't take instructions and the family had to bear the brunt. He was not the sort of man to sacrifice his freedom for the sake of others.

'Most people think that exploding gases do the damage underground,' he says. 'It's not the gases, it is the dust. About three times a year we were compelled to "dust" the whole mine underground.'

He takes the pen Lydia gives him, and licks it. As he speaks, he sketches out a picture of how the fan worked, a portable fan on rails, turn the handle, feed bags of fine ash dust into its shute making the black coal mine white all over.

'Every place must be made safe.'

His hand is still sun-darkened with fingers so engrained with dirt and wear they will never come clean.

'It's all in my service record. What mines, and where. It was law, to document the shifts, so every miner had to have one. Excepting the years from 1935–37, the law changed then, and they didn't have to keep the records'.

'Can I have a copy?' Lydia asks.

'I'll find it for you some time.'

In case the service record does not materialise, Lydia asks him to write it down. His writing flows perpendicularly away from his body across the page. Yet because he has twisted the paper at a strange sort of angle, the lines come out as horizontal more or less, much as you see it here. He writes slowly, in this awkward sprawl, dredging up his memory.

From somewhere beyond the back fence, a late rooster begins to crow.

He breathes in, a-huh a-huh, and settles into the rhythm of a phrase or two. A re-activation of an old silicosis, the doctor's report pronounced. He holds up the X-ray, too, to show grey and white fibres criss-crossing the clear white puff that his lungs used to be, one day long ago when he could speak.

'Why the tattoos,' Lydia blurts out. 'Why did you tattoo yourself? Why the snakes?'

'I don't know why we did it. It was the thing to do then. Just for a change I suppose.'

He struggles through a phrase or two. He gulps a breath and carries on spitting out the words.

'It's popular in Europe too these days,' she says.

'Is that so. Well I never.'

All at once there is the sound of a car pulling to a stop just outside the padlocked gate. A young woman gets out, short blonde-white bristles for hair.

'Coo-ee.'

'Zot,' he huffs.

The old man waves then goes inside to turn off the gate alarm. He has rigged up a siren on the drainpipe, attached to a movement sensor, alongside of the house. Another similar type of set-up sets off a different siren if someone opens the gate. There have been break-ins more than once, he is up and outside waving a stick at the intruders, 'get off of my property,' he shouts, his voice loud despite plunging into wounded lungs for air, cauliflower heads all closed up with the silken webbing roots of his old silicosis. 'Get off or I'll shoot you.'

The blonde-white woman leans against the bonnet of the car, its engine still running, cooler outside the car than in. A shadowy figure sits in the driver's seat pressing now and then on the hooter.

'Zot?' Lydia says. 'I would have passed you in the street without knowing you.'

They embrace. Zot smells of incense and semen, she wears a red bikini top and full-circle flowered skirt. Lydia tries to avoid being jabbed by the twisted moon pierced into her belly. Zot's eyes prey on Lydia, a Qualification. A Doctor. Zot's boyfriend's offers his hand to shake, a rough large hand, surprisingly cold.

The men Zot attracts are *breekers*, men who wear bruised cut eyes like Lydia's Professor husband wears jeans to work after a weekend, unashamed, no one really caring. Lydia asks then forgets his name. Mark? Quinton? Harry?

Zot, like the old man, has tattooed herself. As if it runs in the genes, protest graffiti for those who do not have a voice. While they are settling themselves, Lydia offers to make some tea.

She comes back out from the kitchen. Four large mugs, for he is not the delicate sort for cups and saucers.

'Weak and black for me, with far more sugar than you think,' he says. 'And use a big spoon.

'What about you Zot?'

'I won't have,' she says. 'On a diet.'

'Ever tried "build up"?' he asks his granddaughters. Quinton has disappeared outside.

'Build up? I don't know what it is,' Lydia shakes her head.

'Steve gets it for me, cheaply. Good stuff.'

And turning to Zot, 'You must know it,' he says.

'Build up.' Zot's laughter tinkles and trills. 'Dad swears by it.'

Zot reaches over to squeeze the old man's biceps, thin sticks through his blue-checked shirt.

He shuffles off to the kitchen and brings out a bucket, Mr Universe flexing muscles on the picture.

Harry, or Mark, or Quinton, yes, it's Quinton, Quinton Viveros, Zot informs them, goes out the back lean-to making himself at home amongst the old man's tools. He's going to come in just now and ask to borrow a set of spanners, an old trailer or workbench and that's the last we'll see of it, Lydia thinks. She glances through the list of ingredients on the side label of Mr Universe. Makes a mental note to send him something better.

'Good stuff, but I can't always stomach it,' he says.

Lydia passes him his tea.

'I got used to a lot of sugar in the mines,' he says.

Zot, like him, has the look of growth once stunted never recovered, like something wild that has been tamed, something so alive. She is warm and wholesome. She is managing a restaurant, she says, started out waitressing, worked herself up to this position.

He savours the last dregs of his tea. 'Very nice, thank you.'

He straightens up and starts with his favourite phrase,

'Another thing, did you know . . .'

He likes to tell a technical tale, the hows and whys of rock-plain drilling, how to lay a parquet floor, with matchsticks under to level the blocks, and dig a drain, and a line a pit, and how to fit a lighter on the tailboard of a truck.

'Is it true that every seven years your skin cells die off and are completely replaced?' Zot pushes her bare arm too close to the Doctor's face, stretches the skin either side of her tattoos to show how deep the ink has sunk, the skin's pores each side are still stained blue.

'How do you explain this then? The ink is still here, I had this done more than ten years ago. Who ever said seven years? Some ignorant doctor, medical science,' she scoffs. She still has dimples.

In the Second World War he fought on the side of England in the South African Regiment, Sixth Division, there were six blokes in his unit, no other survivors. He describes it as if it were a holiday, a tour with plenty to see and do and think about. Spent some time in Rest and Recuperation in an American camp; orange juice every morning for breakfast.

Zot bored, saunters out into the yard to join her man. As she passes she can't seem to help an exaggerated lift of alternating hips like a prostitute. Lydia watches her now and then through the kitchen window. She sees how Zot hangs onto the boyfriend, whispering this and that in his ear. Lydia does not like the way that Quinton moves. Something about him seems unnatural. He's on drugs of some sort, Lydia thinks.

'Lydia, ever seen a piece of shrapnel?' the old man interrupts her thoughts.

Lydia takes the object from his hands. Although its shape is unfamiliar, the weight feels satisfying, balanced because it is so heavy, so dense, so much itself. Its outer surfaces carry the perfect tracks of fine machine-calculated engraved lines, like some sort of bolt or screw

looking for a hole, a place, a function, here and there sheared off into
jagged edges, looking to injure, to maim.

'During a "show" one day, I was lying in my trench trying to make
myself as small as possible when I heard something fall beside me with
a thud. White hot, beautiful man, shining like a jewel, I reached out to
pick it up, how could I have been so stupid?'

Lydia wants to hold onto the shrapnel, to keep it for herself. She
gives it back.

'There is no end to the cruelty man inflicts on man.' He shakes his
head and walks away.

When Lydia next turns to the window, she sees Quinton Viveros
grabbing the straps of Zot's top and pulling her backwards to the
ground. Lydia starts, wants to go out to stop this, but the old man is
back beside her, putting his hand on her arm.

'They'll work it out,' he says.

Lydia watches Zot get up, dust herself off. Seeing this, Lydia sees for
the first time how when a woman is under threat, the opposite of an
animal puffing itself up in defence, a woman shrinks.

Zot comes indoors.

'It's time for us to go', Zot says.

'Aren't you staying for supper?'

'Something . . . something has upset Quinton,' she says. 'We'll be
on our way.' And she manages a weak smile, no dimple.

'Suit yourself then,' he says.

They go out to the car to see Zot off.

The old man lifts up the bonnet to pull on a few cables making the
engine roar and shudder. He nods approvingly.

'I can get this babe up to 175 on the open road,' Quinton says, stroking the dashboard fur.

'Bye then.' And with a final hoot they are off.

Lydia intends to leave the following afternoon. She wants to get back
to her home in the city before dark, back to her medical practice, her
family, her children in their private school education, tennis lessons,
ballet, music, the predictable life she has constructed in contrast to all
of this.

He starts putting out some plates for supper.

'Can't you stay a bit longer? Once a week they make me eat Meals on
Wheels. Tonight's the night. A driver comes to drop it off. Horrible
stuff, but I have to promise to eat it. What're you having? There's
plenty of bread.'

'That sounds fine,' Lydia says. 'I'll have bread.'

Over supper he continues his tales of the mines and the War. She has heard some of these before but it doesn't matter to her at all, each time a different embellishment, a different version of the truth.

'In the mines, we always collected the boots,' he says, 'to take them back to the family. The boots are always the first to get blown off. Something to remember, keep your boots on and you will live longer!'

After a while he goes out and comes back in holding a picture.

'Your mother,' he says, propping her up against a slab of margarine.

The child's curly long blonde hair has been moulded into shiny hard ringlets for the picture. She stands buttoned to the chin in a snow white rabbit-skin coat, sent from Italy.

'We were allowed to send home one parcel a month,' he says, 'but I had more money than I knew what to do with. I sent home four or five. That's how it goes.'

The image of that determined and thoughtful child is stamped behind Lydia's eyes, it will keep her awake at night. There is nothing there that remains in the woman Lydia knew as her mother. Where did it get lost? He rarely stumbles for a word, despite that his breath is ebbing away. He leaves few natural gaps, restricted entry for another voice. He cannot tell her. And then he tires, all at once, like a child. Lydia looks across at him. Between the perfect gaps in his holey vest, there is only smooth rose-petal skin, not a single scar of his life visible. He is so perfect now, has turned into the shape of his life, for better or worse.

He walks across the floor to bolt the kitchen door and his joints seem perfectly set, smooth rotation of ball in socket, hinges, long piston-bones; in keeping with his devotion to the mechanical, they do not suffer from lack of grease. Yet their movements are slow and considered, as if telling her that she cannot discount their suffering, it is deep-set, compressed, intrinsic.

'Don't be surprised if the alarm goes off if you open a window,' the last thing he says before retreating down the little passage to his room.

The next morning he is up early, if indeed he slept at all. Lydia brings him his tea at the back where he is cutting up some bits of metal. He plans to make rabbit hutches. Lots of them.

'A good source of protein,' he says.

'Don't the municipality have some kind of law forbidding such a thing?' Lydia asks weakly, knowing he doesn't care.

Then they go to sit in the sun to talk.

'Yes, in the sun please.'

He insists on moving his own chair into position, and hers too. He moves slowly, beautiful, purposeful, like some kind of upright reptile recently evolved into man.

'As children . . . our favourite feast was locusts, great swarms of locusts, sky was black with them, then we would gather as many as we could roast on a shovel and have a feast! Lovely, a taste one does not forget, pulled off their strong back legs and squashed their heads . . .'

The phone rings and he shuffles off. Lydia hears him shout down the phone.

'Strachan Residence. What? Lydia? Wait. Lydia, it's Sylvy, Zot's mother wants you. Don't know what she's mumbling about now.'

Lydia goes to the phone.

'It's Zot,' the voice says. Lydia listens.

Zot had not come home. Her body already recovered. Blue and white by turns. The funeral is on Saturday. Will Lydia stay for Grandpa's sake?

Lydia goes into the bathroom to be alone. Just as it used to, the sign is still hanging there on a single nail on the back of the bathroom door, still covered with coal dust from the mines:

'WE'RE NEVER IN SUCH A HURRY THAT SPEED IS MORE IMPORTANT THAN SAFETY.'

And on the other side, if you flip it over:

'MORE HASTE, LESS SPEED. KEEP OUR SAFETY RECORD.'

Lydia rings home to say she's staying.

Steve, Zot's father, is drunk by ten on the morning of the funeral, weeping for his baby through every orifice, his grief dissolving in booze. Chameleon-grandfather has a whiskey or two in sympathy.

As he passes, he looks at Lydia as if she knows.

She shrugs her shoulders.

'It's okay,' Lydia says. 'We do our best.'

None of Zot's aunts make an appearance at the funeral, not even Lydia's mother. There are certain fractures in this family that have got worse with time.

Before the sun is up on Tuesday, Lydia climbs into her car for the long drive home, a dustbin bag of sweet potatoes on the back seat, heavy as a corpse. They are old and shrivelled, have sat in the ground through too many frosts.

'This thing,' the old man kicks the car fender with the tip of his army boot. When he gets the words out, his voice is soaked through with grief.

'Piece of junk. I hope it gets you home.'

'I've got a cell,' Lydia says. 'I'll call you if I get stuck.'

'You'll be calling me before you've gone 20 k's. Okay? I'll bet you anything you like.'

He turns and walks step by step down to the gate to open it.

As she reverses past him, he sticks his head in the open car window. In the dawn, still full of the sounds of the night, his voice stumbles, has lost some of its sureness.

'Those incidents you're writing down, those stories about my life. How's it going? I've got a few more things I want to tell you.'

'The thing is,' Lydia says, 'these things take time. I'll send you something soon. Bye now.'

She gets home in time for the Immunology Clinic, every Tuesday, 5th Floor. CFS, ME, yuppie flu, neurasthenia. Most of them conditions of unknown cause, and much disputed treatment options. Midway through the clinic Lydia remembers to phone the old man, an unspoken ritual so that he knows she's safely home. She tells the nurse to give her five minutes, shuts the door.

'Strachan Residence.'

'Hi. I'm calling to say I'm back.'

'Everything all right at home?'

'Fine, and you?'

'Listen, the thing with Zot. It's not that boyfriend. He's been cleared. She took her own life.'

'Oh Christ.'

'Lydia, do you believe she could have done that? She was a mixed up kid, but I didn't think . . .'

One by one a list of patients have been taking their places outside.

Lydia leaves the receiver of the telephone dangling and walks over to the window. The blinds are always drawn against the view. She parts one of the horizontal strips as if peering into someone's body, separating tissue from tissue. Down below, a man is pushing a trolley of dirty linen across the service lane. The two tall morgue chimneys send relentless smoke puffs to their fate in the sky, dust to dust, a murky pinkish grey cloud hovers above the skyline.

She feels the colour that has been banking up in her body all these years, reds, yellows, purples, threatening to ricochet across the walls, all over every page. She goes back to the telephone and replaces the receiver. A clear single fingerprint is left on its plastic side; proof, that she, Lydia, has been here. Can the fingers' tips ever be so worn that the fingerprint, that unique identifier of a person, like the nose print of a cow, as the old man once told her, is rubbed out, gone forever? Can a person ever be free of what they were born with, free of the given, a freedom bought by work, by immersion? If anyone's fingerprints are worn down, she thinks, his must be by now. She wonders if he has a fingerprint at all. She thinks of Zot's tattoos too, imagines them still there, swirling into whatever ghost she has become.

The door opens.

'Dr Lydia, your next patient.'

The nurse is holding out a brand-new hospital file.

'Mr Quinton Viveros. Looks as fit as a fiddle but apparently has lymphoma, in remission for three years. Now has recurrence with bone marrow involvement. There is a query here from the oncologist about a hereditary condition. You'd better take a look.'

The nurse hands over the file.

'Will you see him now, Doctor? Are you ready?'

Miscellaneous blues

Graham Carlson

The Lone Ranger stood on the burning porch and surveyed the destruction around him. The roof of the ranch house collapsed in a shower of sparks with a noise like a fat man being punched in the solar plexus. The Lone Ranger flicked his cigarette stub into the flames, swaggered down the smoldering steps and strode towards the corral where a silent figure stood in the flickering shadows, alongside two saddled horses.

'Tonto. Ride into town and see if you can gather some information about this fire. Try the "Smelly Cavern" Tavern – there's always someone there who'll sell their mother for a sniff of something alcoholic.'

'Fuck you, Kimosabi! You want me to ride my redskin ass into a town full of drunk, ethnocentric, hostile Neanderthals and start asking questions about a ranch fire that they probably started because one of them needed a light for his cigarette? You want me to start interrogating a bunch of louts that would rather shoot a man in their path than take the effort to walk round him? Do I look stupid? Do I have "Ignorant savage, will go into town, get beat up so that white dude with an identity crisis can act as a hero" tattooed on my forehead? Do your own dirty work masked man. I ain't goin' nowhere!'

'You can't talk to me like that! He can't talk to me like that . . . can he?'

He turned towards two hitherto unnoticed gentlemen sitting around a campfire. The one was meticulously stirring a small cooking pot over a glowing bed of coals. The other was removing a hypodermic needle from the crook of his arm. He closed his eyes, drew in a sharp breath and slowly let it hiss out between his teeth. 'Aaahhh,' he sighed with contentment and then began to softly sing a surprisingly melodic version of Rodriguez's 'Sugar man'.

'Well, Holmes. Can he?' the Lone Ranger demanded.

'What is it again that I always say, Watson?' Sherlock Holmes enquired of his companion, breaking off from his song.

'I think the phrase you are looking for Holmes is, "when you have eliminated the impossible, whatever remains, however improbable, must be the truth".'

'Yes, that's the one. Whenever you have illuminated the despicable, whatever he contains, however reprehensible, must be aloof.'

The Lone Ranger stared at him blankly for a few seconds, shook his head as if awakening from a daze and turned to a long-haired bearded man on his left. 'You'll go to town for me, won't you J.C.?'

'No way, Ranger dude! One Armenian against a town full of hard cases? They'll crucify me. Besides, I've got to go have a palaver with my old man and Uncle Holy. Catch you later, bro! Ride on!' He pulled a surfboard from the pack on his back and caught a ride skyward on the evening breeze.

'Somebody must want to come with me,' the Lone Ranger said hopefully.

'I'll go with you,' a small voice piped up.

'Uh thanks Goldilocks. Right. Well. Off we go then. Tonto, let's saddle up.'

Tonto opened his mouth, saw the moonlight glinting off the drawn gun in the Lone Ranger's hand and rapidly closed it again. When the party was ready he ventured to ask, 'While we're fixing everybody's problems, shouldn't we check on Bobby Zimmerman?'

'Nah,' said Somebody. 'He's doing fine. Let's go.'

The Lone Ranger pulled back hard on the reins, dug his heels into his horse's side and yelled, 'HIHO SILVER, AWAY. . . Silver . . . Silver . . . oh bugger it.' He climbed off his mount, walked in front of it and signed the words, 'HIHO SILVER, AWAY!' The horse reared onto its back feet, let out a loud whinny and charged off into the darkness leaving the Lone Ranger standing angrily in its wake. 'Bloody horse,' he muttered as he walked to where Tonto sat astride his mount and pulled himself up behind the giggling Indian. 'Buy a deaf horse he says. It'll look good on your employment records, he said. Cheap at the price, he says. Last time I buy anything from Attila the Hun, I don't care how many swords he has at my neck.'

The tiny group slowly set off in the direction of the disappeared horse with the glowering Lone Ranger still muttering angrily to himself.

The town of Little Genocide was nothing more than a dusty main street, a few ramshackle buildings and a couple of empty-looking general stores. One side of the street was dominated by a huge saloon with a hitching post out front, two badly hung swing doors and a barely legible sign that announced it to be "The Smelly Cavern" Tavern. From within came the raucous sounds of debauchery, punctuated by the occasional gunshot and resultant cheers. Goldilocks took one look at this house of ill repute and suddenly remembered that she had left a pot of porridge on the stove and disappeared in a flash. The Lone Ranger, Tonto and Somebody tied their horses to the pole and, after glancing at each other nervously, pushed through the doors and entered the dingy interior. The floor squelched under their footsteps while cigarette smoke, stale beer and the regurgitation of numerous drinks too many had a stand-up fistfight for supremacy. The trio eased their way past the fighting smells and finally managed to reach the bar. A disinterested barkeeper ambled over and grumbled, 'Whatta ya want?'

The Lone Ranger looked at the patron next to him and said, 'We'll have whatever she's drinking, and another for the lady.'

'OK, four poisons coming right up.' After putting on a pair of industrial gloves he reached up and took down an old-fashioned bottle with a large skull and crossbones emblazoned on the front from the shelf behind him. Carefully he poured a small measure of the sickly green contents into four shot glasses. Ramming the cork back into the bottle he replaced it on the shelf and, using a wooden spoon, pushed one of the drinks to the girl. The drink slopped slightly over the side and where it landed on the counter and the spoon, wisps of smoke began to rise. 'Here Juliet. Courtesy of these three young gentlemen.'

'Thanks boys.' She raised the glass to her lips and knocked the drink back. 'These things taste quite good once you've built up the immunity for them. So what are three innocents like yourselves doing in a place like this?'

'We're looking for information.'

'Yeah, well sugar, we're all looking for something! Me, I'm just looking for somebody to love. Ever since that bloody fool Romeo did himself in.'

Somebody's eyes lit up and he moved a little closer. 'Yes, that must have been quite tragic. Why don't you two look around while I try to seduce . . . uh, deduce if Miss Juliet knows anything that could help our investigation.'

Tonto rolled his eyes at the Lone Ranger who shrugged and then wandered over to a group of cowboys, engrossed in a game of 'pin the tail on the donkey'. 'Howdee partners,' he said. The men spun around to see who would dare presume to interrupt their intellectual pursuit and, taking advantage of their lapsed attention, the donkey no tailed it out the door.

''Ere, you've just lost us our donkey. And you're a cheater! Look, Mr Croce. His blindfold has got holes in it!'

The Lone Ranger and Tonto backed away nervously. 'Uhh, look here lads. Didn't mean to interrupt. In fact we were just leaving, isn't that right Tonto.'

'You two ain't going no place,' said old man Croce. 'You don't tug on Superman's cape. You don't spit into the wind. I'm gonna pull the mask off that dumb Lone Ranger cause you don't mess around with Jim! You know, I think there's a song in there somewhere. Hmmm.'

'Mr Croce, it was an accident. Isn't there anything that we can do to make up for it?'

'Well, it has been a mighty long time since we last beat up a hero's Native American sidekick. Leave your pal and you can go!'

Tonto turned to run, but was grabbed by two powerful looking men. 'Ah no, Lone. Don't do this to me. I told you this would happen if I came into town. Lone! Lone! Aaaaaahhhh!'

'It's OK, Tonto. You stay here and entertain your friends. I don't mind doing all the work as usual. Play nicely.' The Lone Ranger turned and slunk away. Spotting a booth in a dingy corner he angled towards it and was gratified to note that it held only one occupant. The woman sitting in the booth was small and petite, wore a huge blue bonnet and held a shepherd's crook in one hand while she wept copiously into a saturated hanky that she held in the other.

'Do you mind if I join you? My name's Lone. Lone Ranger.' When she failed to respond he removed his Stetson, sat down and said, 'I'm trying to investigate a case of arson out at the old MacDonald place. You wouldn't be able to help would you?'

At the mention of MacDonald the woman's wailings became even more agonised and the tears flowed more copiously. 'Miss. Are you alright? I'm sorry I didn't mean to upset you. I'd better go.' He started to rise, but the weeping woman reached across the table with the crook and, hooking it around his neck with practiced ease, forced him back into his seat.

'No, stay. I don't know who set the fire but I wish it were me! My name is Bo Peep. Little Bo Peep. Everyone thinks that I lost my sheep, but I didn't. I got fleeced! They were butchered by that horrible man and sold to the knacker's yard for pittance. You see, Old MacDonald and I were lovers and at first everything was great. We had a nice farm, loads of animals and I had my sheep to look after. But then those bloody pigs took over and started with their 'four legs good, two legs bad' rubbish and before we knew it we were facing a revolution. Old MacDonald was forced to wipe out the entire livestock. Of course my darling sheep had nothing to do with it, but he wouldn't listen to reason. He called in the Ex-Terminator, Arnold someone or other and between them they destroyed the lot. Even Mary's little lamb that I was looking after over the weekend. And after every one he would laugh evilly and say 'Hasta La vista, baby'. It was terrible. I couldn't stay with

Mac after that, so I packed my things and left. The last I heard he had taken up with someone De Ville. Was going into dog breeding or something. Heaven knows where he was going to get the capital to finance a venture like that. I suppose that's no longer a concern.'

'What do you mean?' the Lone Ranger asked.

'Well he's rich now. That old farm of his was insured for millions. Look, it's been nice talking to you, but I really should go. I've taken a new job as a sing-o-gram and I've got a "I'm divorcing you 'cause you've been cheating on me" number to do at the Beckham place at 7 a.m. tomorrow. Or is it "I'm divorcing you and I've been cheating on you"? Hmmm. I'd better check.'

She rose to her feet and without a backward glance or a word of farewell staggered out into the night. It hardly mattered. The Lone Ranger was sitting chuckling to himself and shaking his head, oblivious of the world around him. 'Old MacDonald, you sly fox. Thought you could get away with it, but I'm onto you. I think it's time to pay you and Miss De Ville a visit.' Absent-mindedly he rose to his feet, grabbed Tonto from the midst of a punching melee of men and unceremoniously detached Somebody from Juliet's warm embrace. 'Time to go, boys. We got work to do.' He led them outside and although he raised his eyebrows when Juliet joined them, he refrained from comment. She climbed up behind Somebody on his horse and the four of them rode south out of town towards the De Ville place.

Tonto was sulking, Somebody and Juliet were cuddling together and so the Lone Ranger whistled a happy tune until they arrived at the house. The first fingers of light were beginning to appear on the horizon as Dawn cautiously raised her golden head. She watched the riders ride past her place and then lay back down and went to sleep again. The De Ville house had a machiavellian look to it, all brooding shadows and darkened doorways. They rode right up to the door, dismounted and stood, huddled on the threshold while the Lone Ranger filled them in on what had recently transpired. As he finished bringing them up to date the door flew open and there framed in the light of an old gas lamp stood Old MacDonald, toting an enormous shotgun, dressed in a pair of dirty overalls and gray hair all mussed with sleep.

'Mumble, mumble, mumble!' he said, sneeringly. 'As if I couldn't hear you. Quick all of you, inside, with your hands up.' He stepped back into the hallway and motioned them into the dining room with a wave of his gun. Well if it isn't the old Lone Ranger and his motley crew. You know, apart from all the spotty fur coat and scarves we produce, I've had a rather interesting order for lampshades and chair covers from a Mr Lector. Initially I was a little concerned but now I think I'll be able to fulfill the order. You especially,' he stood gesturing towards Tonto, 'will make a particularly nice pair of shoes. Anyone volunteering to go first.'

'Wait,' cried Juliet pulling a hipflask from her pocket, 'One last shot, before the . . . er . . . last shot.'

'Sure, why not?' MacDonald replied benevolently.

Juliet walked to the side cupboard and poured a small measure into five glasses which she then proceeded to hand around. 'Nostravia,' she said, 'we will never drink so young again,' and proceeded to down the contents.

'Nostravia,' the others echoed, MacDonald a little condescendingly and while he swallowed his the other four threw theirs over their shoulders.

While filing the report at the Sheriff's office a few hours later, Nottingham walked in. 'What was that stuff you gave him to drink?' he asked in amazement. 'Half his lower jaw has dissolved away!'

Juliet smiled sweetly and reached for Somebody's hand. 'Just a little something that I won't be needing anymore,' she said.

The Sheriff stared at her for a while, but on getting no further clarification turned to the Lone Ranger and said, 'You were right. We interrogated Miss De Ville and she confirmed the whole story. She and MacDonald needed the money to finance their Dalmatian project and so they burnt down his farm for the insurance money. She's going away for a long, long time. So now that it's all over what are you going to do?'

'Well,' said Somebody, 'Juliet and I are getting engaged and we're going to live at her father's mansion and become dog breeders. We've already spoken with the SPCA. and they've agreed to let us take all the puppies at De Ville's house.'

After the congratulations had died down, Juliet asked, 'And what about you, Tonto?'

'I've had enough of this ethnic minority sidekick scene. I think I'll change my name to John McLean and become one of those die-hard, Caucasian cops in New York City. It can't be as tough as what I've been doing now! What about you, Lone?'

'It's time I stopped hiding behind my mask and expressed my true identity. I'm going to hook up with an old friend of mine, Robin, and we're going to blow this joint. The craziness in this place is driving me batty. He rose to his feet, hitched his guns more comfortably around his waist and walked out the door. Somebody, Juliet, Tonto and Nottingham trouped behind and watched as he climbed onto his horse, turned it towards the sunset and cried, 'Gotham City here I come! AWAY! Away you stupid horse! Away! Don't make me get down there and sign you . . . away!'

Despair

Bruce Leech

There's nothing really to talk about . . . actually I feel a bit of a fool being here, but my wife said she thought it might help. That it might help me, that is.

Perhaps also us. Perhaps she thinks that it will help us.

She doesn't know that I am here. I don't want her to know either, because then she might make more of it than it is. She might get worried and think that I am in over my head . . . out of my depth . . . that I cannot cope, when in fact I can cope. I most definitely can cope. This is really just a small bump . . . a detour in a path that has otherwise been straight and true. I have always managed.

No! No, not at all. I have definitely done more than just manage – I have done admirably. I have achieved. I am successful. Successful, yes. I have overcome all of life's little trials and tribulations. I am confident, secure, financially prosperous. I have a well-established marriage. Twenty-seven years we've been married – that's quite an investment in this day and age. There are not many today who can boast that record.

Happy? Yes, I believe that I am happy. *We* are happy. Yes, of course we are – we wouldn't have lasted this long otherwise.

Am I supposed to just rattle on like this? Do all of your pati- . . . does everyone just rattle on like I am doing? I have never done anything like this before, you see. But she suggested that I come. Apparently you helped a friend or a friend's husband or someone. She thought that you might help me.

It's quite funny, really. When you look at it all, it's actually quite pathetically funny. I suppose we have to laugh at ourselves, because there's nothing really the matter. You see, I know what the problem is.

Well . . . that's not entirely true either.

I know that I am experiencing problems. I know when those problems first started and I know what happened to me around the time the problems first started. So there we have it – cause and effect. The bugger is, I just don't seem to be able to shake off the effects. It's really the effects that are causing the problem, the incident itself I can live with.

On reflection, no. No, maybe I can't live with the cause. But then, why not? Why should this trouble me so much? After all, it's not as though I knew the man at all.

What was that? What man . . .?

Oh yes, you don't know. You can't know. I haven't told you yet. Funny that, you not knowing. Well then, where do I start?

At the beginning *is* a good place, only, where is the beginning? No that's silly – I know where the beginning is.

It happened on a Tuesday evening. Tuesday 25 June, to be precise.

I finished up at the office at my usual time – around eight o'clock. I was packing some papers into my briefcase to take home to read for an early morning meeting. I suddenly felt very, very tired. Not quite tired even. Something more. It think it was despair. A feeling of complete and utter despair. I thought that it may have been because I had forgotten something – overlooked an important piece of work, or a meeting, or something. I checked my desk, diary and messages and found nothing. Yet I was still not reassured.

I carried this feeling with me down to my motor car and it persisted all the while I was driving home. Not that I got very far, however, before it happened.

I am a commercial solicitor – a highly successful commercial solicitor. I am the senior partner in my firm. When I started at the firm it was nowhere near the size it is now. It was originally a small family practice – grandfather, father, son, that sort of thing. I was articled there, reporting to the then senior partner – the last one of the sons. He was a harmless fellow, really. Too soft to cut it in law and too preoccupied with other interests to make a proper go of running the firm. His son, on whom he absolutely doted, was not interested in the law and so there was no natural successor to take over the family firm. It did not take him long to realise that he didn't need to be there. As soon as he realised *that* the way was open for me to take over and that is precisely what I did. I took the firm from being an old family practice and have turned it into one of the most successful commercial-law partnerships in the city. You can see, then, why I, with some justification, regard myself as successful.

What happened? Oh the incident, the accident, of course. That's what happened.

I left my office around eight-thirty. I know that to be the time because I passed one of the attractive young juniors on the way down to my motor car. She commented on how I was not working late that night. I, in turn, suggested she might want to come with me and that perhaps I could help her with whatever she was busy with over a dinner or something. She laughed and said that her boyfriend was coming to pick her up in half an hour – at nine.

She's an uppity little bitch and I admonished myself on the way down to the basement for having flirted with her. She's the type that could get you into trouble. It happens more and more nowadays. I know. I have seen it with clients and friends; and the sad thing is that the more prominent you are the more likely you are to be targeted.

There has been a complete change in attitudes amongst young women. When I started my career the only women I worked with were clerks, secretaries, receptionists, typists. Most of them left their jobs after their marriages: went off to raise their children, look after their homes, care for their husbands. They were only too glad to be shown a little attention: might even end up finding a husband that way; better prospect than the local lout that they were likely to meet in the pub. My wife worked for me once.

But no longer, that's for sure. Today the women that we employ tend to be ambitious young things with more degrees than there is space on their narrow office walls to hang them on. The only reason they would consider looking at you is if they think there might be a promotion in it for them. Otherwise you are more likely to end up being slapped with a summons than enjoying a little slap and tickle.

Why am I telling you this? Because I feel like with you I can; you are a man, after all; you must understand these things . . .

The incident . . . Yes, the incident. No . . . Yes! Yes, it does relate to the incident. You asked me what time I left the office . . . Well, I was telling you what time I left the office.

I got into my car and drove out of the basement. I turned right as I entered the street and drove in my usual direction towards Main Road that takes me down to Link Road and eventually to my home. It is a route that I have travelled countless times in the past. I have a little routine that I follow: first, I put on some music – usually some Brahms or a little Beethoven, depending on the mood I am in. Then, if I am going straight home, as I pull out I telephone my wife and let her know to expect me. When I put down the phone to her, I turn the music up loud and, once I am out of the basement, I gun the motor and charge down to the main road intersection. The engine is very powerful and, in spite of the size of the car – it is the new Bentley Turbo, standard with surround sound, CD player, all of the gadgets – it accelerates very quickly.

I am probably already doing close to one hundred when I reach Main Road; if not a little faster. You must understand, it is a very short distance.

I never told the police this, of course.

I am listening to the music. Beethoven tonight. The streets are dark. They seem empty. There's a light breeze blowing and it whips up a piece of paper and flicks it across the window, distracting me for a moment from the music and the road. And then he's there! He rolls onto the bonnet. His face smashes into the windscreen just in front of mine. He seems . . . he seems to almost throw himself across the front of the car . . . across from the passenger side . . . he throws himself head first into the windscreen. One minute he is on the side and the next minute . . . the next minute he is on the car. His face is crushed up against the windscreen, the windscreen is bulging in towards me, forming a little crown around the shape of his head. A little crown of silvery spikes.

And then he is gone. He simply disappears again, leaving a trail of saliva and blood on my shattered windscreen. I can see nothing, my vision is gone.

I think that I must have slammed on the brakes. There were no skid marks, of course, the car has superb brakes . . . But I must have slammed on the brakes because I stopped a very short distance away from where it happened. I stopped and pulled over to the side; switched off the engine. And then I just sat there. I sat there and stared at the smear on the glass.

People came and I got out of the car. They asked me if I was hurt and I said, he jumped out in front of me. I said it over and over again, he jumped out in front of me, he jumped out in front of me, he jumped out in front of me . . . What I meant to say, of course, was that he jumped *at* me. But I couldn't.

I stood – halfway between the car and where he lay – watching as a crowd clustered around him. There was a doctor or someone amongst them and he seemed to be doing emergency aid, or emergency care, or whatever you call it. I don't really know because although I was watching I wasn't really looking.

I was still standing there when the ambulance and police car arrived. They covered him then. Such a simple act that . . . seen it many times in the cinema and on the television . . . pulling a blanket over the face. So simple and yet so . . . *definite.* There is an element of the theatrical about my memory of it, as though in a scene from a movie.

And then my mobile phone rang in my pocket. It was my wife. And then a policewoman came over to me.

What, my wife? I don't really know what I told her. I cannot recall. Is it important? Well do you think it could be important, because I can ask her what I said if it is? She is sure to remember. No?

Anyway, there I was standing there like an idiot with this police-woman asking me if I was alright and I said to her that I was fine but that I had to get out of the rain and she said to me, but it isn't raining, sir, and I felt my face and it was wet and I said, but I'm wet, and she said to me, come with me, sir, and then my whole body began to shake with the sobbing and the cold and the shock and she took me away to the ambulance and sat me on the back, between the open doors while they loaded his body onto the stretcher. They put a blanket around my shoulders and I stayed there and cried. This little policewoman stand-ing there, watching me while I cried and making these pathetic noises about how I would be alright. She couldn't have been much older than my daughter. And I just stood there like a silly old sentimental fool and cried.

I cried like a little baby. I cried like I haven't cried since I was a very little boy. I cried like a little boy ashamed of crying . . .

No, no. I'm fine. Really, I'm fine. Just give me a minute to clean up a bit.

They put me in the back of the police car and drove me home.

The garage came and collected the Bentley.

I still have their blanket. Perhaps I should return it to them.

When I got home my wife was waiting, so I must have told her some-thing about what happened. They took some details from her and then left, while I went inside and sat down. She brought me a whiskey and some of my sleeping tablets. I sat there on the edge of my bed with the glass in my hand; shoulders still covered in the thin grey blanket.

My wife must have gone off to her own bed.

I don't know, eventually I must have got into bed myself and I woke up in the morning: still dressed in my suit and socks. I had missed my meeting.

The police came around to the house later that day and took a state-ment. I told them what had happened.

He was my age. Just a bum. No! No, that's not entirely true – he had become a bum; he was a professional of sorts . . . Was a bum, is a bum – it makes no difference really. Well, because he's dead, of course. He must have been quite good at whatever it was he did, because the address that I sent the flowers to was just down the road from my house. What? Oh, to his wife of course. Widow. To his widow.

She telephoned to speak with me – to thank me for the flowers. They had never divorced, although he had lived apart from them – lived on the streets and what not – for the last few years. She hadn't seen him, in fact, for a number of years and then, on the day of the accident, their daughter saw him standing outside the house. He was apparently just standing and watching the house. She said that when she opened the door to speak with him, to call him in, he walked away. He came back later and stood there again, watching. All day. Strange that, isn't it; just to stand and watch your house all day. She thinks that he must have left between half past seven and eight that night.

That means that he must have been on his way from his house to wherever he was going when . . . when I . . . when the accident happened.

It's there. It's there all the time. I can't get rid of it. When I look in the mirror in the morning I see his face staring back at me. I catch a glimpse of him in reflections off windows, shopfronts, shiny surfaces, looking at me out of the corner of his one, squashed eye. I see him when I drive home in my car; when I drive my car anywhere: his face is pressed up against my windscreen. And I cannot make him go away. No matter what I say and do to him, he will not leave me alone. Some-times I find myself shouting at him, shouting out loud – my secretary came into my office the other day.

The daughter? Yes, yes, he had two children. The oldest is the same age as mine. He must have been about my age. Do you know I might even have known him? Well, not really as friends, but it turns out we were at the same university at around about the same time.

I don't know: doctor, architect, engineer . . . does it really make a difference?

No! Not a lawyer. I would have known him if he was a lawyer!

I just would have. We are a relatively small community and we tend to know one another. Not a dime a dozen like you lot are.

She said that he just got tired. That one day a few years ago he woke up and said that he was tired of it all. That he didn't know what it meant anymore . . . didn't know if he could carry on with it anymore the way he had been all those years.

He asked her whether it was all worthwhile. When she asked whether what was all worthwhile he pointed to the things around him and said, all of this.

He left his house that morning – dressed for work with his briefcase – and simply never came home. No phonecall, no message, no word of warning. Just that simple line, that he was tired. She said that he, a few years later, or a few years ago – I forget which – he started to telephone from time to time, but that he would say nothing. She would answer the telephone and there would be no one. At first she thought it was a crank-caller and would hang up, but then later she realised it must be him and she started to talk with him. She would tell him about their children, about how things were, how they were. She would tell him about herself, little things about the house, friends, family . . . As soon as she mentioned him, or the fact that she, that they missed him he would hang-up.

She told me that she never stopped loving him.

It's the problems. The problems are starting. That's really why I have come to see you: the problems, the doubts, the despair. He just will not go away. It will not go away. The despair.

The hideous bride

Jonathan Cumming

Long ago there lived a captain named Abiathar Nhanseb. He claimed to be descended from the crusaders of old, and was chivalrous in all his doings.

Now this Abiathar was in his prime. He had a regal wife, strong sons, comely daughters, a band of skilful warriors and many horses, sheep and goats. He also had a brave friend and lieutenant. This man's name was Gideon. Gideon was a little older than Abiathar, and was known for the power of his silences. It was said that in the presence of Gideon people became aware of the foolishness of most of their words.

While Abiathar's life was prosperous and fertile, Gideon's seemed cursed. For one thing, Gideon's share of any raided livestock would always catch some disease and wither away to nothing. Gideon now refused to keep any animals save a couple of horses; vicious, skeletal nags that no other man could handle or want.

Gideon's wife had died in childbirth. He had never taken another, and had no family except the child – if you could call the creature whose birth had killed his wife a 'child'.

It was not quite human. It had six fingers on its left hand. Worse, it had only one eye. On the left side of its face was a pit where the eye should have been. Some said that the flesh that should have gone to the eye had gone instead into forming the sixth finger.

Many had wanted Gideon to put the newborn thing out into the bush for the hyenas to find, but he would not. He nursed the thing himself, feeding it goat's milk and soothing its strange cries.

The thing was plainly female, and though it could not be christened, it received a secret female name from Gideon. The rest of the clan called it Goat. Goat had been born with grey hair sprouting from her head and back. As she grew older this hair grew with her until it swept her thighs. It served as a kind of clothing, and curtained off her repulsive no-eye.

Nobody expected Goat to live long, but she survived and seemed to grow hardy – as hardy, even, as her namesake-animal. Like some of the more truculent goats, she was given to disappearing into the bush for days. Nobody asked her where she went, except perhaps for Gideon.

Around the time Goat reached the age of fourteen, a rumour began to spread within the clan: a powerful witch, it was said, was living half a day's ride from their main encampment. This witch – so the rumour continued – could cure any ailment. The cost of a witch's cure was Damnation to Hell, but some members of the clan did not mind this.

We will have more to say about the witch later.

The raiding season came. Abiathar rode out with his men, and Gideon rode at Abiathar's side. Abiathar fancied millet porridge for breakfast, so they went to a village that was known to have had a good crop of millet.

The villagers knew of the raiders' arrival in the district. Indeed, they had been preparing for such a visit for some time. Their reputation as farmers had allowed them to buy, on credit, a dozen or so muskets of unusually good quality. Moreover, the trader who sold them the muskets had once been a soldier of some distant monarch. As part of the bargain, he had taught the villagers how to judge the muskets' range, aim and fire in a concerted volley.

The villagers allowed Abiathar and his warriors to enter the main street. Then, from the surrounding dwellings, they ambushed them. Abiathar's horse took a ball in the nose. It reared, threw Abiathar and bolted. Abiathar lay stunned. Gideon dismounted. With astonishing strength he put his arms around Abiathar's waist, lifted him up and set him on his own nag. Abiathar regained consciousness. He looked down at Gideon. A hole appeared in the side of Gideon's neck. Gideon stepped back. Another hole appeared in his chest.

Gideon looked up at Abiathar. He spoke clearly: 'Look after my daughter. Find her a good husband.' Then he dropped.

Abiathar turned Gideon's nag and kicked its flanks. It bolted. Abiathar clung on. The nag hurtled out of the village and took Abiathar with it. Only when the sound of musketry began to fade did the nag slow to a trot, turn its head and bite Abiathar.

Abiathar lost five men that day, and many more were wounded. The rest of that year's raiding season did not go well either.

When the season was over, Abiathar turned his attention to Gideon's request. He gathered his leading men around him and told them the story of how Gideon had saved his life. He repeated Gideon's last words. When he had finished, all were pale. They knew what Abiathar was going to ask.

'Who will undertake this duty?'

No one answered.

'Who will marry my friend's daughter?'

They could not meet Abiathar's eyes.

Abiathar turned to his sons, two of whom were unmarried. 'Enoch? Hamutal? Which of you will step forward first?'

Enoch and Hamutal shook their heads.

'Who will save my honour?'

There was silence.

'Very well,' said Abiathar. 'Though Christ forbids it, I must take a second wife.'

One of the men had been looking thoughtful. Now he said, 'I will marry the girl.'

The man's name was Egret. He was about sixteen years old. Not only was he the most beautiful and gentle of all Abiathar's raiders, he was also one of the finest horsemen, and had the knack of being able to fire a pistol at full gallop and actually hit the target. He was a favourite with almost everyone in the clan. Abiathar had often wished Egret were his son.

'No,' said Abiathar. 'I forbid it. You are too young, Egret. Thank you, but no.'

'Sir,' said Egret. 'Truly.'

'Truly?' said Abiathar.

'Truly.'

Ever since the ambush in the village, a black phantom had been gathering at the back of Abiathar's skull. He had been considering asking his surgeon to drill a small hole to release it. Suddenly, Egret's suggestion seemed to make the drilling unnecessary.

'Very well, Egret,' said Abiathar. 'I will consider it.'

Egret bowed his head to Abiathar. Abiathar nodded back. The meeting moved on to other matters.

For the wedding of Egret to Goat, Abiathar supplied two good gold rings, a suit of white silk for Egret, a white cape, hood and veil that would help conceal Goat, and a feast of mead and spitted sheep for all the clan. He supplied a pavilion, long tables and benches, minstrels, jugglers and a troupe of performing baboons. He organised a sports day and included an egg-and-spoon race for the children.

But the wedding was not joyful. Many of the girls were seen shedding not-so-secret tears, and so were certain matrons and grandmothers. As for the men – their faces were stiff. They gazed impassively at the antics of the baboons.

The children sensed the mood of their parents. Nobody won the egg-and-spoon race because all dropped their eggs. There was gnashing and squabbling between them.

Egret, however, seemed serene. When the moment came to bind himself to Goat, he took the gold ring from Abiathar, took her hand (the one with the ordinary number of fingers) and slipped the ring on as smoothly as if he had been handling one of his pistols. He ducked

under Goat's veil and kissed her with no visible shudder. Later, at the
high table, he offered her a choice slice of mutton and held the mead
cup to her mouth. He might even have whispered something in
her ear.

Everyone tried to forget this day. The fact remained, though, that
Egret was now married to Goat. Still more disturbingly, as the weeks
went by, Egret did not appear unhappy. He remained as cheerful as he
had been before, and was, if anything, more vigorous in his horseman-
ship and his attendance to whatever duties he was given.

One day Abiathar took Egret aside. 'My dear boy,' said Abiathar. 'I
must confess I am a little anxious about you. Are you perfectly well?'

'I was, I think, Sir,' replied Egret. 'But now I feel troubled. Have I
offended, Sir?'

'No, no, of course not!' exclaimed Abiathar. 'I am simply anxious
that the nature of your marriage, so nobly undertaken out of duty to
me, may sap certain of the youthful juices. You do not feel it is so? I can
always arrange a little tryst for you; the better class of girl, naturally . . .'

'Thank you for your concern, Sir,' said Egret, 'yet I am content with
my wife.'

'I am glad of it,' said Abiathar. But in his heart he remained
troubled. That evening he dressed in the black cloak he usually wore
on night raids. He went to Egret's shack but did not knock on the
door. At one window, the curtain-mat fell short to leave an open gap.
Candlelight came through it. Abiathar put his eye to the gap and
watched and listened to Egret and Goat.

Later, Abiathar could not sleep. When dawn began to touch the sky,
he saddled his horse and rode out alone. He followed a map he had
obtained from one of his less reputable warriors. The map led him
along a series of antelope paths and dry riverbeds. He arrived at mid-
morning. A stone's throw from the riverbed was a low cliff, and the
witch's hut was at the base of it. The hut was a dome of woven branches
caulked with mud and patched with skins. It had no windows and no
proper door. Instead, a low, woven tunnel extended from the dome by
about the length of a man and then a little more. To enter the hut, you
would have to crawl through this tunnel on hands and knees.

Abiathar went to the mouth of the tunnel and cleared his throat.

From the depths of the hut came a voice, possibly a woman's: *You
are expected. Come in.*

Abiathar loosened his dagger in its sheath. Then he went down on
all fours and crawled in. He passed through curtains. The hut was better caulked that it had appeared from the outside. It was so dark he

could not see his own hands, no matter how closely he held them to his face.

'*Yes?*' said the voice.

'I am troubled,' whispered Abiathar. 'Perhaps you can help me?'

'*Tell me.*'

Abiathar began to talk. He talked for a long time. He told the witch about Gideon's last request, and how Egret had bound himself to Goat. He hinted at what he had seen and heard in Egret's shack. 'The Goat has bewitched my Egret,' he finished. 'She has put a spell upon his eyes. He cannot see how hideous she is. He was so tender with her . . . I must ask you –'

'*What is your question?*'

'Did the Goat buy a love potion from you?'

'*No. Your Egret loves her because she is the one he has chosen. Besides, in the private moments of love, every woman is beautiful.*'

Abiathar did not reply to this. He said: 'I am afraid for Egret.'

'*What do you fear?*'

'Potion or no potion, bewitchment is bewitchment. I cannot use a warrior who is bewitched. Besides, the pastors will not permit it – and will learn of it soon enough. I must cast Egret aside. But I do not want to.'

There was silence. At last the witch said: '*Return here while dusk is falling. On the flat rock outside, you will find a whistle. The whistle will be made of bone; I can say no more about its origins. You will also find a bracelet of hair. Take the whistle and bracelet. Tomorrow, when Egret is out attending to your business, go to the well just south of your encampment. The one you call Goat will be there. Conceal yourself nearby. Blow the whistle and creep ever deeper into the bush. She will be lured by the whistle's call. When you have her well away from the camp, lay hold of her and force the bracelet onto her wrist. The bracelet will render her docile. Put her on your horse and bring her here. Leave her outside for me. Then go. Do not linger.*'

'What will you do with her?'

'*That is my business.*'

'What payment do you ask?'

'*The girl will be payment enough.*'

Abiathar backed out of the hut. He could still see nothing, but the knees of previous visitors had worn a slight trench into the earth floor, and he was able to feel his way out along this.

He returned at dusk. The whistle and bracelet were on a flat rock outside the hut. He hunched down over the rock and peered at them, wanting to examine before he touched. The bracelet was plaited from hair that could have been either human or from the mane of some

animal. The bone whistle was of a length to match Abiathar's own finger digits. He looked around. Then, quickly, he plucked up the
articles and stuffed them in his pouch.

'Thank you,' he called.

There was no reply.

Everything happened as the witch had said it would. Next day, Goat
was at the southern well. Abiathar mastered his repulsion against the
whistle and put it to his lips. Its note was thin and high as the call of
some predatory bird. Goat raised her head. She seemed not to see
Abiathar, but began all the same to walk towards him. He backed away.
She followed him into the bush. When he grasped her wrist she kicked
him in the shins. He forced the bracelet over her hand. Her arm went
limp. She stood still. He led her to his horse, mounted and pulled her
up behind him. Then he rode with her to the witch's hut.

Outside the hut he dismounted, took Goat by the waist and set her
on her feet. 'Hello,' he called into the mouth of the hut. Again, there
was no reply to his call. He put the whistle on the flat rock. Goat stood
mutely. He hauled himself into his saddle and trotted away. When he
looked back, Goat was standing exactly as he had left her.

That evening, Egret came home from guarding Abiathar's flocks to
find neither his wife nor his supper. He was only a little worried. When
she wandered off into the bush in search of the herbs and small wild
creatures it delighted her to find, he let her be.

But midnight drew near and passed and turned to morning, and
still she did not come. Before it was light he saddled his horse and
rode out to find her. As the sky whitened he began to scan it for vul-
tures, the first sign of a lion kill. He was trembling within.

The morning marched on and the sky turned pure, cloudless blue.
It remained so for most of the day; bright and empty of anything
much.

Day upon day, week upon week, Egret rode out in search of Goat.
Eventually Abiathar had to order him to stop searching and attend to
his work. Egret disobeyed. He had become a fleshless, silent man. He
was no longer a favourite. Abiathar knew that soon he would have to
give the order for Egret to be flogged.

Abiathar went alone one day along the antelope paths and dry riverbeds. He arrived at mid-morning. He stood before the mouth of the
witch's entrance tunnel and cleared his throat.

The hut was silent. Abiathar waited.

At last: *'You are expected. Come.'*

Abiathar loosened his dagger in its sheath. He got on all fours and crawled in. He passed through curtains. He could not see his own hands.

'Yes?'

'I am troubled,' whispered Abiathar. 'Perhaps you can help me?'

'Tell me.'

He told the witch about Egret. 'I beg you,' he finished, 'give me a potion that will make him lust after the village girls. Anything would be better than this pining away.'

'Bring him to me.'

'What will you do to him?'

'I will cure him.'

'At what price?'

'There is no price. I will be glad to be of service to my Captain.'

'He will not come to a witch's abode.'

'Put out your hand. Make a cup with your palm.'

Abiathar put out one hand. He could still see nothing. He wanted to pull his hand away but pride would not let him. Something dropped into the cup of his palm. He made a fist around it. His fingertips told him it was a ring, and gold.

'If you give it to him, he will come.'

'I will try to bring him tomorrow,' said Abiathar.

The witch did not answer. He knew it was time to go. He backed out of the hut. The trench worn by visitors' knees seemed deeper than before.

Outside, he looked at the ring. He remembered it well, for he had supplied it. Egret had, at the moment of binding, slipped it over Goat's finger.

Abiathar returned to the encampment to refresh himself, then went out to the pastures and found Egret. Without attempting an explanation, he handed Egret the ring. Egret turned pale. He could not speak. Abiathar put his hands on Egret's shoulders. 'Ride with me tomorrow,' said Abiathar. 'We must go secretly.'

Egret gazed at him and nodded.

They rode out on the morrow. When Egret saw the low cliff with the witch's hut beneath, he hesitated.

Abiathar looked at Egret, began to speak, and found himself saying: 'She who lives within found the ring by chance . . . Perhaps, by chance, she can help you find what you seek.'

'May Christ forgive me,' said Egret. He kicked his horse forward and rode slightly ahead of Abiathar up to the tunneled mouth of the hut.

There he dismounted. Abiathar came up behind him and cleared his throat.

The now-familiar voice responded immediately: *'Come.'*

'Go in,' said Abiathar.

Egret knelt and crawled into the tunnel mouth.

The voice spoke to Abiathar: *'Ride home, Captain. Do not linger. Provided you do not linger, he will come to no harm.'*

Abiathar rode away. When he thought he was out of sight of the hut, he turned his horse off the path and into a thicket. There he dismounted, tied the horse and stalked back towards the hut. He shuffled on his belly into a hollow beneath a canopy of low thorn branches. From there he watched the hut. He watched till dusk. All the while, Egret's horse stood to one side of the hut, waiting silently, as well-trained raiding horses will.

When the sun dipped below the cliff, Abiathar decided he would go to the hut and tear it down with his bare hands. He imagined how it would be to expose the witch to the last rays of light. He imagined her looking up at him from the feast of Egret's flesh.

As Abiathar began to reverse from his hiding place, Egret emerged from the hut. Egret went to his horse, mounted and began the ride back towards the encampment. His head was high and he was whistling a melody. It seemed to Abiathar that the melody echoed back from the walls of the witch's cliff.

Abiathar did not reveal himself to Egret. He waited till the melody disappeared into the sawing of night crickets, then trailed him home through the twilight.

In the weeks that followed, the flesh began to return to Egret's face. He was seen to laugh with the other young warriors, and they were seen to seek out his company again. Abiathar noticed, however, that Egret was given to disappearing at odd moments from the encampment and his duties. He tracked Egret thrice, and found that the tracks led always towards the witch's hut. It seemed that Egret was once again under some spell. Abiathar could not rid his mind of his vision of the witch feasting on Egret.

At last Abiathar spoke to his chief pastor. He said it had come to his attention that a witch was living in the vicinity.

'We know,' said the pastor. 'We have been waiting for your word on the matter.'

'What action should I take?' asked Abiathar. 'Advise me.'

The pastor's advice was firm.

First Abiathar sent Egret on an errand. There were rumours of rustlers on the northern verges of the clan's territory. He asked Egret to investigate. This meant Egret had to ride out in the direction opposite to that of the witch's hut.

Then Abiathar picked twelve warriors and the chief pastor picked two assistant pastors. They prepared a raid. When the preparations were done, the chief pastor blessed the raiding party. He dipped his forefinger into a bowl of lamb's blood and smeared a cross on each man's forehead.

The party set off slowly. Warriors and pastors alike had loaded bundles of brushwood across the rumps and shoulders of their mounts. Behind came mules carrying yet more brushwood.

Before they reached the witch's hut they fanned out into the bush. The warriors at the front flanked the hut and the cliff, so that the party formed a broad circle around the witch's domain. They stalked in closer; the circle drew tighter. They halted within a paddock-length of the hut. Some of the warriors were on the cliff above.

Of the witch herself there was no sign. It seemed to Abiathar that the mouth of her hut's entrance tunnel gaped emptily at his preparations. He signalled to his warriors. They dismounted, hoisted the brushwood from their horses and mules onto their own shoulders, ran in and began to stack the wood over the hut.

The chief pastor and two warriors stood at the mouth of the entrance tunnel. One of the warriors poised his spear, ready to skewer anything that attempted to dash out. The other warrior, a man known for his physical strength, hugged to his chest the last and fattest brushwood bundle.

'Witch!' called out the chief pastor. 'You are to be cleansed. Reflect while you may upon your sins.'

But the witch, if she was there, remained silent.

The chief pastor allowed the silence to linger just long enough to make the hairs lift on the back of every man's neck. Then he gestured to the warrior hugging the last brushwood bundle. The warrior rammed the bundle into the mouth of the tunnel. The chief pastor struck his tinderbox and put the flame to the base of the bundle. The assistant pastors on either side of the hut struck their tinderboxes also.

Soon the heat was such that the men had to draw away. Flames were gushing up against the top of the cliff.

The pyre collapsed inwards onto the bubble of the hut. They saw, now, the one they had called Goat, all her hair burnt away, standing curiously erect while she roasted.

The sight was so curious, in fact, that none of them saw the horseman till he was in their midst. His horse reared up against the wall of flames and lashed out with its forelegs against the licking agony. He turned the horse, leapt down from the saddle and, with motions of his arms that some later likened to a swimmer's, dove towards his love.

'Remarkable,' murmured the chief pastor, 'how even in death she casts her spell.'

'NO,' roared Abiathar. 'NO . . .'

Pictures

Tebogo C Sengfeng

There's a long pause as I hold an envelope with old pictures inside. My unsteady hands are shaking and my eyes are fixed onto this bunch of memories without a wink. I slowly sit on my bed; collect all my guts to open it. Thing is, I hate pictures . . .

But I can't get rid of this echoing need to reopen my past . . .

I wrestle with my conscience . . . *let me open this for the last time. I'm yearning for it . . . please.*

Ahh . . . here is it. It seems like I'm seeing it for the first time. Mandisa. She displays a beautiful smile. Her eyes are staring at me and I feel a certain vibration from them piercing through into my inner being. I stare back at those eyes and it seems as if she'd wink. I can't help but be mesmerised by the beauty I'm facing here. The beauty of her I never realised before. In fact, I think this is the most beautiful woman I've ever seen. I remember how Mike the cameraman coached her to pose for the picture.

'No . . . no . . . put your right hand over your hip . . . okay, move closer to the flower'.

The flower. A blooming red rose. Even now I can smell its fresh scents.

'Yes . . . closer . . . okay . . . face this way . . . that's it! Now say cheese.'

Mandisa blushes and awkwardly says cheese.

'No! Not like that! You don't want your picture looking like you were just coming from a funeral . . . this will be a memory captured forever . . . now let's try it again. Smile and feel it this time when you say cheese.' Mike demonstrates with his mouth how she should say it.

Mandisa smiles, says cheeeezzzz. Then she laughs. Then a quick light and a snap! And that was it. A smile, a cheeeezzzz, laughter, a light and a snap! Captured here forever.

Ag Mandisa, how I wish you'd been happy like you look here. I feel there's a lot of injustice done to you through this photo. It fails to tell the true story of your reality, because this is not how I remember you at all. Pictures can lie. That's why I hate them.

The next one is that of Ntatemogolo – a wise man in his old age with white beard, holding a stick in his right hand, wearing his glasses. I used to try those spectacles out when he was asleep and I never saw clearly in them. Ntatemogolo had an interesting way of looking into the world and I when I tried to view it through his eyes, the view would be so awkward.

I flip to the next photo, give it one glance and go to the next one. Here I am. I'm about seven or eight, just about a year and a half since Ntatemogolo had died. Dammit I'm such a mess. When Ntatemogolo bought that shirt it was brightly white, now I can't even agree with myself that white was its original colour. And I look so embarrassed – some of the neighbourhood kids had been laughing at me because the shorts was wearing were torn at the back and I wasn't wearing any undies.

'Mandlebe ka lerago le lentsho!' my mates had teased.

Mandlebe is a nickname I got from having big ears. Ntatemogolo used to say that having big ears made me a good listener; therefore I would be a wise kid. Now my friends were teasing me about it and this woman used to pinch them and call me *sana-ma-bish* while banging my big head against the wall. If I cried she encouraged me to cry more *'lla o fokotse metsi a a tletseng mo tlhogong ao!'* and I would cry harder as if I believed her when she said my head was filled with water and crying helped reduce it. I always wondered what *sana-ma-bish* meant until later when I'd learn that this woman had been trying to say *son-of-a-bitch*.

Back to this expression of shame – trying to face away from the camera with mucus around my nose – see, that's another reason why I hate pictures, they remind you of what you were yesterday. Their figures are so fixed and it is this fixity that embarrasses you. There's no way you can wipe that mucus from the nose, or wash that dirty shirt, or hide the cracks on those feet, or wipe the dirt from those legs, or comb that hair. There's no way you can coach that fixed figure of shame and embarrassment to move closer to the rose, to smile and say cheese. It's captured forever, and it stares at you, embarrassing you.

In the next one I'm with my friends and we're carrying *diketi* – we've just tried our luck to shoot flying birds. We always missed but never lost hope. Hai! Childishness! How we would run around with old car tyres for the whole day and go back when my friends' mothers had called them back home, and how I hated that moment of leaving the streets. If I had wings I'd fly away like those birds we'd been trying to shoot during the day. Fly away and feel free. Ntatemogolo had taught me that *'gaabo motho go thebe phatswa'* yet I felt like running away from this . . . this bullshit which was home to the stressed men and women of our township. After a hard day at work they would start off at Nice-time shebeen, as they used to call it, to have some beer or chibuku. On Fridays they'd come to spend the night and make all the noise they couldn't make during the week. At times they would sing some of the church hymns their poor spirits had been longing to sing.

This bullshit was home to men and women with broken hearts. Years later my colleague Harry and I would hear the song *Where do broken hearts go?* by Whitney Houston and I would joke to him and said broken hearts went to a beer bottle. This bullshit was home to those lustful men whose beloved pregnant wives were tired of them in the bedroom, and to those men whose marriages were on the rocks and weren't getting enough from their wives, and to those men who were probably bored by their conservative wives and needed something different and spicy, and to the hopeless romantics who'd just given up on love, earning themselves the title '*mafeta*' . . . oh, and the widowers as well. All these men I used to call them *bo-Malome* – uncles. This woman's bedroom used to be their place of pleasure. They paid for the services anyway. Fair enough. But sometimes they didn't pay and if she shouted to demand her pay they would slap her.

I slept in the next room and sometimes I put tissue in my ears so I wouldn't hear the noises coming from her room. The moans and groans of a slight pain . . . moans that grew louder, and louder and louder . . . *please stop hurting her,* her voice escapes a scream and she tells him not to stop, 'cause she's loving it – screams of a certain pleasure. Sometimes she'd scream and I'd think she's enjoying it, and then she'd tell them it's painful. But most times it would just be silent, except for the complaints from tired mattress springs. After they'd released all their lusts into her I would hear her pouring water into the baby bathtub. One day I slightly opened her door to see her scrubbing herself. As if the uncles had smothered sin onto her she squatted and scrubbed so hard, washing the sin, then rinsing it away, applied a coconut lotion on her beautiful brown-skinned body, used a Sadie roll-on, vanished her face with Ponds and rolled a red lipstick over her lips. She smelled so nice. Almost like a rose outside. Just almost.

One Friday night I've just served the other uncles their beers and I'm sitting in my room, thinking of Ntatemogolo. Malome Joe walks in and closes the door behind him. He sits next to me and says that I'm a very cute boy. I remember how ugly I am with my big ears, but anyway I say thank you and he brushes my cheeks. I get a little uncomfortable, slightly move away from him and he asks if I don't like him touching me and I just keep quiet so he comes closer and I move away from the bed as he moves closer until I can't move anymore because the damn wall blocks me. He tells me I look scared . . . am I scared of him? He says I should relax, he won't hurt me, and we'll just have a little fun. He smiles, tries to unzip my shorts so I try to scream but he quickly blocks my mouth, displays a threatening expression and warns that he doesn't like naughty boys, then he promises to kill me if I make another sound and asks if I understand. I nervously nod my head. He smiles and says good. He puts his hand inside my shorts and I'm not wearing any undies. He touches my balls with his big hand and plays with them so I grin my teeth together, close my eyes and wait for him to finish but no, he is far from getting finished. He takes my hand and makes me touch his balls as well but I can't because my hands are shaking so badly. He then makes me bend over and pushes his thing in there and it's damn well hurting. Before he leaves he warns that I shouldn't tell anyone, even that bitch-woman, otherwise I will die.

Now I understood why this woman – this bitch-woman – used to scrub herself so badly. I didn't sleep that night; I kept on asking Ntate-mogolo why he let this happen to me. He used to tell me that he would be my ancestor and would look out for me when he was in 'the other world'. Where had he been? The following morning I also scrubbed myself and went into this woman's bedroom to steal her coconut lotion. Maybe if I smelled nice I would not feel so dirty. But this woman catches me in the act and asks in a shouting that makes our shack vibrate why I don't use my Vaseline. She pinches my 'big-for-nothing' ears with her long nails because they can't hear and bangs my head against the wall. She then tells me *'lla o fokotse metsi a a mo tlhogong ao, sana-ma-bish!'* This time when I cry. I tell her it's not about the water in my head, but about pains in my heart. Then she says what do you know about pain so I tell her I felt it when Ntatemogolo deserted me and I feel it every time she shouts at and beats me and also when she pinches my big ears and bangs my head against the wall and every time those kids tease my ears.

She doesn't listen, gives me some money for tonight's supply. I tell her I also felt pain last night when Malome Joe visited my room.

'Go buy the beers.' She ignores me. 'I better find cold beer inside the fridge when I get back from town,' she continues.

'Who are you going to see in town? Uncle Sbusiso . . . or Sphiwe . . . oh, I see, the new Malome who's been coming here lately . . . Malome Mandla. Is . . . is that uncle your new boyfriend as well, Mandisa?'

She slaps me and says it's a reminder that she is my mother. I tell her I can't remember her giving birth to me so I can't really be sure if she's my mother.

'*Kare ke mmago, wa nkutlwa*!?' she forces me to acknowledge her as my mother.

Long pause. I hear her breathing. I hear my heartbeat. I feel my blood ragingly running through my veins. I feel that hardness blocking my throat. I smell blood in my nose.

'Malome Joe . . . I . . . I don't like him, Mama.' I'm not surprised I've just called her that. Her voice tones down.

'*Bona fa ngwanaka. Malome Joe ke customer ya rona e tona.* His money helps put pap on our table and buy the clothes we wear.'

I take a look at the clothes I'm wearing and remember how my enthusiasm was embarrassed the previous week when we passed all the nice shops in town and walked inside Khupukani – the ou-klere shop.

'If it weren't for all these uncles, we would be living in the streets right now.'

I'd rather we lived in the streets than in this bullshit.

'But Uncle Joe . . . he . . . he touched me, mama.'

'What do you mean he touched you?'

'He . . . he undressed me and he hurt me.'

She looks surprised, swallows very hard and opens her mouth but nothing comes out.

'I hate him! And I hate all these people who always come here for making noise!'

I heard noises escaping through my mouth from somewhere deep inside me. I was shaking. She sat on my bed, looked up at me and slowly, with patience, explained some things to me. My big ears heard her voice sailing through my head but I didn't hear her words – a voice without language. All I did was stand there, looking back into her eyes. Ntatemogolo used to say that eyes could speak as well. So I decided to turn a deaf ear to her words and tried to find some language from her eyes. Maybe her eyes would express her motherly love for me. I stared so deeply into them, and all I could feel from them was a chilling coldness running down my spine. Without a wink, I kept on searching through her eyes with desperation. Suddenly I realised I was looking into her pupils. And in them I saw me – a tiny little figure shaking with fear. And that's all I found. *What's wrong with you Mandisa? What's wrong with us?* At that very moment, after searching for a mother I never found, I hated her and everything about her, including that little boy I saw in her eyes. I hated me for being borne by her. I hated our world. I hated Ntatemogolo and his theories about ancestors and God. I hated my mates for making fun of my ears. I hated the children at school who used to talk happily about their mothers and fathers. Fathers. I hated a father I never knew. I hated those birds we always tried to shoot for being so free. I hated me and I wanted to die.

Later on Mandisa would confront Uncle Joe for his coming into my room now and then: '*there's nothing for Mahala you know,*' and Uncle Joe would answer her with a brown twenty rand note. That became a part of my normality.

Ahh . . . pictures. They remind me of my hate. That's why I hate them. Slowly, I put them back inside their envelope, close it and put it away. I hate being back in my past.

The phone rings. It's my boss. After talking to him, I call my girl-friend Sibongile to cancel our date, grab my camera, and make sure my notepads will be enough, sharpen my pencil and run off to the scene of the crime.

There she lies. Another victim. I study the scene very well, there's not much difference from the previous one. Rope tight around her neck, a dead red rose next to her body. The typed message on A4 paper is still the same: *this is how I want to remember you.* I get my camera ready – don't get me wrong, I love taking pics. But unlike Mike, my pictures have to tell a story, a true one, even if I have to face a grue-some scene like this. It's what we have to go through as storytellers, you know. I snap my camera from all angles, ask the SAPS that are there a few questions.

'All I can say is we're getting closer to catching him. We have his profile and it's going to help us a lot.'

I write it down, word for word.

'What's in his profile?'

'He could be a teacher, handsome and very very neat, and a smooth-talker as well . . . charming. That's as much as I'm prepared to tell you.'

Two weeks later we get a call in our offices. The killer is in the hands of the community. My colleague, Harry, and I get our things ready and rush off to Gobusamang High School, a little afraid of what we're going to see, desperate with anticipation, so hungry for that story.

Police vans on the side with the SAPS and a bunch of angry people – women waving their hands in the air, men carrying batons. As soon as we step out of the car I start snapping my camera, capturing all their anger onto my camera, with the police handcuffing some of them and throwing them into the SAPS van, Harry asking questions and writing down what they are saying.

'So where is the victim?' Harry asks one of the SAPS.

'A victim?! You call him a victim!' shouts one of the women.

'What about the women he's been raping and killing! As a teacher we trust him with our kids and he ravages their innocence! He's even on bail for rape.'

'Rape?'

'He takes underage children!'

'Oh – you mean statutory rape?'

'Rape is rape and this time we caught him red-handed.'

'Let me get this straight – you caught him raping a woman?'

'In the same bush he's killed those women!'

'But what were you doing in the bush?'

'Patrolling. These police are failing us so we got together and patrolled the bush. He also fits with the profile we've been reading about in the papers.'

I was snapping my camera at her all the time.

'Ke ntja selo se! The police should have left us to finish him off. What we did to him is not yet enough.'

'What exactly did you do to him?'

'We cut it off with a knife and fed it to the barking dogs. You should have heard him bleating like a goat, saying sorry.'

A police officer comes to shackle her hands and put her into the van as well.

'Where is the . . . the alleged culprit?' Harry asks another officer, this time rephrasing his question.

'He's in there, waiting for an ambulance,' he says, pointing at the classroom door.

'But he's in a very bad way . . .' he warns as Harry and I run to the classroom. We step into the classroom and, Jesus Christ! He lies there, unconscious, and smothered with blood all over. I snap my camera from all angles.

Outside, we interview a beautiful female teacher, Miss Sechele, about her colleague. There is just something about her which I feel I need to check out – only later.

How about those pictures again?

Ahh . . . Mandisa, this picture fails to tell about the true story of your reality, because this is not how I remember you at all.

I remember one Friday I'm coming back from school and I'm so excited that Mandisa is not home. It means I can go play soccer for a while or shoot flying birds; I'll go buy tonight's supply later. But as I'm about to step out the door I have this weird feeling that something's wrong. I wait and listen, probably trying to absorb the ominous feeling in our shack. I feel like Mandisa is in trouble – call it sixth sense if you will. I decide to go to check in her bedroom, open her door and the first thing that greets me is the chair thrown to the floor, her legs hanging in the air. Slowly, with my knees shaking, I walk inside. As I look up I see her neck is strangled by a rope, her eyes could almost pop out and her greenish-purple tongue is sticking out with a white foam around her mouth. *Mandisa! What have you done to yourself!?* I quickly run to the kitchen to get a knife, run back to her room and climb on the chair to cut the rope. She falls down.

'Mandisa! Mandisa!'

Maybe a slap will do. Her scared eyes are just staring into space.

'Mandisa!'

Maybe shaking her will do, but she's so numb in my arms.

'Mandisa! Tsoga!'

How about reminding her about the business?

'You have to give me the money to go buy tonight's supply. It's Friday, remember?' A pause. Something stinks and I realise she has shat herself. *What have you done to yourself Mandisa? What have you done to us?* Helplessly, I think of closing her eyes, but something says no. I think of shoving that greenish-purple tongue back into her mouth and wiping the white foam, but something says no.

No suicide note. Mandisa could not write. The only thing next to her – this picture of her standing next to the rose.

When the men and women of our township came for their entertainment that night, they found me holding her so tightly and struggled to get me off her. At her funeral they all cried, except for some uncles and me. There was no more water left in my head.

Mandisa. How I'm craving your picture again. I stare at this picture to view her beauty. I'm craving another of her pictures.

In the meanwhile, since I'll be writing an article on literature I call Miss Sechele (she's a languages teacher) and ask her for an interview.

After the interview I offer her a lift home.

'So, how old are you?' I ask the first question since we got into the car.

'Don't you know? A woman never tells her age.'

Good answer.

'About thirty perhaps?' She's flattered and smiles.

'Okay, somewhere in my forties.'

'You don't say!'

Silence.

'So why aren't you married?' I ask because I don't see a ring on her finger.

'Marriage is not really my scene. I hate commitment.'

'But do you date?'

'Yes.'

Women like her are like Mandisa. They prey on other women's husbands.

'But a woman your age – either you go for a young oke or you hit on married men.' I say that in a more humorous tone.

'I do both. Let's face it, young guys these days want more experienced women. They would like to be educated.' She laughs and continues, 'Would you also like to be educated, Mr Journalist?'

Slut! Bitch!

'So what about married men? You know . . . what do you think about their wives and kids?'

'Married guys tend to get bored by their wives and would like to have a little fun . . .'

I quickly speed the car into the nearby bush and she screams. I suddenly hit the brakes.

'What? Did you lose control or something?'

I just look at her and she reminds me of Mandisa.

'Why are you staring at me like that?'

'I would like to take you up on that offer . . . educate me.'

'Look, I was just flirting with you. It's not like I shag every guy I come across.'

'Bullshit! You are just like her.'

'Who?'

'Mandisa!'

'Who is Mandisa and what's going on?'

'I will educate you who Mandisa is.'

I take out the rose from under my seat and she doesn't take it.

'What? Don't you like your present?'

'A dead rose?'

I quickly put my gloves on, open my door and grab her out from her seat. When she tries to scream I shove a cloth into her mouth. As she fights against me her skirt moves up, revealing her beautiful shiny and brown thighs. My angry manhood is stiffened. Uhh . . . my boiling blood races through my veins and intensifies my muscles, a willingness surges through my body and I'm craving to give her a slight pain, to make her moan and groan. I throw her to the ground and fall between her thighs. I rip off her red G-string. Red – did she know it was my favourite colour? My manhood rages more as if it'd break off my pants. I free it of my pants and thrust into her. The more she fights the more fun it becomes. I thrust deeper and deeper and deeper till I almost scream in ecstasy. *Ahh Mandisa. I've been craving you for so long . . .*

I pick her up, grip her with one hand while I get a rope from the car boot. I tie it around her neck and slowly tighten it. When I'm positive she won't scream I remove the cloth I'd shoved into her mouth so that I can see her saliva dripping out of her mouth, so that I can see her tongue as it gets full in her mouth, and sticks out, as it turns greenish-purple. Her eyes redden and broaden as if they'd pop out of their sockets. I squeeze the rope tighter and tighter. *Ahh Mandisa. This is how I remember you. This is how I want to remember you.*

As I drive off she's facing up, as if looking at something. And I will later come back to this very scene with my camera, notepads and pencil.

Ahh . . . Mandisa.

Hatchlings

Justin Fox

I've never liked guinea fowl. Foul fowl.
Uncle Jacob flew on the night of my flight.

The elements are not connected, but somehow they've become yoked in my memory, lodged in such a way as not to be undone. I've resigned myself to ownership of this combination of tales, much as one does to untruths that, in recollection, sit better with one, and thus become fact. The sum of the parts is greater than the whole.

Stories are like
eggs.

To begin where? With the scholarship? Uncle Jacob, my mother's eldest brother, won a scholarship to read Classics at Cambridge in 1935 after which he enjoyed a distinguished career as a pilot in the Second World War and then as an inspector of aerodromes round South Africa. After Cambridge he returned to South Africa with his wings and a posh English accent. My mother's family is Afrikaans and as a young girl she was in awe of her dashing brother with his British movie-star accent. When I was a child she expressed the hope that I would one day speak English like Uncle Jacob. Perhaps partly because of this, sixty years after Jacob, I was heading for Cambridge, to read Classics, to acquire the posh accent.

Because Uncle Jacob lived in Pretoria during his retirement I did not see him for years at a time, but just before leaving for England, my mother told me he was coming to Cape Town to live in an old-age home in Sea Point. She would be flying up to Gauteng to fetch him. She said he had become senile, but I felt that when I saw Uncle Jacob again I could somehow get through to him and let him know I'd be winging my way to his alma mater, following in his footsteps. When Jacob arrived at our rambling, family home I was shocked to see that the old man could only manage a slow shuffle. His mind was obviously elsewhere and I could not understand his mumbling. I told him about Cambridge, asked about his college, his rugby playing years, his time in North Africa during the war. Nothing.

However my mother did tell me that when they'd boarded the Boeing in Johannesburg, his eyes had sparkled and he'd been all attention. As the aircraft accelerated down the runway he'd craned his neck at the port-hole, his expression a strange look of contentment. I cut down two of my plastic aeroplanes from where they hung on fishing-line from the ceiling in my bedroom. I built dozens of Airfix model aircraft as a child. Only planes from the Second World War mind you: any flying machine of the post-1945 era held no allure. Perhaps with these I would get through to Uncle Jacob.

He'd flown coastal patrol out of Wingfield in Cape Town, but the closest I had to a reconnaissance aircraft was my Consolidated Catalina, a lumbering flying boat that I felt sure Jacob would never have piloted. The Lancaster and Wellington bombers were also unlikely, so I hit on the Dakota. Just about every Allied soldier had flown in a Gooney Bird: surely Jacob had piloted one. My Dakota had United States Air Force transfers on its wings – a Korean War version – but I didn't think this would matter.

I also cut down a Hawker Hurricane, that stalwart fighter of the British and South African Air Forces. When Jacob became a Colonel he had one of these fighters at his disposal and had flown it up and down Italy during 1945. I often imagined him chasing Messerschmitts from an aquamarine sky above the Apennines, although this was certainly far from the truth. The Hurricane had desert colours for my North African collection. Jacob's would have been camouflaged in greens and browns. I felt that this would also not matter: the stocky lines of the fighter were unmistakable.

I found him staring at the wall in his bedroom and placed the two aircraft on the table. I held up the Hurricane and said, 'Uncle Jacob, what kind of fighter is this?'

Was I patronising him? He stared at the model and then at me, looking confused and saying nothing. Damn, the thing's too small, too puny; it doesn't look like any bloody thing at all. I'm treating him like a baby.

The transport plane was bigger, more detailed. It had taken me days to build. Maybe one more try. 'Uncle Jacob. Please, Uncle Jacob, what kind of plane is this?'

He looked me straight in the eyes and said one word quite clearly: 'Dakota.' That was all. Then he tipped back into his interior world.

I could have yelled I was so pleased. Uncle Jacob was fine – if he could remember that old plane I was sure there was lots else we could access. But he only stayed with us a few days before being moved to a frail-care home where his condition deteriorated. When I visited him there he looked like a child out of place in grown-ups' company as he idled up and down the corridors. Within weeks he was bedridden, and things looked bad.

Meanwhile I'd been preparing for my departure, packing crates of books, clothes for the English climate, sporting gear, appliances for my college room. It was a storm of activity in those last weeks before the flight. My feelings were mixed. On the one hand, I tingled with the liberation to come; on the other, there was a dread concerning the many good-byes, perhaps most of all the good-bye to Uncle Jacob.

Just days before my departure Jacob fell seriously ill. He was in a ward on a back corridor. The sterile, institution smell caught in my throat. His face had sunk in upon itself, closed up shop, and his skin was yellow parchment, his breathing erratic and laboured. He was at altitude without oxygen. His eyes did not open when I spoke so I just held his hand.

When it was time to leave I said, 'Uncle Jacob, I'm going to Cambridge, to your old university, your old college, to follow in your footsteps.' I could think of nothing else so I said lamely, 'Get well soon. I will see you when I return.'

On the eve of my departure I was packing suitcases in my attic room, ducking between low-flying Second World War planes, when I heard screams coming from the street. I bounded downstairs and out the kitchen door to find a young boy sprinting up Apple Lane. He was crying and looking over his shoulder. I ran after him, drew the child to a halt and asked him what was the matter.

'Bird!' he blubbered, 'Big bird . . . wanted to kill me . . . I was just walking home to the flats at the bottom of the road . . . it came for me!'

'Are you sure?' I said, 'this is the suburbs. A bird wouldn't harm you. Come, I'll lead the way.'

I took his hand and led him down Apple Lane towards the flats. He was nervous and tugged at my arm. I picked up the satchel he'd discarded in his flight. He began to whimper. I chuckled to myself, imagining a three-metre-tall ostrich bounding up the lane in a flash of black-and-white feathers and a hail of kicks from its reptilian toes. Or maybe a martial eagle had found the idea of schoolboy carpaccio appealing.

Suddenly his nerves got the better of him and he broke free and ran from me. I watched him sprinting away, marvelling at the lad's timidity. When I turned back towards the flats I had just enough time to duck as the thing flew at me, low, like a fighter-bomber.

As I straightened up, the creature banked and I saw the black-and-white spots: it was a guinea fowl, a common enough bird in city suburbs. Did I catch a look of rage in its eyes as the blue-and-red face fixed on mine, coming for the kill, flapping dementedly? I ducked again, but it had seen me do this once before and timed its run to take my evasive measure into account. It wanted my eyes. The bird hit me like a rugby ball kicked hard from up close and its talons nicked my forehead ploughing tiny grooves of flesh and hair.

I covered my head with my hands. Like the boy, I turned and ran up Apple Lane pursued at head altitude by the bird. Out the corner of my eye I glimpsed a squadron of guinea fowl chicks crouched in the shrubbery, fascinated by the dogfight.

It was only afterwards, in the safety of the bathroom and after the ministrations of my mom, that I realised it was simply a mother fulfilling her duty to her young, protecting them until it was time for them to fly the nest, or in this case the shrubbery of number 7 Apple Lane. I'd always thought of guinea fowl as stupid birds, wild chickens, cumbersome in flight, loud and obstinate. They were irritating creatures: each morning I was woken, long before I was ready, by the staccato chipping of their voices. Now, at least, I would view them with more respect.

The rest of the day was a stream of good-byes. Little time for tears and proper leave-takings. No opportunity to see Uncle Jacob one last time. I packed my toys in boxes marked 'toys'. Some were to be given away. The model aeroplanes were to remain hanging and my mother received instructions as to which ones must be kept at all costs if my parents moved house or some covetous child-relation visited and demanded part of my air arm. The Dakota and the Hurricane were top of the 'preserve' list.

That evening, before I could fully grasp what was happening, I was belted into my seat, taxiing down the runway in a Boeing bound for London. My mother and father were driving back along the N2 to the suburbs and I was as good as gone. The northwest wind scoured the airfield, bending the trees. In the dusk, black clouds coursed overhead and broke against Table Mountain like a tidal wave. The aircraft turned and its engines began to breathe deeper, raising their voices to a crescendo. I heard the sound of cracking.

I looked out the window, tears streaked my cheeks, as the bird rumbled along the runway. Memories spooled freely: child-time, boyhood, teenage years and coming-of-age, all in fast forward, accelerating towards the present, the unstoppable now. Dandled on Uncle Jacob's knee, giggling till it hurt . . . El Alamein in the garden with

Stukas and Spitfires, Messerschmitts and Hurricanes, fighting it out
above the roses . . . sprinting breathless at wing towards the corner flag
. . . the splendid news from Cambridge. I felt like I was going to be sick.
It was happening too fast. It was heavy, this yoke, this thing that was
being lifted from me and was lifting me.

The thud of wheels over runway corrugations sounded like the
crushing of shells. Jacob's Hurricane slipped past the jumbo on a parallel runway. Lighter and more nimble, it took to the air, hurtling skyward long before our plane had reached take-off speed. I could see my
young uncle waving from the cockpit, World War Two oxygen mask
clipped over his face – he was going to be flying high tonight.

The nose of the jumbo began to lift and I wanted to howl with the
engines. I imagined Uncle Jacob lying in his cot, his breath rasping
slower, images of flight flickering through his mind. The guinea fowl
dived out of the sun and strafed me full in the face, leaving tears
of blood.

The plane heaved, ungainly, into the air and was swallowed by an
ocean of sky. The egg was broken and I spilled into the night.

War child evacuation

Kyne Nislev Bernstorff

Heavy panting, wheezing. An insistent rhythm pulling at his shoulders. His small, bare chest heaving then collapsing. Pulsating in sweat, it glistens with the late afternoon sun. He stands hidden within the tall elephant grass the winter wind has dried stiff; it rises and sways in the breeze like the panting of a runner.

He tries to calm himself, takes deeper breaths. But he is a child. His feet feel raw, his legs shudder and he can barely stand upright. His eyes threaten to burst. He squeezes them tight, holding them shut so they cannot spill the memory, the dreadful images that spin in his head like tumbleweeds lost to the storm. His heart hammers to be let out. It too is afraid. He tries to clasp his trembling hands together, then places them one on top of the other over his heart, where they bounce to and from his chest. He sucks in a deep breath for strength, and holds it. His head whirls into twilight.

He steps out of the grass and takes the winding path treaded to dust towards the village. He turns off into a thinner track that snakes through the secrets and darkness of the banana grove. His thoughts are nowhere. Memory and instinct show him the way, turning him at the old and bent mango tree onto a footpath where familiar smells make him start to run again. His feet pounding, faster and faster.

He stumbles into the cool familiarity of the hut, and onto the mud floor swept neat. He lies there, huddled and weeping. He shivers into a convulsing frailty and loses himself into the darkness that swallows him.

Large, soft arms curl about him. Their strength grips him, then lifts him into warmth and comfort. His mother squats so she can cradle him deep between her breasts and her thighs and then begins to rock him. He lifts his head and with lips almost kissing her ear, he spills his tears and all the fear, his anguish gasping into echoes that jolt off the mud walls.

She stills, sits suddenly straight, a large stone set.

She drops him out of her hold and stands, staggering towards the entrance of blinding light. She holds onto the doorway, her head heavy upon the wood. Her red and yellow printed wrap and matching doek seem to shimmer in the bright heat. Her T-shirt hangs holed and forgotten. She lifts her sagging arms of flesh and clasps her mouth. Then she wails as her heaving body stumbles forward over the wooden stools and stones and between the pots and pans left to dry in the burning sun.

She clutches her mouth with both hands, yet the wails seep through, determined to fill the air with her untold horror. She mazes her way between the huts and panicking faces of the compound.

A man in blue overalls with the top hanging around his hips to cool his sweating nakedness suddenly stops digging. He rests his fatigue upon his hoe and listens. He hears it between the pounding blows of the others: his wife's wailing. He drops his hoe and runs down from the field in the bush into the compound. His feet beat the dry ground, drumming out his rhythm that quickens with every step. Arms outstretched with hands locked open and wild he follows the dreaded sound. Under the Masasa tree he reaches her and clasps her tight within his anxious embrace.

She lifts up her face, streaked with dusted tears, her eyes rolling red in bewilderment and fear. She rasps and chokes on her tale as she tries to whisper it into his ear.

He shakes his head, disbelieving. She falls against the tree trunk then holds it, sobbing, clinging to its scratching comfort. Her sister comes but no one can calm her hysterical sobs that whoop and splutter out like a river bursting its banks in flood.

He leaves her, stalking his way through the gathering crowd before turning to look at her. He sees only anguish tearing at her face, contorting her features so that for a moment he does not recognise her and wonders who she is. Then he hears her wail rise up through the tree; he turns and runs to the Chieftain's stone hut. The dark entrance gulps his figure as the corrugated-iron door is latched close. The witch doctor is summoned and his chanting and spirit-calling is heard, spiralling out of the grass roof like smoke from a kitchen fire.

The child remains within the darkness, weeping in muffled confusion into the lap of his grandmother. He can still hear the cries of his mother, coming with the wind like an evil spirit possessed of terror. Then the gusts of warm air shift and bring the feral chanting of the witch doctor. These strange melodies spin and dance together, intruding into the deep shadows of the hut and swirl around as if trying to enter their souls. The grandmother will not let them and wraps the boy closer within her body, cocooning him from these winds and songs of torture.

His crying will not cease. He lies curled and shaking, she is afraid his insides will dry, leaving him shrivelled and lifeless. Like the lost skin of a lizard left useless on the sanded trail.

The villagers are grouped around the wailings of a family split and scattered around the compound. Nothing is said to them, yet they continue staring, waiting for the explanation, children worming their way between legs and peering, frightened, from behind long skirts.

After a while the men slowly shuffle away, trembling, to their tasks. The women and children remain in silenced fear.

The sun sighs the last of its red glow and falls to hide behind the far, blue hills. Dusk noises begin to fill all corners, like a drunken jazz-band warming up. The fires are started early as the people know that tonight will be a thief of both light and warmth.

Someone comes and lights a fire outside the entrance to the hut; another enters to wrap a blanket around the grandmother and child who sit solemn in the shadows, entwined in a huddled, disfigured form.

The mother will not be removed, finding the strength to continue sobbing from the tree. Two men build a fire by her as she crouches, hugging the rough bark, her head pressing hard against the trunk, its shadows swallowing her whole. Within the glowing firelight she becomes one with the tree and fire, the colours mix, yellow and red and orange, flickering forlornly.

The villagers will eat their dinners inside their huts tonight. Silence hangs, bitterly cold. The compound creeps into a deepening darkness that even the large trunk fires cannot warm. Fear hangs in the air like a mist entwined within the thick wood smoke. The moon rises, a cautious yet curious guardian, waiting to shine its paleness into the cool, lost shadows, as if trying to chase away any lurking malevolence.

When the crickets are tiring of their musical feats, three figures creep out of the Chief's hut. They stop by the Masasa tree. One holds the woman, lifting her under her arms and moves with her down the path, towards her home. The others follow.

The child is asleep. Gently, they wrap him in a blanket, his head and feet dangling out as if forgotten. His face falls towards the firelight and in the flickering glow looks contorted and swollen from all his tears; all the fear and agony that spilled out has left him featureless and empty. Together with the child they move out of the hut, taking the pot of food someone has left outside. The mother falls against the wall, biting her hand to silence the awakening sobs. She cannot bear to look as they take her child away.

The grandmother picks up the broom of twigs and begins to sweep. Like a wind through the dust, the floor of the hut is left trackless.

The three men walk one behind the other, down the path and across the empty dancing grounds. Gangling silhouettes with bent legs trudging one after the other, their dignified steps muffled by the dust. As they turn, the one in the middle shows a hump; it is he whose hanging shoulders carry the burden. The night is dark and deep, the shadows full of a suffering silence. The moon peeps from behind a cloud, helping them find quiet footsteps.

Amongst the granite boulders they place the child and wait for the call.

It comes, an eerie whistle hummed from within the dense bush. They try to wake the child but he cannot return from his world of slumber. Still asleep, they strap him to the whistler's form. The runner can easily carry the child at a fast pace, even through the thickest bush. The child hangs hunched like a night-ape upon the runner's bare back, his legs latched in the crook of each strong arm. His head lolls against a shoulder. They tie a strip of torn blanket under the seat of the child and across the runner's forehead like a sling comforting something broken. Now hunchbacked, he moves away, slithers like a serpent down the rocks and disappears into the awakening thicket. Without a sound.

The three men close their eyes. The father prays for the safety of his child. The witch doctor asks the spirits for the protection of the boy and his family. The Chief pleads to the ancestors for peace in the village and deliverance from what the child has seen and never shall be spoken of.

As dawn spreads her papaya-pink ripples across the treetops and breezes begin to tickle the leaves, a lone figure trots in determined rhythm through the tall grasses which sway low as he passes, bowing in respectful dance to the body carrying a secret tied fast to his back. The blanketed bundle jolts with every running step, head thudding in beat against the hard muscles of the runner's bare back.

It is the sun warming his body into sweat that causes the boy to open his eyes. He cannot focus clearly as he shakes in rhythm to his carrier's steady panting. The bush and tall grass flee past him as if they, too, wish to escape his presence.

Small tears begin to sting his tired eyes as he thinks of his life now being taken away. He thinks of his mother and wishes for comfort within her large, thick arms. And his grandmother's warm breath that smells like clouds of honeyed beans as she sings him lullabies of long ago.

A heavy stone-like creature is crawling up inside his chest. He tries to swallow hard but it keeps rising. He is afraid he may choke.

Just like yesterday. He had choked then on the vomit that had exploded out of him. It was from all the pain he had seen. He had been walking to set traps for wild rock rabbits and guinea fowl on nests when he had heard a noise. He had moved quietly towards it, only to realise that it was muffled sobs, and then it was too late to escape. He had seen it all.

He was a witness.

He squeezes his eyes hoping the reminiscence will be forced out of his mind, taking with it all that he had seen. But it is already stuck inside his head, a memory vivid and alive as it tears at him, angry and insistent; a monster who will not be forgotten. It sinks its claws into his mind and rips it open, spilling out the images – red, blood, dead, mud . . .

He sees it all over again.

Young soldiers, just boys like him, holding rifles into the mouths, chests and backs of a kneeling family whose terror faced him, stared him in the eyes. Their fear choking them into silenced statues of shock. He had watched five children fall, individually, into a dust which took them like a famished desire. Then the father's head pooled red in helpless pain, his eyes still wide, fixed on his children. The six shots echoed, then the bush shuddered and was quiet. The mother broke the stiffened silence with a scream that sliced the air open. Torture fled from her soul. She held her mouth from which blood flowed from a lipless gape as she stared at her family's slaughter, their life in blood spreading, shimmering in the noonday sun. Her bare breasts dripped red onto her knees. They shot her, several times, into the large, bulging belly she tried to hold, protecting. She fell slowly sideways, still shaking softly. A baby pouched upon her back rasping its screams. They kicked it till the air moaned still.

He had seen them. They knew that.

The darting animal they had heard run away ran on the feet of a child.

He knew that. His mother knew that. And his father. And the Chief with the witch doctor.

The villagers know only that he had seen something. Something too terrible to tell.

He closes his eyes and lets his face fall onto the runner's back. He will never forget. They know that.

He begins to cry, thinking of his family packing up their worldly affairs into a cardboard box and an old, mended sack. Quiet farewells whispering. His grandmother sweeping their hut of all familiar traces.

Carel Alberts has worked in the magazine publishing industry for ten years, after graduating with an LLB from the University of Stellenbosch. He would write in his spare time if any such thing existed. He is married with two children and lives in Johannesburg.

Kyne Nislev Bernstorff was born in Zimbabwe, to Danish parents, and brought up on a farm with a game park. She has studied literature, languages and philosophy in France, London, the USA, Colombia, Denmark and Cape Town, though her soul rests in the African bush. She lives in Cape Town and is married to an organic farmer/fly-fisherman, has a baby son and not enough dogs.

Darrel Bristow-Bovey was born in Durban in 1971 and studied at the University of Cape Town. He has worked in book publishing and as a freelance writer for television and the print media. He has published a collection of his prize-winning newspaper and magazine columns, and his first book for young readers will be published in 2005. He lives in Johannesburg.

Graham Carlson was born in Grahamstown and schooled at St Andrew's College. After completing a degree in Human Movement Studies at Rhodes University, he spent two years living in London, desperately trying to avoid finding a real job and settling down into a career. He returned to South Africa and joined the ranks of professional rugby before taking up the position of Director of Sport at Kingswood College, Grahamstown.

Maxine Case lives in Cape Town and works in marketing for a publishing company. Before that, she was an editor and project manager, but felt that she was no longer suited to that vocation once she found her own writing voice. She has recently completed her first full-length novel and hopes that it will be published soon.

Dinis F da Costa was born in southern Angola and completed his academic studies in Exacts Science at Pre-University School (PUNIV), Luanda. He then taught for two years at Il de Novembro Orphanage High. He has studied Education, Creative Writing and Journalism, and Basic Theology and is a freelance journalist for *Southern Cross* newspaper. Some of his poems have been included in anthologies published by the Poetry Institute of Africa.

Jonathan Cumming was born in Zimbabwe in 1968, and spent much of his childhood in Zimbabwe's remote Sengwa wildlife research area. He was educated at St George's College, Harare, and Rhodes University, Grahamstown. He has worked in professions ranging from 'punt chauffeur' for tourists on the River Cam, to tobacco trade journalist, to corrector of English for a translation company in Tokyo. He now lives in Johannesburg, where he writes scripts for African-adventure-type television series.

Nicholas Dall has lived in Cape Town all of his life, apart from a gap year spent in Italy after finishing high school. He studied for a BA, majoring in English and Italian at the University of Cape Town, where he is currently completing an MA in Creative Writing. If financially viable, he intends writing for the rest of his life.

Jessica Druker matriculated from King David School in Johannesburg and went on to complete an Honours degree in Dramatic Art at the University of the Witwatersrand. She began writing poetry at the age of ten, encouraged by her Speech and Drama teacher, Mrs Maurine Feldman. She is currently studying Copywriting at the AAA School of Advertising.

Justin Fox is a travel writer and photographer for *Getaway* magazine, and is a Mondi journalism award winner. He was a Rhodes Scholar and received a doctorate in English Literature from Oxford University in 1995, after which he was a research fellow at the University of Cape Town, where he currently lectures part-time. His short stories, poems and photographs have appeared in various books and journals.

Silke Heiss has published poems and prose since 1990. In 2002 she received an MA in Creative Writing from the University of Cape Town for a novel, which won second prize in the Ernst van Heerden Creative Writing Competition in the same year. She has been sponsored during 2004–2005 by the South African National Arts Council to complete a collection of short stories.

Liesl Jobson lives and works in Johannesburg as a music teacher. Her writing has appeared in both local and overseas literary journals, as well as in online publications. She is currently studying for an MA in Creative Writing at the University of the Witwatersrand.

Farhad Abdool Kader Sulliman Khoyratty was born in Plen Vert, Mauritius, in 1972. After his postgraduate studies at Cambridge University (UK), he returned to lecture at the University of Mauritius, where he was Coordinator of the English Unit in 2002/3. A finalist of the Prix du Jeune Ecrivain Francophone with "Pourquoi?", he then won the Ministry of Arts and Culture Short-Story Competition with "Shah Jehan". He has served on the Executive Committee of the Mauritian Writers Association and helped organise two of their writers' conferences. He is a member of the President's Fund for Creative Writing in English. He participates actively in the intellectual life of Mauritius and the region, is multilingual and regularly travels to Europe, continental Africa and Asia.

Bruce Leech lives in Johannesburg, where he works as an advocate. He is married and has three children.

Heinrich J Louw was born and raised in Pretoria. He has a BA degree in English from the University of Pretoria, and is currently completing an Honours degree in English. He has a special interest in anything technical, philosophical or literary.

Kirsten Miller was born in Port Elizabeth in 1970. She graduated from the University of Natal (Pietermaritzburg) in 1992, and obtained her Honours degree Cum Laude in Drama Studies in 1993. She has lived in Johannesburg, London and Cape Town, where she worked as a lecturer, teacher and freelance writer. She now lives in Durban, where she spends her time writing, producing art and craft, and working with children. In 2004, her first unpublished novel, *All is Fish*, was shortlisted for the EU Literary Award.

Fatima Fiona Moolla is a Capetonian who, for as long as she can recall, has loved life and loved books. Her penchant for the written word was given a more critical edge with an MA (Lit Studies) from the University of Cape Town. As a mother of two young boys and as a part-time teacher at the University of the Western Cape, her ambition is modest but inspiring: 'to equip those in my care with the skills to discover and enjoy the world in and through texts'.

Huw Morris grew up in the Eastern Cape where he left small marks on institutions in East London and Grahamstown. He is still busy growing up . . . but now in London. 'When I was in

Standard Four at Selborne Primary, I entered a school writing competition and got second prize for a heartfelt story about a panther that got shot in a jungle. Since then I haven't really received any attention for my literary skill, apart from once when I was caught writing rude words on the desk in an examination hall.'

Pier Myburgh was born in Johannesburg in 1965 and has worked there as a journalist and a stockbroker. In July 2003, she moved to Boston with her husband and two small children, where she began to write fiction. 'The long, cold and dark winter of that year probably contributed in part to the dark nature of my stories. Friends have urged me to lighten up, and I plan to do so now that I am back in South Africa, where I hope to continue learning to write.'

Elizabeth Ann Pienaar is an architect by profession, and is interested in esoterics and economics. 'I avoid cooking, but I love food. I live with a gourmet so that works alright. We share a home with a Basset, an Alsatian and one wild little girl. The dogs eat garden furniture. The child eats Beenos. I write because I always have. I believe the root of all art is the search for a reflection, to see ourselves.

Gill Schierhout was born in Zimbabwe in 1967 and has lived in Zimbabwe, South Africa and the UK. She has a PhD in Public Health from the University of Cape Town and works as a public health consultant. She writes poetry and stories and has recently completed a novel. She is currently working on another novel and a biography. She lives in Johannesburg with her husband Theunis Roux and their two daughters, Hannah and Sarah.

Tebogo C Sengfeng is a Motswana who belongs to the Bakgatla clan, whose origins are from booraMotshegwa in Mochudi, Botswana. She was born in Diepkloof, Soweto, but grew up in Matlhako in Bophuthatswana (now North West province). She later moved to Orange Farm where she now lives with her family.

Melanie Wright was born and raised in Johannesburg. She is the only daughter in a family full of boys, and writes to keep herself sane. She has a BA in Dramatic Art from Wits University and has written several plays. She eats too much chocolate, watches too much television, and spends most of her time trying to bring to life the characters in her head.

Thishiwe Ziqubu is in her twentieth year of the institution of life, and studying Scriptwriting and Directing at AFDA in Johannesburg. She is the founding director of ba-Ntu, a sociocultural movement that seeks to bring Africa back to the days of glory, when expression was a part of life, through oral tradition and the arts.

Acknowledgements

Write! Africa Write! We acknowledge that new writers make this book – thank you for your contributions and for some exciting and creative work. Thank you too to those who submitted entries but were not selected. Please try again!

So many people gave their unpaid time, often working long hours, and I would like to thank all of them most sincerely for their contribution to this project and ultimately to literature: Brian Wafawarowa, Professor Geoffrey Haresnape, Dr Marie Philip, members of the editorial board whose acumen, open good humour and considered consensus made working with them a pleasure. JM Coetzee read all the shortlisted stories, and was most gracious and effective in his vital role as prize judge. Readers Elisabeth Anderson, Peter Anderson, James Bisset, Diana Davis, Mark Espin, Dolores Fleischer, Michiel Heyns, Colleen Higgs, Iracema Hromnik, Ashraf Johaardien, Sarah Johnson, Chris Jones, Michael Lawton, Sindiwe Magona, Tony Morphet, David Philip, Marie Philip, Neil Veitch, and Brian Wafawarowa assessed scripts with great care. Lesley Lambert, our media adviser in Johannesburg, 'gave' PEN hours of professional time, with outstanding results.

Drs David and Marie Philip offered wise counsel, practical advice and encouragement throughout the year. My wife, Dolores, co-ordinated the whole project for SA PEN with characteristic skill and thoroughness.

The whole process of recording and circulating entries to readers while maintaining strict author anonymity was the responsibility of SA PEN secretary Deborah Horn-Botha and Margaret Matthews of New Africa Books. Deborah liaised closely with Joan du Plessis of HSBC Bank plc Johannesburg, and I thank all three for their efficiency and cooperation.

SA PEN needs money to manage a project such as this, and I would like to express my deep appreciation to the Anglo American Chairman's Fund, Media 24 and the SC Menell Charitable Trust for their timely grants, and to the National Arts Council, the Oppenheimer Memorial Trust, and Business and Arts South Africa, who have given us financial support this year.

Finally, our sincere gratitude to our lead sponsor HSBC Bank plc, who recognised the potential of the whole project, and Krishna Patel, who gave valuable personal time to it in a very busy life.

Anthony Fleischer
President, SA PEN